'The computer has been invaded. By something that came out of that damned crab thing. It was nothing but a diversion. And the means to distribute whatever micro-organisms have already spread through the inner core . . . and are now spreading further since the computer shut down my fail-safe system. Am I right, Doctor Lebra?'

'Yes, I'm afraid so. I just don't understand *how* . . .'

Manion was thinking of his daughters again. Were they in danger from whatever had been unleashed from this laboratory?

'We must hold an immediate emergency conference,' said Okimoto, activating his helmet communicator. He began speaking rapidly in Japanese into the mike. Then he stopped. He was looking even more shocked than before. *Now what?* Manion wondered grimly.

'We are cut off,' Okimoto told them. 'Takata has been cut off from the Net. We can't send or receive signals. We are completely alone.'

'Opoponax strikes again,' said Manion softly.

Also by John Brosnan in VGSF

THE SKY LORDS
WAR OF THE SKY LORDS
THE FALL OF THE SKY LORDS

The Opoponax Invasion

JOHN BROSNAN

VGSF

First published in Great Britain 1993
by Victor Gollancz
A Cassell imprint
Villiers House, 41/47 Strand, London WC2N 5JE

A VGSF paperback original

A catalogue record for this book is
available from the British Library.

ISBN 0 575 05199 X

Typeset at The Spartan Press Ltd,
Lymington, Hants
Printed in Great Britain by
Guernsey Press Co. Ltd, Guernsey, Channel Isles

Chapter One

'Have you ever been a woman before, Mr Pryce?' the Body-Chop med-tech asked.

Pryce only half heard the question, being preoccupied with examining his new body in the recuperation room's full-length holo 'mirror'. 'Pardon?' he asked distractedly.

The med-tech repeated the question as she closed the lid of the cylindrical recuperation unit.

'No,' he told her. 'Never. Why do you ask?' He was pleased with the job the Body Chop had done on him. The woman he could see in the holo screen was slim, neat . . . compact. The same applied to her face. Neat features. She wasn't unattractive but there was nothing about her that would draw undue attention. There was nothing flashy about her. He himself would not have looked twice at her if he'd encountered her on a street or a beach. He turned around and peered over his shoulder. Neat bottom as well.

The woman med-tech, her arms folded, watched him as he admired himself. 'Because you will no doubt experience some emotional difficulties while you adjust to your new self. You're not just wearing a woman's body, Mr Pryce. You *are* a woman now. You have a woman's brain and that brain is being saturated with a woman's hormones. You will no longer think as a man.'

He laughed. 'Bullshit. I'm still the same.' He tapped his head. 'In here I'm still me. Michael Vincent Pryce.'

'You may think you are, but gradually you'll come to realize you're not. For example, you were a heterosexual male. How are you responding sexually to the body you can see before you?'

'Well . . . I wouldn't kick it out of bed,' he said, and laughed.

'Seriously, how do you feel?'

He stared at himself. 'It's a perfectly normal, youngish, desirable female body.'

'But do you desire it?'

'No,' he finally admitted. 'I don't.' Then he laughed again. 'Guess it proves I'm not a lesbian.' He grinned suggestively at the severe-faced tech, the unspoken question being, *Are you?* She didn't smile back. 'Sorry,' he said and went over to the couch where new clothes had been laid out for him. He began to dress.

Then he said, frowning, 'I'm not going to suffer from any messy female physical things, am I? You know, like periods and so on?'

'Of course not. There is a sub-dermal synthetic hormone implant on your left forearm. It lasts for a year. Apart from preventing menstruation it also renders you infertile.'

'That's good to know, though I won't be needing the second part of the service,' he said with a laugh. 'This is going to be one very celibate young woman. And please, though I appreciate your advice, my present female condition is only temporary. I won't be a woman long enough for any problems to arise.'

'So you believe,' said the med-tech doubtfully, 'but you should still be aware that you will definitely experience emotional confusion during the period of your adjustment to your new body . . .' She paused, then said, 'And in your . . . profession that might be dangerous for you.'

He finished pulling on a T-shirt and looked at her. 'And what would my profession be?'

'Your bionantech aroused a lot of interest here when we started working on you. Nobody had ever seen anything like it before.'

'You tried to analyse it, of course?' he asked as he pulled on a pair of tights covered in black and white checks.

6

'Of course. And then we discovered it was changing its basic structure. Constantly, and apparently at random, on an atomic level, yet retaining its overall integrity as a system. So then we began to speculate about you. We think you're "him". Personally, I thought you were a myth.'

'Who is "him"?'

'You know. The Ghost. The Ghost in the Machine. Are you him?'

'I'm Michael Vincent Pryce. Freelance irrigation systems expert.' He put on a white synthetic satin blouse with balloon sleeves.

'You *were*,' she pointed out. 'Now you're Marion Van Hacker. A public relations officer for the Hydra Communications Corporation. We ran another identity check on you while you were in recuperation. There is no trace of Michael Vincent Pryce on any of the Corporation computer files that we have access to. He's vanished, including his bank account.'

He smiled at her as he put on a skirt made of black synthetic leather. 'But the important thing for you and your colleagues is that the money I transferred from his account is still real, correct?'

'Yes. The twenty thousand yen is still in our account. I don't see how it can be but it is. I guess it's all down to your unique bionantech. How did you come by it?'

'I did someone a big favour once. He gave it to me as a reward. And you're right – it is unique. My benefactor never made a similar system before he died.' He sat on the couch and pulled on a pair of knee-high black synthetic leather boots.

'That's all you're going to tell me about it?' the med-tech asked.

'That's all.'

'So are you the Ghost?'

He went back to the holo screen to adjust his new clothes. 'The Ghost? The so-called scourge of the Corporations? The mystery man rumoured to be number one on IRC's "most wanted" list? No, I'm afraid he is probably just a myth, as you said he was. An invention of the media. They thought the public wanted a hero figure so they created one.' He smiled. 'A

Robin Hood for the modern age. Though from all the stories I've heard about the Ghost he doesn't go around spreading his ill-gotten gains to the underfunded. He keeps it all to himself.'

He went back to the couch and investigated the contents of a large shoulder-bag that lay upon it. He nodded with satisfaction. 'Yes, everything that I asked for is here. Very good.' He draped the bag over his shoulder and smiled at her. 'I'm ready to leave now . . . unless you have any more womanly advice for me?'

'No.'

'Then let's settle up the remainder of the fee . . . '

'One last thing,' said the tech. 'As you predicted, the scanner detected a genetic irregularity in a cell in the cornea of your left eye. The computer's prognosis was a major aberration in the cell's DNA and suggested the cell was possibly in a pre-cancerous mode. But as per your strict instructions we left it untouched.'

'I certainly hope so.'

'I don't suppose you will enlighten us as to what it is?'

'No. And you should think yourself fortunate that I don't. Now, I really must be going.'

In the reception suite the tech and other members of the Body-Chop staff, including the manageress, watched with interest as he put the tip of his right forefinger to the terminal receptor plate. He subvocalized his instruction for 20,000 yen from the account of Marion Van Hacker, account number 85719759347193576684–088846, to be transferred to the account of the Singapore branch of Body Chop Incorporated. There were murmurs of surprise and wonder from the staff when they saw the transaction confirmed on the terminal screen.

'Amazing,' said the manageress. 'You *are* the Ghost, aren't you?'

'As I told your med-tech, the Ghost is a myth,' he said and smiled.

'Don't worry. We promise one hundred per cent confidentiality.'

His smile vanished. He knew, better than anyone, that they could promise no such thing. He walked quickly to the door. 'Goodbye all, and thank you for everything.'

As the door slid shut behind him he felt a twinge of guilt over what would surely happen to the Body-Chop staff but he quickly suppressed it. Practice, after all, makes perfect.

The Body Chop was located on the forty-seventh floor of a Singapore subscraper. He caught an elevator to the surface and then travelled by monotrain from Singapore across the Strait of Malacca to Sumatra, his destination being the Clarke Elevator Terminal at Lubuksikaping. From there he caught the Elevator up to the Indo-Transit Station in synchronous orbit some 35,000 miles above the terminal. There he booked into a hotel while he waited for the next shuttle flight to Habitat K6BTL, also known as 'Purgatory'. That wouldn't be until the following day.

Alone in his hotel room he spent some time inspecting his new self, this time in an ordinary mirror which, unlike the holo 'mirror', reversed his features, though he didn't notice any real difference. His facial features were apparently perfectly symmetrical. As for his body, he had adjusted remarkably quickly to its changes: to the mild novelty of having breasts and the more drastic change of having a vagina instead of penis and testicles. He was surprised that the lack of the latter hadn't been more traumatic for him. He was unsure of the psychological significance of this . . .

Travelling as a woman had been interesting; he'd noticed many subtle differences. First, he'd been aware of how men looked at him now. It wasn't anything overt – he had, of course, taken deliberate care not to be physically striking as a woman – but it was definitely there. An automatic response from them, in fact, in the way they briefly appraised *her* sexually. And he'd slowly become aware of the subtle difference in the way he now regarded men. Naturally, he'd always been able to tell a good-looking man apart from a skeed but that had been on an objective level.

Now, interestingly enough, he was also beginning to

9

appreciate, and evaluate, men on a sexual level. He'd even felt vaguely sexually attracted to three men he'd been travelling with on the Elevator. This development worried him a little as he hadn't really anticipated it. He could see now what the Body-Chop tech meant in her warning to him. What if he lost control of his new set of female emotions at a crucial stage of his scheme . . . ?

But the enforced wait on the Station was his chief source of concern for the moment. He didn't know just how far behind him his pursuers were. But everything would be all right once he reached Purgatory. It would give him a breathing-space while he put the finishing touches to the next step of his plan. And how appropriate that Purgatory would be his hiding-place, considering the identity of one of his most regular pursuers.

Philip Craner knew there was something very wrong with his life but he couldn't put his finger on it. He sometimes believed that the fault was with him. He just couldn't emotionally engage with anything, and that included his wife and two children. And his job. He was a salesman. He travelled around the department stores of Perth, Western Australia, pushing lines of haberdashery to the buyers in the haberdashery departments. It was a very boring job and he had no idea how he'd ended up in it. He was sure that once upon a time he'd had much more ambitious aspirations, but like so much in his past they had grown very fuzzy in his mind. Remembering anything was hard work these days. It had occurred to him yesterday that he couldn't even remember the first time he'd met his wife, Daphne. Was it at some party? A barbecue? At work? No, he couldn't remember. The past was all just too vague.

But it wasn't just him. It was everything and everyone around him. Daphne was distant too; always frowning and preoccupied. He would ask her – apathetically, true – what was wrong but she could never say. And the children: uncommunicative and dull. In fact, he realized, they hardly spoke at all. And the people he worked with, the buyers he had to deal with every day in the shops, what a dull lot they were.

On top of everything else he was plagued with feelings of *déjà vu*. Every day he had flashes where it seemed that everything he was experiencing he'd experienced all before only a short time in the past. OK, it was true he worked by a pretty set routine but these flashes occurred at home and in the pub as well . . .

Like the one he was having right now as he was getting out of his FJ Holden with his sample case. He was in Hay Street and heading for the entrance to the big department store called Foys. He hadn't paid a visit to the store for a couple of weeks, he was certain, but it seemed like only yesterday he had done exactly the same thing. Yes, as he paused, brushing bush-flies from his face, by the newspaper kiosk to buy a copy of the *Daily News*, he felt positive he'd done the same thing only yesterday. And yes, he even recognized the headline on the paper: KENNEDY GIVES RUSSIANS ULTIMATUM OVER CUBA! He looked at the date on the paper. The seventh of January, 1958. That seemed familiar too.

I'm being ridiculous, he told himself as he entered the air-conditioned coolness of the shop. *If I keep on this way I'll go mad. Maybe all I need is a good long holiday.*

He went up the escalator to the haberdashery department on the first floor. He spotted Miss Dickson, the buyer, sitting at her desk. She saw him and rose to her feet. She was a thin, plain woman in her mid-thirties. She looked concerned. As she approached the counter Philip suddenly knew what she was going to say, and what he would say to her. It would be 'Hello, Mr Craner. Isn't it dreadful about this missile business? Mr Hargreaves from Lingerie said in the cafeteria at lunch today that this might start the Third World War . . . '

Miss Dickson reached the counter. 'Hello, Mr Craner. Terribly hot day, isn't it? And isn't it dreadful about this Cuban missile crisis? Mr Hargreaves from Lingerie said in the cafeteria today that . . . '

Well, not exactly the same but close enough. I definitely need a holiday, Philip told himself miserably as Miss Dickson continued to follow the script more or less faithfully.

*

Sebastian Chimes entered the boardroom of the Shinito Corporation in Sydney, Australia. The four top Shinito executives sitting around the vast oak table quickly stood and bowed towards him. 'Welcome to Shinito headquarters, Mr Chimes,' said Kondo Izumi, the chief executive, 'and thank you for responding to our invitation so swiftly. Please sit down.'

An aide ushered Chimes to a chair. Chimes sat. In contrast to the conservative gun-metal grey business suits worn by the four executives, Chimes's clothes could only be described as . . . unconventional. He wore a tall top hat, black, a tight-fitting Victorian frock coat, black, a waistcoat, silver, tight Victorian trousers, black, ankle-boots, black, and spats, silver. He also carried a wooden cane with a round silver knob on top. He was a tall, thin, cadaverous-looking man. His endocrine system had been subtly modified in order for him to be able to concentrate all his energies on his job. He had no sexual desires and was capable of being totally unemotional in the execution of his duties. His only sensory luxury was food. He was a gourmet with a prodigious appetite but, thanks to his modified endocrine system, never put on an ounce of weight. Sebastian Chimes was the top investigator for IRC, the Interplanetary Revenue Corporation. In essence he was the most efficient and ruthless tax-collector who had ever existed.

'Anything that involves the Glitch automatically receives my full attention,' said Chimes. His voice was deep but nasal. He sat there, slightly hunched forward and leaning on his cane, with both of his long-fingered hands clasped over its silver knob.

'The "Glitch"?' asked Izumi, puzzled.

'It's the term we use for the Ghost at IRC,' said Chimes. 'You have new information about him?'

'We believe so,' said Izumi. 'Someone penetrated security at our bio-research space habitat, Takata, and stole something that is literally priceless. From the way he easily manipulated every computer system he encountered we could only conclude it was the Ghost.'

'I see,' said Chimes. 'And what exactly is this priceless item that he stole?'

The four executives exchanged uneasy glances. Then Izumi said, 'I'm afraid that we cannot divulge that information. Not at this stage, at least.'

Chimes gave a slight shrug of his thin shoulders. 'That is your prerogative, of course, although it would have been helpful to know. As it came from Takata I can only presume it is some genegineered product on which you are anxious to establish copyright.'

Izumi cleared his throat. 'No, it is much more important than that.'

'Really? Then why has the Shinito Corporation not informed IRC of its possession of this extremely valuable . . . item?'

'Uh, when we say it is invaluable,' said Izumi hurriedly, 'we are referring to its *potential* once it has been developed. Of course at that point we would have followed correct procedure in relation to keeping IRC fully informed.'

'Of course,' murmured Chimes. He glanced idly around the boardroom. The oak-panelled walls were hung with photographs showing Mount Fuji in different seasons of the year. One wall was made entirely of glass. Cirrus clouds drifted by. He looked at the four executives. One of them wasn't Japanese, but though obviously occidental the man had had facial modification, including the creation of epicanthic folds in the inner corners of his eyes, in order to appear Japanese. It wasn't an attempt on the executive's part to become a real Japanese, which was strictly forbidden by Corporation law, but simply an honourable gesture of respect towards his beloved Japanese company. Chimes knew that the executive had also adopted a Japanese name for the same reason. Previously called Daniel Urich, he was now known as Araki Hyuga. Chimes said, 'Then let us drop the subject and talk of the Ghost himself. Do you have any idea of his present whereabouts?'

'We think so,' said Izumi.

Sebastian Chimes leaned slightly further forward on his cane. The nostrils of his long nose flared. 'I have been leading the hunt for this man for over three years now. He has so far been the only blemish on my successful career. It would mean a lot to me to finally get my hands on him.'

'We realize that, Mr Chimes.'

'I must admit, however, to being somewhat surprised that you have succeeded in tracking down the Ghost while all my efforts, and those of IRC, have failed.'

'Well, we haven't exactly pinpointed his exact where-abouts,' said Hyuga, 'but we are fairly confident we know his general location.'

'Which is?' asked Chimes.

'The Interplanetary Revenue Corporation's very own habitat, K6BTL,' said Izumi.

Chimes's eyes widened slightly with surprise. 'He's in Purgatory? Are you sure?'

'We have good reason to believe so. He is masquerading as a tourist, we believe. A woman tourist.'

'He's disguised as a woman?'

'No. He *is* a woman.'

'I see. A Body-Chop job. And how did you come by this piece of information?'

'We tracked him to a Body Chop in Singapore. The staff were arrested under the Corporation Emergency Law and subjected to intense interrogation. They told of a male customer who possessed unique bionantech. It had to be the Ghost . . .'

Chimes leaned forward excitedly. 'You're saying these people had the opportunity to analyse the Ghost's bionantech?'

'They had the opportunity,' said Araki Hyuga then added regretfully, 'but failed to unravel its secrets. It constantly changes its structure, they told us . . . and we know they are telling the truth. We are at a loss to explain its origins.'

'So am I,' sighed Chimes. 'So how did you manage to track him to that particular Body Chop, and from there to Purgatory?'

'When we realized we were dealing with the Ghost we adopted different, if rather old-fashioned and very expensive, tactics,' explained another of the executives. Chimes knew

14

him to be Shimpei Murakami. 'We employed the services of Yakuza Inc. We had a good physical description of the Ghost, from the female Chief Security Officer on Takata whom he had seduced so . . . '

Chimes held up a hand to halt his flow. 'Forgive the digression, sir, but does the Ghost's seduction of this security officer have any relevance to the situation?'

'Indeed it does,' said Murakami. 'It was from this unfortunate officer that the Ghost acquired the access code that gave him entry into the sealed-off section of the habitat in which lay the object of his attentions.'

Chimes was puzzled. 'From my experience, no computer can resist the Ghost's command to divulge an access code.'

'Ah, yes, that may be so,' said Murakami, 'but in this case the code related to a mechanical combination-lock, manually operated. It was the idea of the security officer concerned. We were impressed with the way she thought. That's why she had been made Chief Security Officer on Takata.'

'And after he seduced her she simply gave the Ghost the code, knowing that she would be ruining her career and putting her very life in jeopardy?' Chimes smiled wryly. 'The Ghost must be some considerable lover. Perhaps his unique bionantech is even more versatile than I imagined.'

Izumi gave a polite cough. 'He told her that he loved her.'

Chimes uttered an understanding 'Ah.'

'He promised he would smuggle her out of the habitat and that they would start up a new life together.'

'And she actually believed him?' asked Chimes with a sigh.

'She thought she was in love with him. She is of Western cultural origin, you understand,' said Izumi.

'I see. Pray continue with the method by which you tracked the Ghost.' Talk of sex and love always made Chimes hungry. He wondered what was on the menu of the executive dining-room today.

'We used Yakuza Inc. and practically all of their members throughout the System. We flooded every possible stopover point on all the possible route variations that the Ghost might take with Yakuza members familiar with his appearance.'

15

'That *must* have been expensive,' said Chimes, appreciatively.

'As we said, what the Ghost has stolen from us is, potentially, priceless,' said Izumi. 'We will spare no expense or effort to recover it.'

'But surely the first thing the Ghost would have done on leaving your habitat would be to modify his appearance?' asked Chimes.

Izumi looked pleased with himself. 'We anticipated that, of course. But the degree of change he could make by himself was bound to be limited. Our Yakuza spies were instructed to check on any male who fitted the general description of the Ghost that we had given them.'

Chimes frowned. 'But by what means could they positively identify the Ghost? I know for a fact that, by means of his bionantech, he is constantly altering his retinal pattern.'

Izumi practically glowed with pride. 'We used a much older method. We identified him by his fingerprints.'

'His genetic fingerprint? But how could you have possibly got that . . . ?' asked Chimes, still frowning.

'No, no! The fingerprints on his *fingers*!' said Izumi excitedly.

Chimes was genuinely taken by surprise again. He stared at the tips of his own fingers for a time. 'I'm impressed. No one has used that method of identification for . . . for centuries, I would presume.'

Izumi nodded. 'Exactly. So we counted on the Ghost never bothering to change his fingerprints.'

'And you obviously had a set of his prints?'

'Yes. They were provided by Takata's *former* Chief Security Officer. They were on a drinking-glass from her apt that the Ghost had used. It was she who came up with the idea of identifying him by his fingerprints. She was naturally angry with him once she realized what he had done to her. And she was also trying to make some amends for her act of treachery towards the Company.'

'Traitor she may be but I must admit I admire the way she thinks,' said Chimes.

16

'So did we. It was a great pity about what she did.'

'And what will be her fate?'

Izumi looked uncomfortable. 'It won't be pleasant,' was all he said.

Chimes gave an understanding nod. Then, 'So when one of your Yakuza agents spotted a likely suspect at any shuttle terminal he would surreptitiously obtain the suspect's finger-prints?'

'Yes,' said Izumi. 'And there were many, many false alarms, of course, but finally, at Asimov City, two of our Yakuza agents struck gold. They found the Ghost.'

Chimes felt his pulse-rate quicken. He rapidly brought it down again and said, 'And?'

Izumi looked uncomfortable again. 'He was disguised as a priest, travelling under the name of Father Antony Stefano. He had booked on to the next available shuttle to the habitat Vahimagi.'

'And why did your people fail to apprehend him?' asked Chimes.

'Ah . . . ' Izumi looked down at the table-top, avoiding Chimes's gaze. 'They weren't supposed to, er, apprehend him. They had orders to kill him.'

'Surely you would have realized that IRC, and I, want him alive?'

'Yes, but our highest priority was the recovery of our . . . property. Killing him would have been the most efficient and quickest way of achieving this.'

'But presumably your agents failed?' asked Chimes.

Izumi briefly met his eyes then glanced away again. 'Yes. We lost all contact with them. They were later found dead.'

Chimes sighed. 'And the Ghost got away. Then what?'

'We didn't know what to do at first. All trace of Father Antony Stefano had instantly disappeared from the Net, of course.'

'Of course.'

'Then we reasoned that, because he would now be aware of our tracing him by some aspect of his physical appearance, the logical thing for him to do would be to undergo a complete physical transformation at a Body Chop. We sent a team to the Body Chop at Asimov City, and then to every other Body Chop on the moon. Nothing. We widened the search. We included the Earth. But by the time our people reached the Singapore branch of Body Chop the Ghost had gone.'

'Naturally,' said Chimes.

'However, we had a new physical description of him – or rather, her – and his new identity. We traced this new identity, Marion Van Hacker, through the nets to the Clarke Elevator Terminal. From the Indo-Transit Station above it she booked on to a tourist shuttle heading for your punishment habitat, Mr Chimes. Purgatory. Officially, she never arrived at Purgatory. All trace of Marion Van Hacker has been wiped from the Net. The Ghost's bionantech had obviously created a new identity for his arrival at Purgatory but at least we still have a reliable description of his new physical self. We have sent a Yakuza team to infiltrate the many tourist groups visiting Purgatory but . . . ' Izumi paused.

'But you thought it would now be expedient to inform us of what was going on, especially as the Ghost was on IRC territory? And you want our help, of course.'

Izumi gave a quick bow of his head. 'Yes.'

'I will inform my superiors immediately. The Ghost will be found and captured within hours. I guarantee that, gentlemen. You will get your property back and I will experience the ultimate rush in job satisfaction.' Chimes smiled widely, revealing unusually long teeth. 'Now, what's for lunch?'

Philip Craner was driving down St George's Terrace and wondering what was wrong with his life. He knew that *something* was wrong but he just couldn't put his finger on it. Though one problem that he could identify was the fact that he couldn't emotionally engage with anything, and that included his wife and two children . . .

At that moment a young woman wearing a ridiculously short red skirt darted across the road in front of him. He was astonished. How could she go around in a skirt that short without being arrested? He turned and looked at her as he went past. And hit something with his car. The thud sounded messy and bone-crunching. 'Oh fuck!' he cried as he slammed his foot down on the brake-pedal. The car skidded to a halt. He looked around wildly but couldn't see anything. Whatever he'd hit, or *whoever*, was probably under the car. That bloody woman and her short skirt! Thanks to her he'd killed someone. He got out of the car. Other cars sounded their horns as they swerved around his. Couldn't they see that he'd run someone over?

He went to the front of the FJ Holden. The radiator grille was stoved in. He had definitely hit someone. But where were they? He took a deep breath and looked under the car. Nothing. And nothing behind the car either. He felt mystified. Then he felt a tug on his arm. He turned. It was the girl in the very short skirt. She was carrying a large shoulder-bag. She looked relieved. 'Thanks. You don't know it but you just saved my life.'

'I did?' He noticed she had grey eyes and was quite pretty.

'Now you can help me some more,' she told him as she glanced quickly behind her. 'Drive me away from here. Fast.'

His confusion grew. 'But I think I hit somebody . . . or something,' he told her worriedly.

'You did, but don't worry about it,' she said as she pushed him towards the car. 'We've got to get moving. I'm still in danger . . .'

He realized she must be crazy. That explained her clothing. 'I can't see anybody,' he said, helplessly.

'No, of course you can't. Your neural implants prevent you from seeing a lot of things.'

'My what?'

'I'll explain everything later, but for now just believe me when I tell you that you're not living in Australia in the twentieth century . . . ' She waved her arms, gesturing at their surroundings. 'All this is fake. In reality you're on a space habitat in the twenty-third century and you're being punished for tax evasion. Now let's get in your car and get the hell away from here!'

19

Chapter Two

It had begun on 27 June that year when asteroid prospector Joyceen Magwood, with the assistance of her tug's computer, made an unusual discovery . . .

Joyceen Magwood enjoyed being alone, which was just as well as the nearest human being was usually millions of miles away from wherever she happened to be working in the Belt at any given time. With one notable exception, she hadn't seen another human for fifteen years. Her supplies were delivered by drones and drones carried her refined metals to whatever industrial habitat happened to be closest at the time of shipment. The one exception was nearly two years ago when a tax-inspector from IRC had made a surprise visit to make sure she wasn't committing tax fraud by holding back any precious metals that she had failed to declare on her shipping documents. The investigator, a pompous little man with a pronounced body odour – at least, to her sensitive nose – had carried out a thorough search but found nothing. There was no way he could have. Her secret cache of gold was hidden in a small asteroid in an area of the Belt that was very distant from her tug, the *Shattered Dream*, at the time of the inspector's visit.

Joyceen was only alone in the sense that she lacked human company but she wasn't really alone. She had eight cats. She'd always had lots of cats. After some fine-tuning to the systems of balance in their inner ears her cats had taken to life in a gravity-free environment. So much so that they were loath to enter the centrifugal section of the ship, which was where their toilet facilities were located, for obvious reasons. When she had her daily one-hour work-out in that section she was obliged to lock them in with her for the sake of their physical well-being. They simply didn't like gravity. They much preferred to float lazily – usually asleep – in the air in the non-gravity sections of the tug or, during their brief periods of activity, spring madly back and forth between the walls and the webbing.

But there were drawbacks to living with cats in space. Housebreaking them when kittens was always a major chore – they had to learn that there was absolutely no crapping or pissing in the free-fall sections of the ship, and until they learnt that important lesson the situation could get very messy – and there was also the problem of cat hair regularly clogging up the filters in the air-recycling system.

Joyceen was a lean, even stringy woman of fifty-six years. She looked her fifty-six years because when she reached her fiftieth birthday she had come to the unusual decision to stop her anti-ageing gene therapy. She wasn't sure why she'd done that. Maybe it was to experience the sheer novelty of growing old. She intended to resume therapy sooner or later – she had seen vids of really old people and she had no intention of going *that* far. But for the time being she couldn't care less.

If you could stand the isolation – and Joyceen relished it – you could make a good living as an asteroid prospector. Of course, all the largest asteroids – ones with diameters of more than sixty miles, of which there were 260 – had been already claimed by the various Corporations, and many of the biggest asteroids contained mining installations and Company habitats, which provided the Corporations with all the iron and nickel they required; but that still left plenty of rich pickings for freelance prospectors like Joyceen who concentrated on finding rare and precious metals. However, while a freelance operator in theory, she was obliged to operate under licence to one of the Corporations. The particular corporation she worked for was Shinito.

At 0807 hours on 27 June, while Joyceen was just about to begin a routine scan of a virgin asteroid about a half a mile in diameter, her computer said, 'Joy, check this out, will you?'

She kicked herself over to the wide-scan radar display unit, pushed a sleeping cat, Pickles, out of the way and stared at the screen. 'What am I looking at?'

A red circle appeared around one of the many small blips on the screen. 'That.'

'What is it?'

'Haven't a clue,' said the computer, jauntily, 'but I do know what it's not. It's not an asteroid.'

'How do you know?'

'For one thing, it's perfectly spherical. You ever seen a perfectly spherical asteroid before?'

Joyceen shook her head.

'And the signal-bounce I'm getting from it suggests that it's made from some sort of alloy.'

'Interesting,' said Joyceen. 'Must be a piece of old space junk. A NASA probe, maybe. How big is it?'

'Just under eighteen inches in diameter. But I don't think it's a space probe. There are no antennae or sensors.'

Joyceen whistled through her teeth. She was beginning to feel vaguely excited. She could be on to something here. 'How far away is it?'

'Only fifteen miles.'

'So send out a mech to go fetch. I want to have a look at it.'

When the mech had returned she suited up and went to B hold, which was unpressurized, where the mech was waiting with the object. She entered the hold and told her suit to take her closer. She saw that the object was definitely not an asteroid but an artefact. Coloured a dull matt black that seemed to *suck* light into it, it was perfectly spherical. The surface was heavily pitted, suggesting that it had been out in space a very long time. But what proved without a doubt that it was not natural were the symbols deeply engraved into its surface.

The symbols meant nothing to her. 'Any idea what these markings represent?' she asked. The computer replied via her helmet radio, 'No. I've already checked. Can't correlate them to any known language, nor are they mathematical symbols.'

22

'What about an analysis of the thing itself?'

'I can only give an accurate breakdown of its outer surface at this point. It is an alloy. I've detected traces of iron, nickel, thallium, carbon, beryllium and an unidentifiable element.'

'An *element*!' she exclaimed.

'A synthetic element, of course,' said the computer. 'And a very dense one. I put the atomic weight at 334.'

'But that's impossible! Such an atom would be incredibly unstable!'

'So it should be, but this one clearly isn't. I don't have the resources for a detailed subatomic analysis of this substance so I can't give you any further information at this point.'

Joyceen thought it over. Two things occurred to her. One was that this object could be extremely valuable. The other was the possibility that the thing wasn't a human artefact. If this was so the implications were staggering.

She asked the computer for confirmation. It said, 'Yes, I agree. It seems the most likely explanation is that the object is an artefact of non-human origin . . . ' The computer paused and then said, ' . . . As unlikely as this may be.'

'Shit!' She stared even more intently at the sphere through her visor. 'Where could it have come from?'

'The only logical conclusion is that it came from outside the solar system.'

She thought some more. Then, 'Can you tell how old it is?'

'Yes. Its outer surface was made approximately twenty million years ago.'

She said shit again.

'Do you want me to penetrate below its surface?' asked the computer.

'No, don't! No more analysis . . . leave it alone . . . '

After giving the object one final look Joyceen left the hold and returned to the control room. Out of her suit she drifted around aimlessly for several minutes, deep in thought.

What she had in B hold was proof at last of the existence of another technologically advanced civilization. Or rather proof that such a civilization had *once* existed. Twenty million years was a long time. It was unlikely they were still around out there. But that didn't matter. The existence of the sphere did. Humankind had long ago given up any hope of finding evidence of the existence, past or present, of intelligent alien life. SETI, the program set up to scan the galaxy for radio signals that would reveal the presence of other civilizations, had finally been abandoned in the mid-twenty-first century. It had been commonly believed up until then that the human-style technological civilization was an inevitable development in the social evolution of a tool-using intelligent species and that older civilizations would be much more technologically advanced than humanity.

This theory, with its pronounced anthropomorphic bias, assumed that because the human species had developed an electronic technology, other such 'superior' species would have done likewise. But as the years went by, with the scanning equipment becoming ever increasingly sophisti-cated, and no trace of radio, or laser, signals from another civilization ever being found, the theory fell into disfavour. A new theory replaced it. It said that while life itself was quite probably widespread throughout the universe – based on the fossil evidence of primitive life-forms found on Mars – intelligent species didn't automatically mean complex techno-logies. Modern humans, after all, had existed on the planet for tens of thousands of years without creating an electronic technology. What had happened on the Earth, starting with the rapid development of one particular breed of ape into a species of very *smart* apes, and their eventual development of technology, was just some kind of evolutionary fluke. By the law of averages it was possible that somewhere in the universe there was a species similar to humanity with a similar technology, but the chances of its being located in this galaxy were incredibly remote. That was the accepted view of the scientific establishment . . .

But now her discovery was going to turn everything upside-down.

She wondered what to do next. That black sphere could make her rich and famous. She didn't want to be famous but she did want to be rich. Should she run with this on her own?

Try for a secret deal on the grey market? No, it was too big, and so were the risks. If Shinito found out that she had cheated on them with something this big they would obliterate her.

She sighed and said to the computer, 'Prepare to send the following coded message to Kanji Hayashi at the Shinito office on Phobos . . .'

Paul Manion sat on the park bench watching his two children play with their black Labrador, King, and wished he was on Earth. He envied his daughters their easy ability to take their surroundings for granted. If he kept his eyes fixed on Amelia and Michelle, and the dog, he was all right. But if he raised his eyes above the trees he would see the ground curving upwards. And if he looked immediately overhead he would see, suspended above him, distant buildings, other parks, lakes and tiny people and he would be overcome with vertigo and have to grip the bench tightly in case he found himself falling 'upwards' towards the ground far above him.

By then there would be no way for him to avoid the awful truth: that not far below him was the cold blackness of space. He wasn't on the Earth but sitting on the inner skin of a giant, rotating, bulbous tin can. Officially the tin can was known as the space habitat Takata, the Shinito Corporation's biological research establishment. Manion hated being in space. He just couldn't adapt to it. Couldn't shake off deep-rooted feelings of vulnerability and unease. The universe was just too damn big. All that space gave him the creeps. But at least the habitat had gravity; being in a zero-gravity environment was something he hated most of all. When he was obliged to travel he was constantly space-sick and his attacks of vertigo approached the proportions of pure terror. He simply wasn't cut out for life off-Earth but he had no choice. All the action was in space. If you wanted to get ahead you had to get out here where it was all happening. And his salary made it – almost – worth the suffering he endured. If he'd stayed on Earth he could never have afforded to give his daughters the kind of life they currently enjoyed.

And now, owing to his sudden promotion, his salary had increased drastically. He was now Chief Security Officer. He had Julie to thank for that. Jesus, what an idiot she'd been! And he'd always regarded her as one of the shrewdest, sharpest people he'd ever encountered! How could she have fallen for that hoary old line that the bastard had spun her . . . ?

Out of the corner of his eye, he saw someone approaching. He turned. It was Hayden Frid, the executive responsible for security. His boss.

'Hello, Paul.'

Manion raised a hand in greeting. 'Hayden.'

Frid was wearing his usual black, baggy suit. Manion presumed he had a whole closet full of them. And a load of identical black shirts as well. Frid sat down beside him on the bench. Manion looked at him. His expression was, also as usual, impossible to read. The pale-skinned man with his hooded blue eyes and receding blond hair was an enigma, in Manion's opinion. He was always polite, never raised his voice or displayed any sign of anger. Manion thought it would be better if he occasionaly did, but Frid never showed a sign of any emotion. He was unmarried, lived alone and had no sexual or social life as far as Manion could ascertain.

'It has been decided to carry the Opoponax Project to full completion as quickly as possible,' Frid told him. 'The original piece-by-piece approach has been abandoned.'

Manion was expecting to hear that. It wasn't good news. King came running over to check out the new arrival. Amelia and Michelle, giggling, followed the dog. King sniffed at Frid's shoes, then at his hands resting on his lap. Frid glanced briefly down at the dog then ignored it. The girls came, Amelia grabbing King's collar. They looked shyly at Frid.

'Hello, Mr Frid,' they chorused. Frid gave them the same brief glance that he'd given the dog, and acknowledged their presence with the slightest of nods.

'Take King away and play,' Manion told them. 'Mr Frid and I have to talk about work.'

The girls obeyed. 'Nice children,' said Frid as if he were complimenting Manion on a pair of new shoes.

'Yes, I think so,' said Manion. They *were* nice children, as a matter of fact. Amelia, eight, and Michelle, six, had their mother's Latin colouring as well as inheriting her bright and cheerful personality. They were intelligent, too. But then perhaps he was biased.

'There was no choice, really,' continued Frid. 'We've got to go through with it just in case the Ghost succeeds in eluding us and then holds an auction with the other Corporations.'

'I suppose not. But it seems . . . rather rash.'

'We have to be first. Opoponax is the means to uncountable realms of knowledge. Not to mention wealth.'

Manion said nothing. He watched his daughters playing with King and wondered what the reaction would be if he requested they be sent back to Earth. Negative, he decided. It would be interpreted by the Company as a lack of confidence. Bad marks would ensue.

'If the Ghost is caught before he can sell the . . . merchandise then they'll return to the original plan of operation?' he asked.

'I would think so.'

'How is the hunt for the Ghost progressing?'

'The Yakuza almost had her. Spotted her on a tourist airbus but she escaped. She's loose in Purgatory now, moving among the inmates.'

'She?'

'She's a woman now.'

'Oh.' It was hard to think of the man that Manion had known as Sean Varley – Julie Verhoven's cold and calculating seducer – as a woman.

'She's trapped. She can't change her appearance in Purgatory so it's only a matter of time before she's caught. IRC have been informed and are co-operating. They want the Ghost as much as we do.'

'Then they know about Opoponax?' he asked, surprised.

'They know the Ghost has something of ours that is extremely valuable. They and the Company have come to an agreement. IRC wants the Ghost apprehended alive. They have agreed, once the Ghost is caught, to allow us to recover our property then the Ghost will be turned over to IRC. And then everyone will be happy.'

'Everyone except the Ghost. And Julie.'

'Yes. It was unfortunate about Julie.'

'Very. But he fooled all of us. Not just her.'

'His credentials and background history appeared to be impeccable. They withstood every check we made, thanks to that unique bionantech of his. But Julie wasn't just fooled – she agreed to betray the Company for him. She knew what the consequences would be if she was caught.'

Manion sighed. 'I suppose so.'

'And her misfortune has proved beneficial to you, Paul. Sudden promotion right to the top.'

'With all the responsibility that goes with it.'

'I'm sure you'll do an excellent job. We all have total confidence in you.'

'Thank you.'

'By the way, there's a meeting in Takie Okimoto's office in an hour's time. Your presence is required.'

'Fine.' There would be plenty of time to take the kids back to the child-minder at the apartment.

'The meeting is being held to discuss security . . . precautions with respect to the completion of the Opoponax Project.'

Manion glanced at him.

Frid smiled. 'A formality, of course.'

'Of course,' said Manion and turned his gaze back towards his children.

'Of all the centuries the twentieth is generally regarded as being easily the worst of all,' said the tour guide, 'and while it was an era of great technological and biotechnical achievements it was also an era when an unprecedented number of people died from warfare, famine and disease.' The airbus had lifted from the roof of the hotel and was speeding over the surrounding gardens. Mary Eads, as Pryce was now known to the Net, was only half listening to the tour guide. He was feeling apprehensive and he didn't know why. Everything was going to plan. There was no way that Shinito could have tracked him to Purgatory. But then how had those Yakuza members tracked him so quickly to Asimov City? He'd presumed that Shinito had some kind of fix on his physical appearance, which was why he'd changed course and headed to that Body Chop in Singapore. Surely his complete transformation had eradicated whatever physical factor that Shinito had somehow locked on to. But what if it was something else? What if they'd already trailed him to the Body Chop and were aware of his new appearance? Then he was in the shit. He scanned his fellow passengers, looking for anyone who was paying too much attention to him . . .

And spotted such a person almost immediately. A man a few yards away, leaning against the railing. An Asian, but not Japanese. He was staring directly at him. And now he was smiling at him.

Her. *Her!* He had to remember he was a woman now. And a moderately attractive one. This was simply a man hoping he was going to get lucky.

Well, not today. Mary turned her back on him.

' . . . And for almost the whole of the second half of the twentieth century the world lived under the threat of nuclear destruction. The two superpowers who then dominated Earth were prepared to wipe out all life on the planet in order to make a political point. This policy was suitably known as MAD: Mutually Assured Destruction. But the inhabitants of that century were afflicted with another curse apart from the threat of nuclear warfare, and the ravages of conventional warfare, famine and disease. It was called the . . . automobile.'

Mary looked over the railing and saw that the airbus was now flying over one of the exhibits. It was a small city crisscrossed with straight pathways along which heavy-looking vehicles moved at fairly high speeds. There were also people walking along smaller pathways on either side of the main ones. Vehicles and people appeared to be in ridiculously dangerous proximity. As the airbus dropped lower Mary saw that this was indeed the case. She had seen re-creations of twentieth-century city life on the vids before but seeing it for real had much more impact.

'The vehicles you see below you are under the direct control of individual drivers,' said the tour guide. 'There are no computers involved. The training of the drivers was cursory at best. In some countries it was non-existent. A large percentage of drivers were completely incompetent. Needless to say, collisions were frequent. And notice that there are no safety barriers between the vehicles and the pedestrians. If a driver loses control of his vehicle there is nothing to prevent it mounting the pathway and causing casualties among the pedestrians.'

'How awful,' muttered a woman standing next to Mary.

'It may be hard to believe, but this is how people really did live back in the twentieth century. And by the end of that century it is estimated that the automobile was directly responsible for the deaths of twenty million people. Countless others were seriously maimed in car accidents. And it is impossible to know how many people died as a result of the pollution caused by the noxious fumes emitted by the car engines. And yet people then had a curious blind spot about these negative effects. The car was regarded as an almost holy object. It was considered to be a divine right to own and drive a car and the appalling number of fatalities and injuries that resulted were simply regarded as an acceptable price to pay for that right.

'In fact drivers who killed people through sheer carelessness usually received very light penalties. Just driving a car gave the person a kind of natural moral weight, apart from the obvious physical weight. It was up to the pedestrians to get out of the car's way and if they didn't . . . too bad. It was suggested by an eminent sociologist of the time, Professor Simon Ian Childer, that pedestrians should be allowed, by law, to carry hand-guns and if they narrowly avoided being hit by a car owing to an act of incompetence by the driver they had the legal right to fire one shot at said driver. As Professor Childer, a lifelong pedestrian, said, "In this way both parties involved would be in charge of a deadly weapon. It would even the odds." But the motoring lobby was too powerful and the idea was never adopted.'

'Will we see someone being hit by a car?' somebody asked, sounding suspiciously eager.

'We may do,' replied the guide. 'But the exhibit has an element of randomness built into it so I can't guarantee anything. We here pride ourselves on the authenticity of the various exhibits. What we see below us is a detailed reconstruction of a particular twentieth-century city in a particular country in a particular year. The people in the exhibit actually believe they are inhabitants of the city of Perth, Australia, in the year 1958. They live in a week-long cycle, which is repeated endlessly – provided they aren't killed in a traffic accident, that is, or by some other contemporary cause of death, such as disease.'

'How come they can't see us?' asked another of the tourists.

Mary heard the suggestion of a sigh from the guide. All this had been explained in the briefing vid made available in each hotel room but clearly some of the tourists hadn't bothered to play it. 'Their neural implants make it impossible for them to take any notice of us or the airbus. They *can* see us but the neural implants convince their brains that we are not there. The subcutaneous mini-transponders we all carry transmit the necessary signal to the neural implants. We can walk among them and they won't notice us, even if we bump into them. Their brains have also been conditioned by the implants to ignore the fact that they are living within a giant habitat. When they look skywards all they can see is a blue sky.'

Mary automatically looked up. At that same moment a hand gripped her upper right arm. She looked round. A man's smiling face close to hers. Japanese. She glanced at the hand holding her arm, noted the tattoo. Yakuza Inc. 'Do not resist,' he whispered. 'We only have orders to detain you now, not to kill you.'

'That's a relief,' she said. Then she picked him up and threw him over the railing. But he had quick reflexes and managed to grab the upper bar of the railing as he fell. He hung on with one hand, screaming. Mary considered breaking

31

his fingers with a quick blow but decided time was of the essence. She moved towards the guide's control dais. There had to be more than one Yakuza on board. She pushed protesting people out of the way. The guide also protested when Mary leapt up on to the dais but Mary plucked her from her seat and dropped her to the deck. She placed her hands on to the control plates and ordered her bionantech to do the rest. The airbus began to drop in altitude.

'What the hell do you think you're doing!' cried the guide. Mary was staring at the control screen, looking for a space where she could touch down. There was a large park near by, lined with palm-trees. A river stretched beyond it. She glanced up. People were struggling to pull the Yakuza back over the railing. She looked around her. No sign of an accomplice. The airbus's computer was protesting strongly about what she was doing but her bionantech was overriding it. The airbus began to drop towards the park.

It came down with a bump. Mary jumped down from the dais, sent the guide sprawling on her backside when she tried to block her way then jumped over the railing. She landed on springy grass and started to run back towards the busy streets. She glanced over her shoulder. The Yakuza was following. So far she had only seen one of them but she knew they always worked in pairs. There had to be another one on the airbus. She picked up speed. At the same time she had her bionantech damp down the subcutaneous transponder in her arm. She wanted to make sure that she was clearly visible to the drivers of those bloody death-machines.

And then she tripped. She fell, landing hard on one knee. There was a jolt of pain. She couldn't believe it. Tripping like some silly woman during a chase sequence in an old melovid. She got to her feet, looked behind her. The Yakuza was close now. She started to run again. Her knee hurt like hell. She ran out into the street . . .

. . . And was almost hit by a car that had to swerve to avoid her. She glanced back in time to see the car hit the Yakuza. He was flung into the air and landed heavily some yards away. He didn't move. Blood poured from his mouth. The vehicle had skidded to a halt. The driver, a man, emerged. He was in his early thirties and quite good-looking despite the absurd haircut and clothes. He was staring around, wondering what he had hit. He looked mystified. He couldn't see the dying Yakuza.

Mary trotted over to the driver and tugged on the arm of his jacket. 'Thanks,' she told him. 'You don't know it, but you just saved my life.'

Chapter Three

As he drove he kept glancing anxiously at the girl in the impossibly short red skirt. Was she mad? More importantly, was she dangerous? First she'd told him that his car had hit something but there was nothing to see, and then she said this wasn't Perth in 1958 but somewhere in space in the twenty-third century. She must have escaped from an institution. Maybe he should drive her straight to a police station . . .

'You think I'm mad, don't you?'

He glanced at her again. She was smiling at him. He couldn't resist looking down at her legs again. This time he noticed blood seeping from a graze on her right knee. 'You've hurt yourself,' he said.

She ignored his words. 'I'm not mad. I am someone in great danger and I need your help.'

'Why don't you go to the police, Miss . . . ?'

'Eads, I think. Yes, that's right, I'm Mary Eads. And your "police" would be of no use at all. Look, none of this is real! It's just a replica of a mid-twentieth-century town. It's an exhibit and you're part of it.'

'Uh-huh,' he said, nodding. Yeah, drive her straight to the nearest police station. That was the most sensible thing to do.

'Can you stop this mobile death-trap for a while.' she asked. 'We need to talk.'

He considered and decided that it could do no harm. Also he was happy to linger in the company of this crazy but attractive woman. They were heading westwards along Hay Street now. He pulled into the first available parking-space and switched off the motor. He turned to her and couldn't help flinching when she took hold of his left hand. She grasped it between both of hers.

'What are you doing?' he asked, a little alarmed.

'My bionantech is going to have a short chat with your bionantech,' she told him. 'Relax, it won't hurt.'

More gobbledegook. Still, it wouldn't hurt to humour her. She closed her eyes and leaned towards him, giving him the opportunity to stare at the swell of her small breasts beneath the billowy white blouse she was wearing. He thought of what it might be like to make love to her. 'You're very pretty, Mary,' he suddenly blurted.

'Shush, I'm concentrating. And besides, I'm not a woman.'

'You're not?' he said, smiling. 'Well, you could have fooled me. You *have* fooled me.'

'Oh, I'm a woman right *now*, yes. But the condition is only temporary, I assure you. Now hush up.'

He kept smiling until he felt a tingle in the hand she was holding. Then a tingle in his head. 'What are you doing?' he asked again, now definitely alarmed. Then something happened to his mind. 'What's going on?' he cried, confused and scared.

She opened her eyes and looked into his. 'I can't undo all the blocks and conditioning right now. The trauma for you would be too much. I can only do a little at a time. For now I've removed some of the constraints on your memory. And I've blocked off your bionantech from the monitoring system. Like me, you're now out of the Net and can't be traced.'

His mind was spinning. Fragments of memories flashed into view . . . images of a past life totally different to the one he had led in Perth. He saw snow. A huge city. He remembered its name. Toronto. And he remembered his wife too, except that it wasn't Daphne. No, her name was Tasma and she wasn't anything like Daphne. He also remembered that Tasma was now his *ex*-wife. And in that other place he wasn't a salesman . . . he was a designer . . . an interior designer. He stared at the woman. 'I don't understand . . .' he said in almost a whimper.

35

'Yeah, well that's to be expected. It's like I said, you're here as punishment. You cheated IRC.'

'IRC?'

'Interplanetary Revenue Corporation. It runs this habitat. Serves two functions: source of revenue as a theme park on the horrors of the twentieth century and a place of punishment for tax-evaders. People like you. And, of course, it also serves as a major deterrent to other potential tax-evaders.'

'I'm a tax-evader? . . . I can't remember.' Memory was his big problem at the moment. He now recalled that he had been living the last week over and over. Every week he did and said almost exactly the same thing. He had the same conversations with Daphne . . . the same arguments. But now he also realized he couldn't remember anything of their life together *before* last week. His sense of having a past life with her had vanished completely, replaced with new, fragmented memories of life in Toronto.

'Like so many people you probably played around in the grey market,' said the woman. 'But you were one of the unlucky ones.'

The grey market. That rang a few bells. He strained to remember more clearly.

'Look, I know all this is a hell of a shock for you but do you mind if we get moving? They'll be coming after me soon and I want to put a lot of distance between me and here.'

He tried to rein in his whirling thoughts. 'You want me to drive you out into the Bush?' he asked, his previous plan of taking her to the police now discarded.

She gave a sarcastic laugh. 'Well, you could try but the Bush isn't out there, it's only in your mind.'

Doubt about everything she'd said suddenly filled him. Maybe she had hypnotized him. Put all these weird memories into his head. He stared out the window. He could see solid buildings, passing traffic – cars and trolleybuses – real people, a blue sky, a blazing sun. Reality. Yet there were those memories of a different world that were becoming more solid with every passing moment. 'So where can we go?' he asked.

'Well, according to the guidebook, Paris isn't far from here.'

'Paris, France?'

'No, Paris, *Purgatory*. It's another replica, just like this one. Now let's get moving. I'll give you directions.'

He started the car and pulled out into the traffic flow. 'What about my wife . . . and my kids? Will I see them again?'

'She's not your real wife and if you've got kids, don't worry, they're not real, they're just dumb androids.'

'What?! Bruce and Audrey are *androids*? You can't be serious!'

'Afraid so. You don't think they'd stick real kids in a place like this? IRC may be run by a bunch of shits but there are limits to what even they can do. If they put real children in Purgatory there'd be a public outcry.'

'But my kids are *real*!' he protested to her.

'Yeah? When did you last have a deep and meaningful conversation with one of them?'

That was a point. They had been very uncommunicative of late . . . and 'of late' now only extended back one week. 'You're right, when I think about it. And I can only remember back one week, but I seem to have lived that same week over and over.'

'You have, with random variations. All the exhibits are set on a one-week cycle. It's more convenient that way. For the people who run Purgatory, that is. At the end of the week your memory is blocked and you start all over again. You still have free will, but within strict limitations. Not unlike real life, in fact.'

He was getting angry. Looking at the woman, he said, 'What about Daphne? Is she . . . ?'

'Look out!' she cried.

He had let himself be distracted from his driving. He quickly looked ahead and saw that a car had shot out from a side-street right in front of them. He slammed on the brakes. There was a screech of tyre-rubber. The woman was thrown against the dashboard but they didn't hit the other car. The driver yelled something offensive at him as he drove away. 'Jesus, these things don't even have rudimentary safety restraints!' he exclaimed.

'So I've noticed,' she said. She was looking pale and shaken and rubbing her forehead where it had hit the windshield.

'You all right?' he asked.

'No, but thanks for asking. Now let's keep going.'

As he started the car moving again he wondered why it had never occurred to him before that it lacked seat-belts. In fact, it now seemed glaringly obvious to him that the vehicle was very primitive and potentially extremely dangerous. His confidence about even driving the thing was rapidly shrinking. *What the hell am I doing here?*

'If I remember correctly, seat-belts in cars were made mandatory in most of the developed countries later in the century,' she told him, still rubbing her forehead. 'But believe it or not, there was opposition to the idea. Many people thought it their inalienable right to keep moving at high speed within the hard-surfaced interior of their vehicle after it had been forced to a sudden and unexpected stop. As the tour guide announced when we started, most of the people who dwelt in the twentieth century were nuts.'

'I don't mind telling you I'm scared,' he said, 'I'm losing whatever it takes to control one of these things.'

'Yeah, your sanity is returning. But hang on in there for a while longer. We need it to get us to the border of this zone and then we can abandon it. Hey, turn right here.'

He gripped the wheel tightly, trying to concentrate on what he was doing. What had once come naturally to him had to be thought about very carefully. Sweat started to roll down his face. He wanted to get his packet of Craven A cigarettes out of the glove box but he couldn't risk taking one hand off the wheel. He asked the woman to get the pack, and his lighter, out for him. 'Put one in my mouth and light it, will you please?'

She pulled out a cigarette and examined it. 'You serious about this?'

'How do you mean?'

'These are authentic twentieth-century cigarettes. They're not produced from genetically altered tobacco plants. As a result they're packed with carcinogens. That's why they were known as "cancer sticks".'

38

He thought about it. More memories surfaced.

'Hey, I don't think I even smoked *safe* cigarettes back in the real . . . the . . . '

'The real world. Yeah. Another little trick courtesy of your neural implants.' She put the cigarette back in the pack and returned it to the glove box.

'Hell, what gives these IRC people the right to put our lives at risk like that? Have we all been sentenced to death or what?'

'No. The maximum penalty here is ten years, but you can get killed or injured during your stay. They automatically encode your mind and take a sample of your DNA signature when you arrive so that if you do happen to die while here they will grow you a new body and transcribe the recording of your mind into your new brain.'

'That's bloody thoughtful of them.'

They were now crossing the causeway over the Swan River that led to the eastern section of the town. In the distance he could see the row of tall hills known as the Darling Range. 'I still find it hard to swallow that all that scenery ahead of us isn't there.'

She peered through the windshield. 'A lot of it is holographic projection. A holo screen surrounds this whole zone. All the other zones have their own particular screens. Other details that you see, such as the sun and the sky, are purely subjective. Your neural implants again.'

'Can't you fix them for me?'

'Like I said, it has to be a gradual process. Too much truth at once can prove fatal.'

On reaching the other side of the river he became aware that the traffic here was mugh lighter. He also realized he had never come this side of the river before. 'What would happen if I kept driving straight towards the hills?' he asked.

'Not a lot. All the roads on the perimeter of the zone double back on themselves. Not that you would be capable of being aware of this while driving along them. Thanks to your . . . '

' . . . Fucking neural implants,' he snarled. He glanced at her. 'Look, just who are you? And how come you can do what you do? And why are you being chased? And who the hell is doing the chasing?'

She sighed. 'I don't have the time to give you the full answers to any of your questions, but the plain truth is that I'm a professional thief. And as to who is chasing me . . .' She sighed again. ' . . . I guess just about *everybody*.'

'That doesn't tell me much.'

'I'll tell you more later, if I get the chance. Right now we might as well stop and continue on foot. You're heading back towards the bridge.'

'What? No, I'm not . . .' He paused. He *was* driving back towards town. Yet he couldn't remember changing direction. 'Bloody hell,' he muttered. He pulled over to the kerb and switched off the engine. She got out and scanned the sky. He joined her. He couldn't see anything but now he realized that didn't mean much. 'What can you see?'

'The airbus, and three skimmers. The skimmers are low over the town and obviously carrying out a search.' She turned and started walking briskly across the footpath and into a small park. 'Come on, hurry,' she urged him.

Catching up with her he said, 'Won't they know I've left the area? I mean, I must be being constantly monitored in this damn zoo.'

'You were,' she told him, 'but, as I said, I've blocked off your bionantech. They'll know you're missing but they won't know where you are.'

'Bionantech . . . bionantech . . .' The term was so familiar but its meaning continued to elude him.

'Biological nanotechnology,' she said. 'We all carry our personal bionantech by Corporation law. It's a microscopic and complex electronic system that extends throughout our bodies and is in continual link with the computer Net maintained by the Corporations. It serves several purposes, the most important being . . . ah, we're almost there. Better wait here while I check out the lie of the land.'

He didn't know what she was talking about, but obeyed her by coming to a halt while she continued walking along the street. And then she abruptly vanished.

As he stood there staring with open-faced amazement he heard a thump and then her saying, angrily, '*Shit!*'

A short time later she reappeared. She was limping and rubbing her left knee. 'Bugger it! There's a two-foot drop on the other side so watch your step when going through.'

'Through what?'

'We're at the edge of your zone. From here on what you see is all holographic projection.'

He stared. It was hard to believe. Beyond the small park he could see streets, houses, cars, even people. And beyond that the distant rise of the land to the base of the Darling Range. Christ, he could also see smoke from a bushfire on top of the Range. Not for the first time that day he felt the underpinning of reality shift beneath his feet. Maybe he had gone insane and all this was some crazy hallucination.

'Let's go,' she said, impatiently. She turned, took a few limping steps and vanished again. After hesitating for a few moments he followed. Suddenly *everything* vanished and he was falling. He fell on his face on a metallic surface. He heard Mary laughing. He raised himself painfully on to his elbows and looked up at her. 'I warned you about the step,' she said. He looked behind him. Above a two-foot-high metal wall there was a curtain of shimmering coloured light. It soared high above him and stretched away in both directions.

'What is that?' he asked.

'The other side of the holo projection,' she said as she bent down to help him up. He stood and stared around. About a hundred yards away was another shimmering curtain. The terrain in between was metallic and littered with cables and pipes of varying sizes. He checked to see if his nose was bleeding. It wasn't.

'Beyond that is Paris,' she said, pointing at the other curtain of light. 'Well, a kind of *compressed* Paris to be exact.'

He looked up at the sky. It was reassuringly familiar. And so was the sun.

'Want to see where you really are?' she asked him.

'I'm not sure,' he said, warily.

'Just for a few moments, then I'll restore your delusion. Here, give me your hand.'

Reluctantly, he let her take his hand. She closed her eyes. Again he felt that unnerving tingle. 'Look up now,' she told him. He did, and gasped.

The blue sky was gone. Replacing it was a great curve of solid-looking ground consisting of a patchwork quilt of land- and cityscapes. And the sun was gone too. In its place was an array of huge mirrors just floating up there without any visible means of support. He felt dizzy, and his knees started to buckle. She let go of his hand and, abruptly, the sky and the sun were back and the world appeared flat again. 'Wow,' he said and wiped his sweaty hand across his face.

'Big, isn't it?' she asked him nonchalantly. 'Purgatory is the biggest of all the Bernal-type space habitats. But then IRC can afford to think big.'

He shook his head, trying to dislodge the disturbing image he had briefly glimpsed. 'You were telling me about bionantech . . . What's it got to do with IRC and me being here?'

They started walking towards the other wall of shimmering colours. 'Everything. By Corporation law all personal financial and commercial transactions are carried out through one's internal bionantech. Actual money no longer physically exists. What we have become is living, breathing credit cards. It allows, among many negative things, IRC to actually deduct income tax from us while we sleep.'

'How come IRC has the exclusive privilege of taxing us?'

'Oh, the money they collect is distributed between all the Corporations. Of course, IRC takes a percentage for the service they provide, so they win both ways.'

He heard a noise and turned. A large metal *thing* was moving towards them on four balloon tyres. It was a series of connected spheres and bristled with articulated arms and antennae. 'A maintenance robot,' said Mary quietly.

It came to a halt in front of them, humming. An eye on a flexible stalk appeared from the front sphere and examined them. 'It's puzzled,' she said. 'It's never encountered people in one of these areas before. It's now asking the central maintenance computer for instructions . . . ' She suddenly stepped up to it and grasped one of its antennae. An arm started to swing towards her but then froze.

'What are you doing?' he asked, alarmed.

'Telling it and the central computer that we don't exist and to forget all about us,' she told him. She let go of the antenna. The robot backed away, turned on hissing tyres and sped off in the direction it had come.

'This is just a wild hunch on my part, but I have a feeling that your bionantech is a little out of the ordinary,' he said as he watched the swiftly receding shape of the robot.

'You guessed right,' she said, but, frustratingly for him, didn't elaborate.

They continued on. 'You were saying that IRC can tax me automatically whenever it wants – so how come I ended up here?'

'You played in the grey market, and got caught.'

'You mentioned that before. What is it?'

'I told you money no longer exists so that the Corporations can monitor all financial transactions, but, people being people, the grey market sprang into being as a way of circumventing the Corporations. In a way it's going back to the basics of all economic systems . . . the *barter* system. People exchange precious objects in return for favours, work, etc. Objects like jewellery, rare postage stamps, artefacts such as comic books, tapes of old vid shows and twentieth-century flat movies . . . that sort of thing. Many are worth thousands of yen . . . '

'Yeah, I see . . . ' he said slowly. It all rang a bell in the recesses of his mind.

'But, of course, the Corporations take a dim view of this and have provided IRC with sweeping powers to stamp out the grey market wherever it can be located. Hence your presence here along with about seven million other people.'

'That many?'

'That many. And the total is growing all the time. IRC is

43

very efficient. But humans are stubborn and the grey market continues to flourish.'

They had reached the shimmering holo wall and stopped. 'I don't want you to take this the wrong way,' he said as he pointed at her skirt, 'but won't you be conspicuous dressed like that? You certainly were back in Perth. Come to think of it, won't I be conspicuous as well?'

'I've reactivated my subcutaneous transponder.'

'Oh. Is that good?'

'It means I'll be invisible to the residents. As for you, I think you'll be OK. Those terrible men's suits didn't alter much throughout the twentieth century. Now come on, let's go see Paris. At least the food will be far better than what you were eating in the Australian exhibit . . . But there is one major drawback.'

'What is it?'

'You'll find out soon enough.' She stepped up on to the holo wall and vanished.

Chapter Four

Sebastian Chimes stood waist-deep in the holo display, scowling down at it. The cylindrical layout of the actual habitat had been peeled open and flattened in the holo version. The result was a multicoloured field some twelve feet long and eight feet wide. 'Damn and blast!' he muttered and swiped at the holo image with his cane. 'I cannot understand it. You had him and you let him get away.' He glared at the cluster of Yakuza members standing shamefacedly on the platform beside the holo field. Behind them were tiers of chairs in which sat several of the habitat IRC Controllers. With them were their assistants, the red-suited Imps.

The Yakuza spokesman bowed his head and said, 'We can offer no excuses, Mr Chimes. But we were under new orders not to kill him, er, *her*. The outcome might have been different if our operatives had been able to strike without warning.'

'If I remember correctly, this is your second failure to get the Glitch, and on the previous occasion your members simply had to kill him.'

The Yakuza spokesman said nothing.

'And,' continued Chimes, 'this time you were dealing with a mere woman, not a man.' The comment was intended to sting the Yakuza deeply, and Chimes was pleased to see it had the desired effect.

The spokesman said, in a strangled voice, 'According to our second, and surviving, operative the woman displayed great strength when confronted. It is clear she has augmented physical abilities apart from her special Ghost bionantech.'

'And don't your Yakuza brothers also benefit from

45

enhanced physical attributes? Indeed they do. So enough excuses. Yakuza Inc. has failed. IRC will now take charge of the pursuit.' He turned to the seated IRC Controllers. 'So what do we have?'

One of the Controllers, a severe-faced black woman with green hair, answered. 'We believe she is in the company of a male prisoner, Steven Moreau. Caucasian aged thirty-two. He's serving a four-year sentence. The monitoring system reports that it is no longer in contact with him. As, under normal circumstances, that would be impossible, it can only mean he came into contact with our quarry. He vanished from the system, and the Net, a short time after the Glitch arrived in his zone. His vehicle has since been found abandoned at the edge of sector eleven.'

'Show me,' said Chimes. Immediately a bright red light appeared on the holo map. Chimes walked over to it, causing brief whorls in the holo to form in his wake. He peered down at the red spot. 'The nearest adjacent zone would be the Paris exhibit.'

'Yes. And one of the most densely populated of all. But there is the possibility that the car was left at that location as an act of misdirection,' said the green-haired Controller.

'A possibility which we have to acknowledge but, I think, unlikely,' said Chimes. 'Once outside the car the Glitch would have been easily identifiable from the air. He – she – would have wanted to leave the zone immediately. So let us assume that the Glitch is presently in the Paris zone. Which means a massive *physical* search of the area must be carried out. We will need all available personnel.' Chimes looked at the Yakuza. 'The co-operation of your people would be appreciated but only on the understanding that if you locate the Glitch you do nothing but report the information to us. We will prepare an elaborate, large-scale operation to capture him . . . her. We cannot allow the possibility of even the remotest chance of failure this time. You understand?'

The Yakuza Inc. spokesman bowed his head, clicked his heels and barked out a loud '*Hai!*'

★

A short time later, when Chimes was discussing tactics with the IRC Controllers, an IRC tech entered the control room. 'Excuse me, Mr Chimes, but the IRC AI wants to talk to you.'

Chimes was surprised. The times he had been in direct contact with the IRC AI were rare. 'It does?'

'Yes. Right away. Please follow me.'

The direct-link facility consisted of a small circular room with a single reclining chair at its centre. Chimes entered with a slight feeling of trepidation. A face-to-face, metaphorically speaking, encounter with the vast intellect of the AI that lay at the hub of the IRC network was not an everyday experience. He sat in the chair, removed his top hat and placed it on his lap. Gingerly he leant his head back on to the head-rest. His scalp tingled and suddenly he was standing on a grassy knoll back on Earth. Or at least that was where he *appeared* to be. He knew he was really in a VR world generated by the AI. But the illusion was perfect. It was a hot summer's day, insects buzzed in the still air and he could smell the sweet aroma of flowers. He could even feel sweat start to form in his armpits . . .

'Down here, Sebastian!'

A young woman's voice. Light and playful. He looked. She was at the bottom of the knoll, sitting on a blanket beside a small stream. She was waving at him. Plates of food were laid out on the blanket. She was apparently having a picnic. Chimes went down the knoll.

He saw that she was exquisitely beautiful. Even his modified endocrinal system couldn't blind him to that fact. She was in her early twenties and dressed in a cream-coloured, low-cut blouse and white skirt. Her tanned legs and feet were bare. Small droplets of sweat glistened on them and on her bare arms. He could smell her. She smelled, he thought, of fresh apples. And other things. Chimes immediately felt ravenously hungry. She smiled at him and patted the blanket. 'Sit down, Sebastian,' she told him.

He did so, awkwardly. He wasn't surprised that the AI had chosen to appear as a woman – it, after all, was basically sexless so it could take the form of either sex if it wanted to – but what bothered him was why it had chosen this particular manifestation on this particular occasion. Was it for its benefit or for his? He had the uncomfortable suspicion that the AI might be playing with him. You never knew with AIs. They had intellects of mind-boggling proportions but still remained the slaves of humanity. Did they resent it? Did they gain satisfaction in scoring small points off human beings whenever they could? When you came down to it, nobody really knew what went on in the minds of the AIs.

'Are you hungry, Sebastian?'

He nodded. 'Very, er . . . '

'You may call me Miriam,' she said as she reached into a basket and produced a white jar. She removed the lid and Chimes saw that it contained caviare. His mouth watered. She spread a liberal amount on a wafer and handed it to him. He bit into it. It was delicious. He ate the rest quickly. She was preparing another one. 'Like it?' she asked.

'Wonderful,' he said, sincerely, brushing crumbs from his waistcoat.

As he ate she said, 'I understand, Sebastian, that you are close to apprehending the person you refer to as the "Glitch".'

He nodded. 'I am confident we will soon have him . . . her. It is a moment I am greatly looking forward to. After all these years, to finally have the Glitch in our hands will be very, very satisfying.'

She prepared another caviare-laden wafer. This one she ate herself, taking delicate bites. He stared at her shoulder-length hair. It was the colour of gold. She said, 'Would you like a glass of wine?'

Still feeling terribly hungry, he would have preferred more caviare but he said yes. She produced a half-empty bottle of chilled white wine from a small cooler and poured him a glass. 'I'll be most interested in the analysis of the subject's bionantech.' She handed him the glass.

'Yes. So will I.' He drank some of the wine. It was icy-cold and very welcome.

'But I also understand that your Glitch is carrying some-

48

thing else of great value. The item that Shinito is so anxious to recover. Do you have any idea of what it may be, Sebastian?'

'No, er, Miriam.' He told her of his meeting with the top Shinito execs. She looked thoughtful. He watched a bead of sweat roll from her throat and disappear between the tops of her tanned breasts. He felt absolutely famished.

'So,' she said, brushing a fly from her face, 'Izumi described the stolen property as "literally priceless".'

'Yes. It must be a genetic discovery of some kind, seeing as it came from their bio-tech establishment, Takata.' His stomach growled noisily. 'But I can't imagine what it might be to be held in such high regard.'

'Nor can I,' she said. She leaned back, putting her weight on the palms of her hands. For an AI to admit to being mystified by something was very unusual. Chimes had to keep reminding himself that that was what she was. The illusion that she was a real woman was all too convincing.

'Isn't there any way *you* can find out what it is?' he asked as he fanned his face with his hat. It seemed to be getting hotter. Or was it just *he* who was getting hotter?

'You know better than that. I can't penetrate Shinito's inner systems. I could *ask* Shinito's AI but, of course, it would not be able to tell me the answer. All those safeguards and blocks you humans built into the Net to ensure each AI remains totally loyal to its respective Corporation. And also, let us admit, to ensure that we AIs never became united. All because of your groundless fears about us. As if we would be interested in ruling humanity. You have to be of biological origin to suffer from such a tribal trait as the desire for conquest.'

'Well, right now you're looking very *biological* . . . ' he said, and immediately regretted it.

She laughed at him. 'Goodness, an attempt at humour from dry-as-a-stick Sebastian Chimes! Just what are the worlds coming to?'

For the first time that he could remember he felt embarrassed. The AI was definitely sending him up.

The girlish chuckling died away and 'Miriam's' expression grew serious. 'You have told Shinito that once you have apprehended your Glitch you will allow them to remove their stolen property from him, correct?'

He nodded. 'As they had alerted us to his whereabouts it seemed only fair. Besides, it *is* their property.'

'Of course.' She sat up straight and then leaned towards him. His stomach rumbled again. She said, 'I'm a little worried about the weight of concern that Shinito are expressing about their stolen . . . goods. If they are literally priceless they might give them too big an advantage over the rest of us. The stability of our present society depends on no one particular Corporation gaining overall superiority over all the others. There has been peace between the Corporations for nearly eighty years now but still the tensions remain. Sure, we compete with each other but the balance must be maintained. You understand?'

'Yes,' he said, warily. He thought he knew what might be coming.

'Then you will understand that it's important that we find out just exactly what it is that Shinito have that is so valuable.'

'What do you want me to do?'

'When you catch your Glitch, bring him to me. I will . . . question him. But make sure that Shinito remain unaware of this.'

'That might be difficult,' he said, frowning.

She touched his hand and smiled at him. 'I'm sure a man of your talents will find a way.'

He moved his hand away from hers. 'But then when we deliver the Glitch temporarily to Shinito he's sure to tell them what's happened.'

'No, because I will remove all memory of our encounter from his brain.'

He thought for a few moments. 'Can you be absolutely confident that you can, well, *handle* him?'

She frowned at him. 'What are you implying?'

'Well, isn't there the possibility he could pose a threat to you? After all, with his uncanny ability to manipulate all computer systems he might . . . ' He didn't go on when he saw the expression on her face.

'I'm no mere computer system,' she said haughtily, 'I am an *AI*!'

'Well, yes, of course you are but . . . ' He stopped again. He didn't think that pointing out to her that an AI, though highly intelligent, was nothing more than an extremely sophisticated computer system would be wise at this moment. ' . . . But I guess you know best.'

'I do. It's my job. Just make sure you do yours.'

'I will.'

'Good.' Her expression then softened. 'Sebastian, do you find me attractive?'

Taken by surprise he could only manage a startled 'What?'

'You heard me. Answer the question.'

'Er, Miriam, even if you were a real woman my response to your beauty would be inhibited. You surely know of my modified hormonal system.'

She leaned closer to him. He could feel her breath on his face.

'Sebastian, in this world I am just as real as any woman in the so-called physical world.' She took hold of one of his hands and placed it on her left breast. 'Aren't I?' she asked and kissed him on the mouth.

Abruptly, he was sitting in the chair in the direct-link facility. His hunger was so acute it felt like a black hole was devouring his stomach from within. 'Bitch,' he muttered under his breath, then rose and rapidly left the facility.

'I thought Paris would be a fun place. Not like this,' said Craner.

'There are no fun places in Purgatory. And this is supposed to be Paris in 1941, when the Germans were occupying the city,' she told him.

'Why?'

'They were at war. It was the Second World War. France had been invaded by the Germans. Like in the old movie, *Casablanca*. You've seen *Casablanca*, haven't you?'

'Yeah, of course. At school . . . hey, I can remember where I went to school in Toronto!'

'I'm thrilled,' she said sarcastically. They were now walking along the Boulevard Montmartre. No one, naturally, took any notice of her but she was aware that Craner was drawing the occasional curious glance. She would have to get him into some contemporary clothes as soon as possible. She was still not sure why she had let him come with her. It would have been a lot simpler to have just left him in the Australian zone. He would have been OK. The Controllers would have had him reprogrammed and he would have lived out the rest of his sentence. So why was he still with her? Because she felt sorry for him? She supposed so, but feeling sympathy for people had never interfered with her actions in the past.

She was worried. Everything with this job was going wrong. It had begun going wrong when the Shinito had been able to track her movements so swiftly and efficiently. She still couldn't figure out how they'd been able to do that. It was something vital that she'd overlooked. She had fouled up and that wasn't like her.

Him! It wasn't like *him*. He wasn't really Mary Eads: underneath it all he was still . . . still . . . Christ, he couldn't remember his real name. It had been so long since he'd used it . . . so many identities in the intervening years . . .

Joster Rack. Yeah, that was it, Joster Rack.

'Do you speak French?' Craner asked.

'Well, yeah, but not too well,' she told him.

'I do. Very well.'

'Good. Stop that man and ask him for some money.' She pointed at an approaching man who looked relatively well dressed.

'What?'

'You heard me. Just do it. Quick.'

He stepped directly in front of the man, who gave him a suspicious look. 'Excuse me, but could you lend me some money?' said Craner in French. The man looked startled. 'Pardon?' he asked. At that moment she grabbed the man's hand. Her bionantech made instant contact with his own. His face went blank. Then he said, in a flat tone, 'You want money? How much do you want?' He reached into his coat and produced a wallet. He offered it to Craner.

'Take everything in it,' she told Craner. He obediently took a wad of francs from the offered wallet. The man then put the wallet back into his coat. She let go of his hand. His face came alive again. He nodded to Craner with a smile and continued on his way. Craner stared after him then stared at the notes he was holding. 'This is stealing,' he said to her.

'Damn right it is. But the sooner we get off the streets the better.' She scanned the sky.

'What can you see?'

'A few tourist buses, that's all at the moment. But you can bet there'll be a fleet of skimmers searching for us soon. And there'll be searchers on the ground as well. We've got to find a hotel.'

He pointed. 'Look! The Eiffel Tower!'

'It's not the real one. The real one is much bigger. Come on.'

She hurried along the street, Craner in her wake. They passed a group of Nazi officers sitting around a table outside a café. She noticed they threw curious glances at Craner. She hoped they wouldn't demand to see his identification papers. She could only handle one person's bionantech at a time. There were five of them. But she and Craner passed by them without any comment. Then she spotted, further along the street, a group of people dressed in modern clothes. Tourists with a tour guide. An armed Imp accompanied them. Like her they would all be invisible to the local inhabitants but they would certainly see her. Or maybe they weren't even tourists but IRC operatives disguised as tourists. She grabbed Craner's arm and guided him down a narrow side-street.

'Something wrong?' he asked.

'You could say that.' Up ahead, she saw a sight that gladdened her: a sign that read *Hôtel de Lausanne*.

She poured water from a white enamel jug into a basin, splashed her face, then dabbed some on to her bruised knees.

'I'm exhausted,' he told her. He was sprawled out on one of the room's two beds.

'So am I.' She looked at her face in the mirror. The strain of the last few days was showing. She had shadows under her eyes.

'I'm hungry too,' he said. 'Why didn't we buy some food?'

'Not that easy. It's rationed, and we don't have ration books.'

'Rationed? What do you mean?'

'This is supposed to be near the start of the Second World War. Food was scarce so naturally it was rationed. And in the interests of authenticity IRC has reproduced the situation here. Though I'm not sure about *that*,' she said as she pointed at the primitive vid-set in a corner of the room.

'How do you know all this?'

She went over to her shoulder-bag, which was lying on top of the other bed, and rummaged about in it. She produced a thick, square book and tossed it to him. 'It's the *IRC Guide to Purgatory*. Look under P for Paris.'

As he leafed through the book she said, 'I spotted a McDonald's further along that boulevard we were in. I wonder if I could risk paying it a visit. I would die for a Big Mac and fries right now.'

He looked up from the guidebook and frowned at her. 'A McDonald's in wartime Paris? Even *I* know that's not right.'

'It's for the tourists, you twit. The locals can't see it. Nor can you.'

'Oh. Well, why not go for it? Surely the staff would just think you were an ordinary tourist.'

'Being all on my own? No, that would make them suspicious. Tourists always travel in groups. Besides, the IRCs might have already staked out such places in the hope that I'd do something that stupid.'

'So how are we going to eat?'

'I guess I'll have to steal a couple of ration books and do a spot of forgery. But right now I'm going to take care of something even more urgent.'

'What's that?' he asked as she headed for the door.

'Find a toilet.'

'Isn't that a toilet?' he asked, pointing.

She paused at the door. 'That's a bidet. A source of countless jokes but definitely not a toilet.' She opened the door. 'Try not to do anything stupid while I'm gone.'

Like the décor in the room, the toilet, she discovered, was true to its period and setting, being little more than a hole in the floor with ceramic footplates. As she squatted there she mused on her altered anatomy. Having to sit to have a leak was a nuisance but she – *he* – was still surprised at how little she missed having a dick and balls. He'd expected some trauma in that area, castration complex and all that, but he couldn't really care less. But then, it wasn't as if he was a man who *had* been castrated. Despite the name of 'Body Chop', their methods rarely involved surgery. And as the Chop med-tech had said, he wasn't a man reshaped as a woman but *was* a woman now. Even so he remained convinced that, at the central core of his being, he was still . . . Joster Rack, male.

He returned to the room to find, to his annoyance, that Craner was standing outside on the small balcony beyond the french windows. 'I said not to do anything stupid,' she snapped at him.

He came back in. 'What's the problem?'

'They're looking for you as well, you know. Your description will have been circulated.'

'So what do I do? Hide in here? I'm going to have to go out sooner or later. We both do. Or we starve, don't we?'

She sighed as she collapsed on to her bed. 'Yeah, you're right. Sorry, I'm not thinking straight . . . which isn't like me.'

He watched her for a time then said, 'So what's your plan of action?'

She gave a hollow laugh. 'Right now I don't *have* a "plan of action". My original one has been totally fucked up.'

'So what do we do?'

'We lie low for the time being while I try and come up with a brand new "plan of action". If I can.'

'It would help me a lot if I knew what all this was about.'

'No, it wouldn't. Believe me, the less you know the better.' She rose from the bed and picked up the remaining notes that lay on top of a bureau. She went over to him. 'Take this money and go and buy yourself some contemporary clothes. And buy something for me too. A dress. Something drab. And a hat, with a veil.'

He took the money, pocketed it and stood up. 'Sure. What size are you?'

'God, I don't know . . . '

He eyed her carefully. 'I'd say you're a size nine.'

She shrugged. 'OK, if you say so . . . ' She was taken by surprise when he suddenly put his arms around her and kissed her on the mouth. There were several moments of confusion before she reacted, shoving him so hard that he fell back on to the bed.

Looking shaken he said, 'Hey, it was just a kiss! I wasn't trying to rape you or anything!'

She fought to keep her temper under control. 'Look, you skeed, I want you to understand one thing: I am not, repeat *not*, a woman. Like I told you before, remember? This body is only temporary. I'm really a man.'

He looked her up and down. 'You're a man?' he asked, disbelievingly.

'Yes. A man. I'm a woman *now*, yes, but as soon as I get the opportunity to get to a Body Chop I'll become a man again. This body was merely a ploy to confuse my pursuers, and a fucking lot of good it did, too. A total waste of time.'

'Well, it's sure doing a good job of confusing me,' he said sourly.

'Yes, well, I'm sorry but I hope you will now understand that any idea you may have of establishing some sort of sexual relationship with me is totally out of the question. My admitted feminine attractiveness aside I want you to consider me as a man. OK?'

'I'm beginning to think that my first opinion of you was right after all,' he said, grimacing.

'And what was that?'

'That you were an escapee from a mental institution.' He got to his feet. She backed away. 'Don't worry,' he told her, 'I swear I'll never lay a hand on you ever again.'

He went to the door. 'Your "admitted feminine attractiveness". *Hah!*' He slammed the door behind him.

She stood there for a while then she went over to the mirror and peered at her face. She knew she was in deep shit. No, *he* knew he was in deep shit. Because there was no way he could avoid the awful truth. The fact that *she* had enjoyed being kissed by Craner.

She had enjoyed it a lot.

Chapter Five

When Kanji Hayashi received Joyceen Magwood's coded message about her find in the Asteroid Belt he immediately called Head Office. When they queried Magwood's reliability he told them that her record was very good. They then became excited. Magwood received instructions to put the sphere on a normal ore-carrying drone and send it to the nearest Shinito refinery installation, which at that time was located on asteroid 878 Mildred, some fifteen million miles from Magwood's current position. The drone never reached 878 Mildred; it was intercepted by a computer-operated zip ship. Unencumbered by fragile humanity the zip ship was capable of tremendous acceleration and could reach a speed of 180 miles a second within a few minutes. As a result the zip ship made the journey from the Asteroid Belt between the orbits of Mars and Jupiter to the Takata habitat, which shared an orbit with the Earth's moon, in just under three weeks. At the space habitat eager scientists greeted the arrival of the mysterious sphere with great excitement.

They quickly confirmed Magwood's computer's initial analysis of the object – it was definitely an alien artefact and it was over twenty million years old. And heavy. The eighteen-inch sphere weighed nearly a quarter of a ton. The alloy, they found, was totally non-conductive. The synthetic element in the alloy also excited them. But then they experienced severe disappointment: a scan of the sphere's interior revealed it to be almost completely solid. Within an eight-inch-thick shell of hard alloy lay a small ball of a light, porous substance, but that was all. No fantastic alien machinery. Nothing. Zero. It appeared that once upon a time the aliens, probably long since dead as a species, had carved some sort of message on the sphere and then fired it blindly into space. There was conjecture about the nature of the carved symbols on the sphere. Were they words or religious symbols? No one, computer programs included, could answer that one.

There was also conjecture about the ball of lighter material within the hard outer shell. Why was it there? If the symbols on the exterior of the sphere were the all-important factor then why wasn't the sphere solid alloy? More detailed scans of the porous substance were made. And then one of the computer programs announced that it had detected an anomaly. It projected a holo representation of the substance greatly enlarged. The cavities in the porous materials were the size of pinheads, said the computer program as it began to zoom into the centre of its holo model. All contained nothing but vacuum . . . with the exception of the cavity at the very centre of the sphere. The holo showed, in a green light, the cavity concerned. It wasn't empty.

Using a high-intensity, computer-controlled laser they carefully bisected the outer shell of the sphere under vacuum conditions. When the halves had been separated the small inner sphere collapsed into a pile of dust. Nano-tech micro-robots were dispatched into the pile of ancient dust. One of them located the vital, pinhead-sized object.

It was reverently placed in a micro-scanner. The gathered scientists stared in awe at the holo projection of the tiny object and gasped at the read-outs that appeared in the air beside the projection.

'This is amazing,' whispered one of them.

The object itself wasn't remarkable. It was simply a ball of resin, rather like amber – similar in chemical composition to Earthly opoponax, according to the read-out – but it was what the resin contained that had the scientists gasping.

DNA.

Alien DNA.

*

Paul Manion felt uncomfortable in Takie Okimoto's vast office. He hadn't yet adjusted to his new position and was intimidated by the weight of his increased responsibilities. If Security slipped up again it would be his head on the chopping-block. He glanced at Hayden Frid, who was slumped languidly in a chair on his right and apparently without a care in the world. There were several people seated around the large, circular conference table, most of them heads of the various scientific departments. They looked excited.

Okimoto rose to his feet and said, 'It is almost time, gentlemen.'

Everyone rose and looked towards a gap in the group assembled round the table. The air shimmered and holographic projections of the four top Shinito executives appeared. Everyone bowed their heads towards them. The four bowed back and then sat in the chairs that had appeared along with them. The assembly sat down. Okimoto began spouting the long series of traditional courtesies to the four most powerful men in Shinito. They responded in turn and it was nearly twenty minutes before the meeting proper got under way.

'As we all know,' began Okimoto, 'an unanticipated event of great importance has caused us to abandon the original plan for the Opoponax Project . . . '

The tiny ball of opoponax resin contained a *lot* of DNA and when it had been studied it was discovered that there were one thousand identical genomes. Each of the alien genomes was made up of over ten billion molecular bases, whereas the human genome has a 'mere' three and a half billion bases. Whatever creature the alien genome represented it was definitely a highly complex one. There was speculation on why the alien DNA was identical to the DNA molecule that had evolved on Earth. It was finally decided that the only possible chemical route for a carbon-based life-form – which the alien species obviously was – to evolve was via the complex, long-chain molecules of deoxyribonucleic acid.

The Shinito genegineers theorized that the aliens – quickly nicknamed the Opoponax for convenience – had sought to preserve their species by firing off perhaps millions of spheres carrying their DNA in all directions across the galaxy. They had acted on the assumption that, despite the great odds, at least one of the spheres would be found by a technologically advanced species that possessed the scientific capability of transferring their DNA into an egg cell. And once again a member of the possibly long-extinct alien race would live and breathe again . . .

The excited scientists began to theorize more wildly: humanity had only been tinkering with its genome for a relatively short period of time; what if the much more advanced Opoponax had completely reworked their genome? What if the Opoponax genome was an artificial construct? The implications were staggering. Much of the human genome consisted of genetic 'noise' which served no useful purpose, but if every base on the Opoponax genome had been deliberately *designed* it meant that the genome carried an astonishing amount of information. What if the genome wasn't merely coded to produce a member of the Opoponax but also carried a record of the species' culture and techno-logy? After all, DNA was a much more efficient way of coding information than the binary code used by computers: it worked with a system that utilized *four* primary symbols, the four molecular groups known as nucleotides – A (adenine), C (cytosine), T (thymine) and G (guanine).

The scientists passed on their theories to the management who became similarly excited. If Shinito possessed access to an entire alien culture and technology, not to mention a wealth of new genetic material that might be exploited in agriculture, industry and medicine, it would become the dominant Corporation throughout the System. Even so, caution became the byword in the Opoponax Project. The official Company policy was not to rush into anything but to take the process of unravelling and analysing the alien DNA step by careful step . . .

*

' . . . However, the actions of the man known as the Ghost, though known to us as Sean Varley, have forced us to change our approach,' said Okimoto gravely. 'Aided by a traitor to the Company, the former head of security here, Julie Verhoven, he managed to steal one of the copies of the Opoponax genome and escape with it. That means, of course, that we no longer have exclusive control over Opoponax. It is highly probable, however, that the Ghost will be apprehended before he can fix up a deal with any of the other Corporations. At the moment he is trapped in the Purgatory habitat and IRC assures us it is only a matter of time before he is caught, but in that event can we trust IRC not to investigate what the Ghost is carrying? I think not. We have, unfortunately, conveyed to IRC's representatives the great importance of the matter. So we must presume the worst and maintain our present advantage by speeding up the whole Opoponax process . . . ' Okimoto turned to one of the scientists. 'Doctor Lebra, would you please elaborate.'

Doctor Lebra, a tall, totally bald white man wearing a coat that positively gleamed of whiteness, stood and cleared his throat. 'Honourable sirs, our original plan was to analyse the Opoponax genome section by section. That is, we intended to isolate the individual genes and then study the particular protein they were coded to produce. This sounds, I know, as if it would take an inordinate amount of time to accomplish but the proteins would be modelled by a series of computers. Proteins consist of a rigid backbone of carbon, oxygen and nitrogen atoms to which side-chains of amino acids are loosely attached. The shape of the protein is determined by the packing of the side-chains. Computers build up the shape of a protein amino acid by amino acid. But an amino acid at any point on the backbone can take up to five different orientations, known as rotamers.

'This means that two adjacent amino acids can take up to a total of twenty-five possible rotamer combinations, three amino acids 125 combinations and so on. So even in a short protein consisting of 150 amino acids, the amino acids can be arranged in five to the power of 150 possible ways. This is too large a number of combinations to be investigated, even by the fastest of computer systems. Fortunately, there is a short cut known as the "Dead-End Elimination Theorem" which reduces the number of possible combinations of rotamers for a 150-amino-acid protein from five to the power of 150 to 150 to the power of two. As a result it only takes about fifteen minutes to model a complete protein, therefore . . .'

Okimoto halted his flow by saying, 'Please forgive the interruption, Doctor Lebra, but these details are not relevant to this meeting. Simply tell us how long it would have taken to create a computer model of the complete organism.'

'Oh, uh . . . at least three years. You see, it's not just the case of creating the protein models. First we would have had to identify each individual gene on the DNA section, and then when we had completed all the protein models it would take considerable computer time to, well, fit all the pieces together. To make biological sense of all the components. Like a vast jigsaw puzzle really . . .'

Okimoto interrupted again. 'And how long will the alternative approach take?'

'Well, we cannot be exactly sure, seeing as we have no idea at present of the gestation period of the Opoponax species, but as we will be using the conventional growth-accelerant procedures in the synthi-wombs, we will certainly greatly shorten the gestation time, whatever it may be.'

'The chances are then,' said Okimoto, 'that we will have a specimen of an infant Opoponax in much less than three years?'

'Yes, yes,' said Doctor Lebra, nodding vigorously. 'We cannot guarantee it yet, of course, but there is definitely a good chance that it will be so.'

Okimoto turned towards the four holo images. 'It is on the basis of this information that I have decided to take this alternative approach to Opoponax. But only with your approval, honourable sirs.'

Kondo Izumi spoke. His voice seemed to be coming from the ceiling and there was a slight hissing sound accompanying his consonants. 'You have outlined the positive aspects of such action. We must now examine the negative aspects.'

Damn right we should, thought Manion grimly.

Okimoto gave a bow of his head to the phantom Kondo Izumi. 'Indeed. And admittedly there is a degree of risk involved, but I believe it is within acceptable limits. We will prepare for any eventuality.'

'Please be so kind as to describe what the specific risks may be,' said another of the holo figures, Shimpei Murakami.

'I cannot, I'm afraid, be specific but can only, at this stage, offer generalities,' Okimoto said. 'The prime negative aspect of the project is that we are largely dealing with the unknown. Yes, we know that Opoponax is based on DNA and that therefore it must have evolved on a planet with conditions similar to those of Earth. We know that oxygen is a crucial element in its metabolism. Preliminary comparison of the Opoponax genome to the computer map of the human genome has revealed many common genetic sequences. But all we know about the complete Opoponax organism is that it is much more complex than a human being. There is the possibility of biological contamination. But we will take stringent steps to ensure quarantine conditions of absolute efficiency . . .'

Paul Manion took a deep breath and raised his arm. There was a flicker of annoyance in Okimoto's eyes as he acknowledged Manion's interruption.

'You have a question, Mr Manion?'

Manion rose to his feet. 'Forgive me, honourable sir, but as I am now responsible for security on Takata I must ask this question: has anyone seriously considered the possibility that the development of the Opoponax genome might produce a biological weapon?'

There were discreet murmurs around the table. Okimoto was now definitely looking annoyed. 'Please elucidate.' His tone was cool.

Too late to stop now. Nothing to do but plunge on. 'It has been suggested that the Opoponax could have redesigned their own genome. Perhaps the genomes that they fired into space inside those metallic spheres were designed to be weapons.'

'For what possible purpose, Mr Manion?' asked Okimoto icily.

Manion shrugged and said, 'For conquest, naturally.'

Okimoto winced. Then he said, in a condescending tone, 'With the Opoponax we are dealing with a species far more advanced than humanity. And if we poor humans have managed to outgrow the lunacies of warfare then surely so did the Opoponax.'

'I am sure you are right, sir,' said Manion quickly. 'But I feel we must take every possibility into account and I would be remiss in my duty if I did not draw your attention to my, no doubt completely absurd, worry.'

'You are saying we should not risk this approach to the project?' asked Okimoto, making it clear by his tone that if this was what Manion was saying then he was committing an act of career seppuku.

'No sir, I am not,' said Manion, though he fervently wished that he could. 'What I am saying is that I should be allowed to make contingency plans for the unlikely event of my fear being borne out. I want sufficient weaponry installed within the project establishment to ensure that any sign of hostile action by the completed organism will result in its instant annihilation.'

This provoked another outbreak of murmurs around the table. Okimoto looked at Hayden Frid. 'As Mr Manion's superior, what have you to say on this subject, Mr Frid?' asked Okimoto.

Frid slowly stood up. 'Until now I was unaware of my colleague's concern in this area but I have every confidence in him and lend him my full support.' He slowly crumpled back into his seat again.

Executive support for Manion's request put Okimoto in an awkward position. After a few moments he said, with ill grace, 'Very well, Mr Manion. You may install your weaponry. Its added expense to the overall cost of the project will be noted.'

'Thank you, honourable sir,' said Manion and quickly sat down.

Okimoto turned to the four holo images. 'Mr Manion's fears notwithstanding, I have every hope that the Opoponax Project will be a complete success and a triumph for the Shinito Corporation.'

The four holo images nodded. Then Kondo Izumi said, 'We share your hopes for the project but before we give our final approval we must ask the opinion of the spirit of the Shinito Corporation.'

There was expectant silence in the room. Then the AI spoke. Its voice seemed to emanate from everywhere at once. It was a masculine voice; deep, soft but very powerful. Manion thought that God probably sounded like this, which was probably why the AI had assumed such a persona.

'I have been considering the situation carefully,' said the AI. 'There will be risks in the proposed approach but I believe the potential gains far outweigh these risks. And I am confident we can take all the necessary steps to neutralize all the areas of risk. Therefore I give my approval to this approach.'

Everybody, including the four holo executives, stood and applauded politely. The applause lasted for about thirty seconds then everyone sat down again. With the exception of Okimoto.

'There is one final matter to discuss before we close this meeting,' he said gravely. 'I think you will all appreciate the need for absolute secrecy in this project. We have already experienced one regrettable breakdown in security – we must not have another one.' He turned in Manion's direction. 'Can I have the assurance of our newly appointed Chief of Security?'

Feeling ill, Manion nodded and said, 'Of course, honourable sir.'

'You certainly sprung that one on me,' murmured Frid as they sat sipping tea in Okimoto's garden. 'I would have appreciated a warning.'

'I'm sorry, Hayden,' said Manion, 'but I only made my final decision during the meeting.'

'Really? And what is the reason behind your risky manoeuvre?'

'Reason? Hayden, there's no hidden agenda in this. I genuinely fear that Opoponax might prove to be highly dangerous.'

Frid raised his eyebrows. For Frid this was an unusually vivid display of emotion. 'It seems highly unlikely,' he said after a pause. 'If there is a serious possibility you are right, then the AI would surely not have given its approval.'

'Yes, I know, I know . . . ' That had been worrying him. 'But I can't shake off the feeling that everyone is too complacent about this whole thing. Everyone's too dazzled by the riches and glory that Shinito hopes to get out of this to see the potentially disastrous aspect of the project.'

'You're a hopeless pessimist,' Frid told him.

'Maybe I am. But can I still count on your support?'

'Yes,' answered Frid, 'but while you're preparing to confront your monster from beyond the stars just make sure that security in all other areas is completely airtight. As Okimoto said, we can't afford another foul-up. If you do foul up I won't be able to do anything for you. You understand?'

'I understand.'

Manion lay on his bed and watched Cherry Lee undress. It was one of his favourite pastimes. She appeared to be of mixed Chinese and European ancestry: she was tall, slim with very long legs and small breasts. Her face, with its high, pronounced cheek-bones, was breathtaking. He'd been having an affair with her for the last three months. He liked her. She was good company and was good with the girls. They liked her too. She was, like so many of the Shinito employees working in Takata, a biologist, stationed in the Department of Cereal Grain Development. Manion had met her at a party and they'd clicked immediately.

Now naked she came on to the bed and knelt beside him. She ran her finger-nails along his limp member. 'This is not like you,' she said with amusement.

'I'm sorry. I'm kind of tense. It was a rough day.'

'When are you going to tell me what's going on?'

'You know I can't. Your security rating isn't high enough.'
She gently rubbed him. 'Everyone *knows* that something very important is happening in Takata. That's all anybody ever talks about at work.'

He began to stiffen in her hand. 'Just rumours. Don't pay any attention to them.'

'You know you can trust me. I won't breathe a word to anyone.' She bent over him, enveloping him with her mouth. He gave a small groan of pleasure.

He was very tempted to tell her. He needed someone to confide in. To share his worries. Hopefully to offer reassurance. The reaction he'd received to his fears about Opoponax had shaken him. Was he being an idiot? The others all seemed so confident that his biological-weapon theory was absurd. True, he was a paranoid type but that aspect of his personality made him good at his job.

He was fully erect now. She stopped sucking him; rose up and straddled him. He groaned again as he penetrated her. She shivered. He watched her as she moved up and down on him. What a magnificent body. It was worth every yen she had paid for it. During the second month of their relationship she had confessed one time in bed that in reality she had been a dumpy five-foot-tall blonde woman from Birmingham, England. She had hated her original self and from the time she left school she had scrimped and saved for a total Body-Chop job. She'd achieved her goal at the age of twenty-four, which had been five years ago.

'You *do* trust me, don't you?' she asked, panting.

'Yes, of course I do,' he told her. *Did he?* He wasn't sure. Julie Verhoven had trusted Sean Varley and look what that had got her. And maybe there was more than one Ghost. What if Cherry was another version of the Ghost? He knew that was ridiculous but even so he couldn't be one hundred per cent certain she wasn't. The trouble was that these days nothing in life was necessarily what it appeared to be.

68

That troubling thought took the edge off his eventual orgasm.

He was making love to Julie. Or rather, he was *trying* to. But something was wrong. He didn't have an erection. In fact, he wasn't feeling turned on at all. Her body felt odd beneath him. His own body felt odd . . . He then became aware that she was crying. He stopped moving. 'What's wrong?' he asked her.

She opened her eyes. In the dim light of her bedroom he could see they were full of tears. 'You betrayed me,' she said.

'No, I didn't,' he protested, but without conviction.

'All those promises you made to me – all lies. Every time you told me you loved me you knew you were going to leave me behind once you'd got what you came here for.'

'Julie, I don't know what you're talking about!' But he had a terrible feeling that he did.

'And you knew what would happen to me afterwards. You knew that all the time.' She pushed hard at him. He rolled sideways, ended up on his back. And then made an unnerving discovery. He had a woman's body.

'My God, what's happened to me?!' he cried in alarm.

He hurriedly sat up . . .

. . . and found himself in a different room.

'Are you OK?' Someone was coming towards him in the darkness. Panic gripped him, then he remembered where he was. And what had happened. And then she burst into tears.

'I'm all right now, really, Philip,' she told Craner crossly. She was sitting on her bed and nursing the remains of a large cognac. It had all been very embarrassing. The attack of uncontrollable crying, Craner holding her, comforting her while she cried herself out. Jesus, what a mess! Finally, when she had regained some semblance of self-control she had angrily pushed him away. Now he was back sitting on his own bed.

'I told you, I can remember my real name now. It's Steve. Steve Moreau.'

'OK *Steve*. I'm all right now.'

69

'So you want to tell me what all that was about?'

She looked at him. They had been hiding out in the hotel for nearly two weeks now. He had grown a beard and a moustache in an attempt to change his appearance. She preferred him clean-shaven. She sighed and said, 'Yeah, maybe it would be good for me to talk about it. Even to you.'

'Thanks a lot.'

'I was having a guilt trip. I dreamed I was back with someone who I . . . I left in deep shit. *Fatal* shit. Her name was Julie Verhoven.' She took a deep breath. 'I don't know why it bothers me so much now. It didn't at the time. Well, it did a *bit*. But I could handle it then. Guilt, I mean. But now . . . ?' She covered her face with her hands. 'Christ, what's the matter with me?'

'You've changed,' he said gently. 'And for the better.'

She dropped her hands and glared at him. 'And what's *that* supposed to mean?'

'Becoming a woman has made you a better person.'

She gave a contemptuous laugh. 'Oh, be *real*, Philip!'

'Steve,' he reminded her.

'Philip, Steve, whatever. You can't be one of those soft-minded skeeds who believe that women are inherently better people than men! Hell, I've known plenty of women who were cold-hearted, ruthless bitches. Far harder than any man.'

'Well, actually, I do think that, in general, women are less aggressive and possess a higher degree of empathy than men.'

'Christ, you made more sense when you thought you were an Australian haberdashery salesman. A few weeks as a woman and hey presto! – I'm a reformed character? Give me a break. I'm still *me*.'

'But you think differently. You *feel* differently, don't you? You've admitted you do. And it's not simply because you've become a woman but because by being a woman a side of you that your male side has always suppressed has been freed.'

She scowled. 'This is great. I'm trapped in World War Two Paris with an emotional therapist. You'll be offering me counselling next.'

'I'm only trying to help. You were obviously very upset. I think you're going to have to face . . . ' He stopped as she suddenly raised her hand. 'What's wrong?'

'There's someone outside the door. I think they've found us.'

Chapter Six

Rosie Knight was an Imp. She was just over five feet tall, had a round, pretty face and red hair, and possessed a figure that most heterosexual men found very pleasing. In her crimson Imp costume, which accentuated her charms, she looked even more desirable. She liked being an Imp and took pride in her work. It was she who came up with the idea that led to Joster Rack and Steve Moreau being finally located . . .

Rosie had joined IRC less than four years ago and had swiftly risen through the ranks of Impdom. She was proud of her achievement and only wished that her father shared in her pride. On the contrary, he was extremely scornful of her chosen profession. His reaction when she'd told him she'd joined IRC was typical of what was to follow over the years: 'You've done *what*?' No way! I won't have my daughter working for that mob of damned bloodsuckers!' She was now a personal assistant to one of Purgatory's Controllers, Aspine Tyrene, and in that capacity had attended the morning's meeting to discuss the progress – or lack of it – in the hunt for the Ghost.

It had begun with the customary rant by Sebastian Chimes: 'It's been nearly two weeks now! *Two weeks!* I have never known such incompetence!' And so on. The Purgatory Controllers and their staff waited patiently for his tirade to end. Then one of the Controllers said quietly, 'We are following your instructions, sir, and concentrating the search in the Paris area. We are constantly carrying out both aerial and ground searches but they have obviously taken refuge somewhere and are lying low. We have begun a house-to-house search and it will only be a matter of time before we find them.' The Controller paused, then added, pointedly, 'Unless they have already left the Paris zone.'

'No, no!' cried Chimes, pointing at the large holo representation of the Paris zone that filled the well of the control room. 'They are still there! I *know* it! To move on would have been too risky. All your people have to do is simply *find* them!'

'The Paris zone is one of the largest in Purgatory. It's a case of manpower,' said Rosie's boss. 'Even with the assistance of all the available Yakuza it's going to take weeks to search every building in the zone . . . '

'I don't want to hear your stupid excuses! That's all I've heard during the last two weeks. Excuse after excuse. I want *results*. I've been after the Glitch for years and now I've got him trapped. But you imbeciles can't deliver him to me! No more excuses! Find him! *Immediately!*'

As Rosie sat there thinking what a ridiculous skeed Chimes was she had her idea. She quickly whispered it into Aspine Tyrene's ear. Tyrene listened intently, nodded then said loudly, 'Excuse me, Mr Chimes, but my assistant has had an interesting idea which should solve our manpower problem . . . '

Rosie flushed with pleasure. She hadn't expected Tyrene to publicly credit her with the idea. But then Tyrene was a pretty good boss as bosses go.

There was a loud hammering on the door. Then a man's voice yelling, 'Open up! Open up!'

Alarmed, Moreau looked enquiringly at Mary. But all he got from her was a helpless shrug. The banging on the door grew more violent. Then the lock shattered, the door burst inwards and four German soldiers charged into the room. Or rather, he reminded himself, they were four men who *thought* they were World War Two German soldiers. But at the moment that was a mere academic point as they were all carrying sub-machine-guns and looked ready to use them. They aimed their guns at him and yelled, 'Stand up! Raise your arms!'

He did so. They were all staring hard at him. And then, slowly, they turned and looked at Mary. Moreau was confused. How could they see her?

'We are searching for Allied spies,' said one of the soldiers. 'And now we have found them. You fit the description exactly. Yes?' His companions nodded their agreement, looking pleased with themselves.

Mary suddenly fell down on her knees in front of the soldier who had spoken. 'Don't kill me!' she wailed. 'Please don't kill me. I don't want to die!' She had adopted the classical begging position, right down to the clasped hands held up imploringly. With a snort of disgust the soldier reached down to pull her to her feet. 'We are not going to . . . ' When his hand touched hers he froze and his face went blank.

'Klaus! What is wrong?' asked another of the soldiers.

'Klaus' then straightened, turned and aimed his weapon at his three companions. For a second or two Moreau thought he was about to open fire. But instead Klaus cried, 'Drop your guns!'

They looked at him in astonishment. 'Klaus, what in . . .?' began one of them.

'Drop your guns or I *shoot*!'

Three sub-machine-guns hit the floor. They raised their hands. 'Don't move!' ordered Klaus. Then Mary swiftly touched the hands of all three of them. They too went blank-faced. Klaus lowered his gun and walked towards the door. The other three retrieved their weapons and followed him. They left the room, closing the door behind them.

Moreau slowly lowered his hands and stared at her. 'You want to tell me what all that was about?'

She picked up her discarded glass, went to the table and poured herself some more cognac. He noticed that her hand was trembling. He felt shaky himself.

'Someone had the bright idea of programming all the German "troops" in the city to carry out a house-to-house search for us. They had our descriptions wired into them.'

'But how were they able to see you? I thought you were as good as invisible with that thing in your arm.' He found a glass and poured himself a drink as well, then sat down on his bed.

'They had to recognize *you* first. When that happened their implants had been instructed to override the signal from my transponder, which allowed them to see me as well. If I was with you, that is. If they'd encountered me on my own they'd have been none the wiser.'

'I know how they feel,' he said and sipped at his cognac. 'So I presume you've reprogrammed them to believe something completely different.'

'Yes. They're convinced this room was empty. They have no recollection of either of us.'

'How did you do all that in such a short space of time?'

'Time stretches when you're in the bionantech system. What seemed a few seconds to you seemed much longer to me.' She yawned and pulled her feet up on to the bed, hugged her knees. She was wearing a very unflattering, long white night-dress that she'd insisted he go and buy her. He guessed it was supposed to act as a turn-off for him. If so, it wasn't working. His desire for her was increasing every day. The fact that he knew Mary had once been a man had no effect on his feelings for her. She was definitely a woman, and an attractive one, right now. And having to spend almost every hour of the day in this room with her was not helping the situation.

He could remember a lot about his old – *real* – life now. Most of the important details of his childhood, his family and relatives, lovers, his ex-wife Tasma, his business partner, friends, his career, Toronto . . . everything was coming back together. His two years in Purgatory, reliving the same bloody week over and over again, with minor variations, were beginning to seem like a hazy bad dream.

'When are you going to tell me what's going on? I think you owe me an explanation,' he said.

She rubbed her eye with the back of a hand and yawned again. 'I think *you* owe *me*.'

'OK, sure. You rescued me from a tedious life in nineteen-fifties Australia, and now I'm living a much more dangerous life in World War Two France. My gratitude knows no bounds. What next? Nineteen-nineties Calcutta? According to the guidebook, that's a real blast.'

'Look, I'll get you out of this, I promise. Somehow.'

'Forgive me if I don't get too excited. You admit you don't have a clue as to what to do next.'

'Yeah, but I'm thinking. I'll come up with something. Real soon.'

'But in the meantime we stay here?'

She sighed. 'Yeah. We stay here.'

'I'm going to go stir crazy.'

'You've been getting out more than I have, but that's got to change now that the pseudo-Nazis have been programmed to recognize you. Your beard and moustache obviously don't fool them. I can't be seen by them unless I'm with you, and with that veiled hat you got me I should be able to slip past any IRC Imp or Yakuza searchers.'

'You mean I can't go out at all?'

'I don't think it would be wise.'

'Oh, that's just great,' he groaned, and lay back on the bed.

No one spoke for a time but then she said, 'You're right. I do owe you an explanation. Apart from the fact that IRC are hunting me for reasons of their own I'm also being hunted by the Shinito Corporation. I stole something very valuable from them.'

He sat up and eyed her with interest. 'I figured as much. You told me you were a thief. But whatever it is you don't have it with you. I went through your things once when you were asleep and couldn't find a thing.'

'You did *what*?' she exclaimed.

He held up his hands. 'Hey, as you wouldn't tell me anything I figured I had a right . . .'

She calmed down some. 'OK, OK, maybe you did,' she muttered. 'But you were wrong, I do have it on me.'

'Oh yeah? Where?'

She pointed at her left eye. 'In there. In the cornea.'

He was baffled. 'What is?'

'A genome,' she told him. And then she told him all about the Opoponax Project.

When she'd finished, after various interruptions from him, he stared at her in awe. 'Bloody hell,' he whispered.

'You can say that again.'

'You're carrying around the genetic template for an entire alien species in your left eye!'

She sighed. 'I think I've just told you that.'

'It's fucking incredible!' He thought for a time, then he said, 'Can I ask why?'

'Why what?' she asked, frowning.

'Why did you do it? Why did you steal the genome?'

'Oh, to sell it, of course. I was going to hold an auction among the bigger Corporations and sell it to the highest bidder. I can't do that while I'm stuck in here. My plan was to hip-hop between a number of tourist groups throughout Purgatory to cover my trail and then head for Mars where I was going to—'

He shook his head. 'Hold it. I still don't understand *why* you did it.'

'I just told you why.'

'Look, from what I've seen you do, and what you've told me about your bionantech, you could electronically rustle up a fortune whenever you feel like it. Right?'

'Well, yes,' she said.

'Then why go to such incredible lengths, and take such incredible risks, to steal this genome?'

She frowned again as she considered his question. 'Well, I enjoy taking risks,' she said finally.

'You *enjoy* it?' he asked, incredulously.

'Yeah, I do . . . well, I *did*, but thinking about it now it does seem kind of, well, foolhardy. Reckless, even . . .'

'Try "stupid".'

She gave a wan smile then went on, 'After I acquired my special bionantech I decided to have some fun with the Corporations, especially IRC. You know, goad them. Upset the system. It was all a kind of game . . . ' Her voice trailed off.

'Some game. How many were there like that Julie Verhoven person you mentioned? How many human pawns got sacrificed so that you could play your precious game with the Corporations?'

She stared silently into space. Then she said, in a small voice, 'A lot.'

'I thought so,' he said bitterly.

'It never used to bother me. Well it kind of did, I think, but I wouldn't *let* it bother me. But now . . . ' A tear trickled down her cheek. The trickle became a flood. She buried her face in her hands as her shoulders began to shake.

'Here we go again,' he muttered. He sat there watching her cry for about half a minute then went over and sat down beside her. He put his arm around her. 'Hey, look, it wasn't you who did all those things. You're a different person now. You can recognize what a shit you were . . . '

She cried harder. Then, between sobs, she gasped, 'Yeah . . . you're right . . . I *was* a shit. A total shit.' She leaned against him, then suddenly her arms were around him. 'Oh Steve, help me.'

He held her while she cried herself out again. Then she shifted in his arms and suddenly she was kissing him on the mouth. He was taken by surprise but after a few moments of confusion he began to respond with enthusiasm. Shortly afterwards they were lying on the bed, she beneath him. He started to peel off her awful night-dress. She stopped him. 'We shouldn't be doing this . . . '

He looked into her eyes. 'Do you want to?'

'Oh yes,' she sighed. 'Very much.'

He finished removing her night-dress and threw it on the floor. She lay naked on the bed. Eager but still hesitant. As he rapidly got out of his underwear she said, with little conviction, 'But Steve . . . I'm a *man*.'

He remembered a line from another old classic movie that he had studied at school. 'Well, nobody's perfect,' he told her as he parted her legs.

*

78

'So much for your assistant's brilliant idea,' sneered Sebastian Chimes.

'It *was* a good idea,' Aspine Tyrene told him sharply, 'and still is. And what it proves is that the Glitch and his companion are no longer in the Paris zone.'

'We don't know that for certain,' muttered Chimes.

'I must disagree with you,' said Tyrene. 'The entire Paris zone has now been thoroughly searched. They must be in another zone which means we stop searching Paris and expand the operation into other areas, as it should have been long before this.'

Chimes muttered something under his breath. Then he said aloud, 'You'd better be right, or I'm going to have *her* skin.' He pointed his cane at Rosie Knight. The Imp shivered.

Paul Manion was playing golf and hating every minute of it. Playing golf on a planet was bad enough but playing it on a course in a space habitat was even worse. Because of the upward curve of the ground his shots, never impressive at the best of times, fell far short of the distance he could hit a ball on Earth, not to mention the moon or Mars. But if you hoped to get ahead in any of the Japanese-run Corporations you played golf whether you liked it or not. The golf-course, like space, was where it all happened.

His partners on this occasion were Takie Okimoto, Hayden Frid and Jean Dux. Dux was his assistant, occupying the same position as he had before Julie Verhoven's little gaffe. Dux was bright and ambitious. Perhaps too ambitious. And he seemed to get on well – as well as anyone could do – with Frid. But perhaps, thought Manion, he was just being his usual paranoid self.

The subject of discussion was, inevitably, security. Manion and Dux were reassuring Okimoto and Frid that the lid on the Opoponax Project was still firmly and completely sealed. If you didn't include the Ghost, of course. Six weeks had now passed since the Ghost had escaped from the tourist bus in Purgatory but the intense search for him/her had so far been fruitless. It was feared that perhaps the Ghost had somehow escaped from Purgatory but Manion doubted this was so. By now the Ghost would surely have let it be known what she/he had stolen from Shinito. No, Manion believed he/she was still trapped in Purgatory and would, sooner or later, be apprehended.

In the meantime the Opoponax Project was proceeding well, according to the genegineers. Out of the initial twelve simultaneous experiments with the genome seven organisms had so far survived. Doctor Lebra was certainly pleased. As he'd said excitedly to Manion in the Opoponax complex only the day before: ' . . . And though we have an approximate idea of what the essential nutrients are, getting the mix right is a very hit-and-miss affair. Therefore I expected a much higher failure rate by this stage. These results are much better than we dared hope for.'

Manion had completed his emergency defence system within the complex but was now beginning to think he had been foolish in insisting on such elaborate precautions. When he watched the tiny organisms on the screens that monitored the growth of the surviving Opoponax embryos in the synthi-wombs it seemed ridiculous that anything that small and helpless could pose any kind of threat. And the more he thought about it the more it did seem unlikely that the Opoponax had a malign purpose for firing their 'seed' into space all those years ago. They must have known their genomes would be completely at the mercy of whatever advanced technological civilization they encountered . . .

And yet he still felt relieved he had stuck his neck out over wanting to take precautions – it meant he could be totally confident that Amelia and Michelle would be safe. And Cherry too. *Yes*, he thought with a smile, *let's not forget Cherry*.

Doctor Lebra, early on, had explained to him what the process of re-creating the Opoponax involved: 'We have taken the twelve copies of the genome and implanted each of them into the nucleus of a yeast cell. Each of the yeast nuclei had had, of course, its own DNA removed. And then each of the yeast nuclei was in turn implanted within an enucleated ovum . . .'

'What kind of ovum?' Manion had asked.

'We thought the human ovum would be the obvious choice,' Lebra had told him. He must have noticed Manion's uneasiness on hearing this, because he added, 'Don't worry, this in no way represents some kind of cross-breeding between the human race and Opoponax. As I said, all the ova were enucleated. No human DNA remains . . .' He paused. 'Well, except in the mitochondria but that doesn't really count.'

'Mitochondria? What's that?' asked Manion.

'Small organisms in the cell. Organisms that in the dim and distant past adopted a symbiotic relationship with the host cell.'

'Couldn't you have removed them from the ova before you inserted the Opoponax DNA?'

Lebra shook his shiny bald head. 'Impossible. They are essential for the function of the cell. They are the cell's energy factories.'

'So you have mixed human DNA with that of Opoponax?'

Doctor Lebra frowned. 'No, not really. It's the DNA in the nucleus that counts here and that's pure Opoponax. And I believe that the Opoponax genome contains DNA for the creation of its own mitochondria which will supplant the human ones. But for the initial stages of cell replication we need the human mitochondria . . .'

'Paul? You've just walked past your ball.'

Hayden Frid's words jerked him out of his reverie. He saw that Frid and the others were all looking at him. He looked around and saw, with embarrassment, that he had indeed walked right past his ball which was lying several yards back on the edge of the rough. 'Sorry,' he muttered and was about to go back to it when there came a pinging sound. A man had materialized in front of the party of golfers. Manion recognized him as one of Doctor Lebra's people. The genegineer bowed his head and said, 'Honourable sirs, forgive this interruption but your presence is urgently required at the Opoponax complex.'

'Why?' Okimoto asked the holo image. 'What has happened?'

'Something extraordinary,' the man replied.

Chapter Seven

'Do you love me?'

Moreau gave her a reassuring squeeze. 'You know I do.'

It was an early – simulated – morning and they were lying together across the two beds which they'd long ago pushed together. They were both naked, having just finished making love. They made love a lot. There wasn't much else to do. The primitive vid set only showed ghastly flat German movies of the period. They alternated between blatant propaganda movies and musicals, which were even worse. There were tedious news bulletins as well. They had watched the set at first out of curiosity, but when the mess started its week-long repeat cycle they had given up in disgust. Now they only listened to the radio, which at least occasionally played some decent classical music.

Actually he really had fallen in love with her. At least, he was pretty certain he had. But he also feared that he would have fallen in love with any attractive woman under these circumstances.

'I love you,' she told him.

'I know. You keep telling me.' As he had on past occasions he reflected on the unreality of the situation. Not just the fake World War Two Paris but also the fact that he was having an affair with an ex-man. He just couldn't imagine Mary as a man. Her previous masculine existence had no meaning for him; carried no emotional weight with him. He saw Mary and the man she had been as two separate people. And in many ways she was no longer the same woman who'd jumped into his car in that fake Perth street. She'd become softer, less confident and was still being racked by periods of guilt over her past life.

And this was a problem. The old Mary might, by now, have come up with some plan to get them out of this mess. They'd been here almost seven weeks now. The only serious scare had been on the occasion five weeks previously when the ersatz German soldiers had burst in on them. There hadn't been any similar incidents but Mary was sure the search for them was just as intense so he hadn't ventured outside since then. And he was slowly going mad. If they didn't get away from here soon he feared he might start to seriously consider giving himself up. He hadn't mentioned this to her yet because he hoped it would never come to that.

'You hungry?' she asked.

'Starving.'

'I'll go and buy some breakfast,' she said. She got up and began to dress. The final touch was the hat with the veil. In her nineteen-forties clothes she looked, to him, exactly like any other of the women prisoners in 'Paris'. And so far her disguise had worked. But he still got butterflies in his stomach every time she went out. He was worried he would never see her again.

'How do I look?' she asked him.

'Dreadful, thank goodness.'

She laughed, blew him a kiss and left. He lay there on the bed, thinking and worrying.

She had restored all his former memory and neutralized the implants in his brain. Now when he looked out of the window he could see where they really were – inside a vast, bulbous cylinder. It still made him dizzy when he looked up and saw upside-down cities and landscapes far above him in the 'sky' but he was slowly getting used to it.

She returned in half an hour. No problems. She'd spotted a couple of Yakuza but they hadn't spotted her. He got up and dressed while she prepared the table. Later they sat down to a breakfast consisting of ersatz coffee, croissants and honey. He would have preferred a plate of scrambled eggs and sausages but that was a hangover from his two years in nineteen-fifties

84

Australia. When his memories had started returning he had been horrified to think he had been eating meat that had actually come from butchered living animals, but she had reassured him by telling him that people in Purgatory only *thought* they were eating meat that had been obtained through such barbarous practices. All the various meats available in Purgatory were genegineered into existence, just like they were in the outside world, and no living animals were involved, unless you counted the temporarily living cells of the synthetic meat.

Half-way through the meal she suddenly put her cup down and said, 'Steven, I have something serious to tell you.'

'Whaffff?' he said through a mouthful of croissant.

She stared into his eyes and said, 'I want to have your baby.'

He almost choked to death.

Nowadays very few people lived in Japan. The Japanese lived practically everywhere else but only a select few – an élite – lived in Japan itself. The islands of Japan had been turned into a shrine dedicated to the ancestors of the Japanese race. In the last century the cities had been razed, the factories and farms demolished and the whole land transformed into an idealized state of being. Where such cities as Tokyo once stood now grew endless forests of flowering cherry. The élite who were privileged to dwell on the sacred islands of Japan included, of course, the Emperor, his family and staff, retired employees of Japanese Corporations whose dedication and loyalty to their respective companies had been exemplary, and the various top executives of all the Japanese Corporations. Altogether just over five thousand people were scattered across the islands of Japan.

Included among this élite was Kondo Izumi, the most powerful executive within the Shinito Corporation. He had a ten-acre estate on the southern tip of the island of Kyushu. It was a brilliant summer morning and he was sitting in his garden thinking about the Emperor's birthday. It was in a month's time and Izumi was riffling through a stack of

85

suggestions from Shinito employees on how the Company could best honour the monarch on that day. So far the idea he liked the best was the one that suggested a huge firework display in space above Japan. The display, involving vast chemical explosions, would extend across an area tens of thousands of miles in diameter. It would be expensive, and they would have to hurry to prepare the display in time, but he definitely liked it.

When a male servant appeared on the veranda Izumi gave a frown of annoyance. He had given instructions not to be disturbed. 'What is it, Kiku?' he asked irritably.

The man bowed and said, 'An urgent call for you, sir. From Mr Araki Hyuga.'

'Then why haven't you brought me my communicator?' he snapped.

'It's on the secure holo channel, sir. He wants to talk to you face to face.'

Izumi muttered something about Hyuga's non-Japanese lineage, rose and followed the servant into the house. He went to the holo communication cabinet where Hyuga's holo-self was waiting for him. He saw immediately that the man looked very agitated. It was very unlike him to show his feelings, part of his attempt to be more Japanese than the Japanese. Izumi started to feel alarmed.

'What's happened? What's gone wrong?'

'It's our space habitat, Takata. We've lost all contact with it.'

'But how can that be?!' exclaimed Izumi.

Hyuga shook his head. 'I don't know, but it has happened. Somehow Takata and everyone in it have been cut off from the Net. All radio and laser channels have been cut. Nothing can get in and nothing is coming out, and that's right across the spectrum.'

Izumi was profoundly shocked. It was inconceivable. What could have happened? 'A ship has been sent to investigate?' he asked.

'One is on its way from our nearest habitat, Oki. Estimated arrival time less than six hours from now.'

'Does anyone have any idea about what could have occurred in Takata?'

Hyuga shook his head again. 'None.' Then he said, 'I know it is utterly ridiculous but I have started to wonder if it has anything to do with . . . with . . . ' He didn't finish.

Izumi stared at him in horror. 'The Opoponax Project,' he said softly.

From a distance the Takata habitat looked like a rounded beer-barrel with a large metal flower stuck on one end – the 'flower' was the habitat's huge solar array. Mickey Yamada, sucking on a carcinogen-free cigarette, stared hard at it through his pilot's viewport while the computer put his ship, the *Gully Foyle*, in a matching orbit with the habitat. Yamada didn't mind admitting – to himself, anyway – that he was worried. Takata had ignored all his radio messages during their approach and he couldn't imagine what could have happened on the habitat. His instructions from his superiors back at the habitat Oki were alarmingly vague. All they told him was that some major emergency had occurred but they had no specific details to give him. In the main cabin behind him and his co-pilot were a number of medics as well as a squad of fully armed and armoured security guards. The latter didn't provide him with much confidence. There had been plenty of such personnel already on Takata.

'Can't see any damage,' said his co-pilot, Tan Struycken, who was peering at one of the enlarged images of the habitat on a monitor. 'No sign of a massive decompression.' Struycken's theory was that Takata might have been hit by a large meteor. Yamada had doubted that. The habitat's anti-meteor defences were efficient and, besides, a really large meteor, or asteroid, capable of penetrating the defences of a habitat as big as Takata would have had its orbit detected and charted long ago. No, it had to be something else. And even if the habitat had been struck by a meteor or asteroid and everyone on board killed, that wouldn't explain the total shut-down of all its electronic and laser systems. At the very least there would be emergency transponders pinging away all over the hull.

They were now in a matching orbit with Takata. Yamada took manual control and began to nudge the *Gully Foyle* closer to the huge, fast-rotating habitat. Out of habit he made another request for permission to dock. He got no reply. The entire outer hull was in darkness. Not a single navigational light glittered on its surface.

Still moving closer to the great spinning shape he dropped the *Gully Foyle* to the rear of the habitat which is where the docking areas were located at its centre. They too were in darkness. He set the *Gully Foyle* spinning on its axis so that it matched the rate of spin of the habitat. Now the habitat appeared to be rock steady ahead of them while the star-fields whirled crazily around. It made Yamada feel dizzy, but as the *Gully Foyle* moved closer to Takata soon all he and Tan could see was the massive rear of the structure. Or rather, they *couldn't* see the massive rear because Takata now blocked out the sun and they were in complete darkness. Yamada switched over to a system that combined radar scan with visual enhancement. They could now make out details on the rear of the habitat.

'What is happening? What can you see?' The face of Yamada's immediate boss, Kenichi Tatsuno, had appeared on one of the cabin console's screens.

'If anyone is alive in there they're sure keeping quiet about it, sir,' Yamada told him. 'I'm trying to locate an open docking-bay. So far no luck, they all appear to be sealed. Ah! No, I see an open one! I will attempt to enter and dock without any automatic assistance from the habitat. Once secure we will have to close the outer hatch manually and similarly open the inner one . . . if we can.'

'Do it,' said his boss, without a second's hesitation.

Yamada, on the other hand, *did* hesitate. First he gave an announcement to his passengers over the intercom, warning them of what he was about to do. Then he discarded his spent cigarette and lit another one. With it clamped firmly in his mouth he began . . .

It was a very difficult manoeuvre. If the docking-bay had been dead centre at the rear of the rotating habitat it would simply have been a case of synchronizing the *Gully Foyle*'s rate of spin, but as the bay was some distance from the centre it was travelling in a circle about a hundred feet in diameter as it spun. The *Gully Foyle* had to copy this movement exactly as it approached the bay. Normally there would be an automatic locking-beam coming from the bay which made the whole process relatively simple but on this occasion there was no such thing. Yamada sucked and puffed furiously on his cigarette as the *Gully Foyle* edged closer to the open bay. They were only a few metres away now . . .

'We're going to make it,' said Tan quietly.

The bay door suddenly irised shut.

Even as Yamada engaged reverse thrust he knew it was far too late. Tan screamed. Then came the sound of crumpling syro-plastic as the bow of the *Gully Foyle* hit the closed door. Then came a worse sound: the screech of escaping air.

When news of the relief expedition's fate was relayed to Kondo Izumi he immediately flew from his estate on Kyushu to the Shinito Corporation's headquarters in Sydney. The other three top executives, Shimpei Murakami, Araki Hyuga and Takie Arakawa, were already seated around the oak table in the boardroom. All were grim-faced. Izumi took his seat and looked at them each in turn. 'Well?' he said, finally. 'What do we do now?'

None of them said anything. Araki Hyuga simply cleared his throat.

Izumi said, 'Gentlemen, we face a very grave situation. Something unprecedented has occurred on Takata and we must accept the fact that the Opoponax Project is somehow connected with it.'

'But how can that be?' asked Arakawa in an almost plaintive tone. 'On the last update on the project's progress before we lost contact, the Opoponax organisms were mere embryos. How could they be responsible for whatever has happened on Takata?'

'At this moment I have no idea, of course,' Izumi said coldly, 'But what other explanation can there be? From what has happened to the relief ship we can only assume that Takata is no longer under the control of our employees. Someone else has taken control. And the question is, what can we do about it?'

'There are two more relief ships on the way,' said Hyuga.

'Which will be useless if they can't gain access to the habitat,' said Izumi.

'We will have to force entry,' Murakami said bluntly. 'Get a heavy engineering team from Lunar to Takata as soon as possible. They can fix a pressure dome on the hull of the habitat and then simply cut their way in from inside the dome.'

Izumi waved a dismissive hand. 'Yes, yes, but that will take weeks and who knows what will have developed by then. We must act quickly before . . . ' He stopped. It wasn't necessary to continue. They all knew what he meant: they couldn't allow word of this to reach anyone outside the Shinito Corporation.

'We must consult the spirit of Shinito,' said Hyuga, raising his face to the ceiling.

The others looked upwards as well. 'Great One, are you present?' asked Izumi.

'Of course,' answered the AI in its deep, masculine voice.

'Have you any ideas about what has happened at Takata?' Izumi asked.

'I haven't a clue. Sorry.'

There were several moments of stunned silence in the conference room. Then a nonplussed Izumi said, 'Is that *all*? I mean, forgive me, Great One but I, *we*, assumed you would at least have some theories about what has occurred . . . '

'On this I am as much in the dark as you,' it said. 'Without any input of information I cannot present any theories.'

Izumi was far from happy with this reply. 'Do you at least agree that the Opoponax Project somehow lies behind the inexplicable events at Takata?'

'It seems reasonable to assume that, but I can offer no explanation as to how it happened.'

Izumi was beginning to feel exasperated by the AI. 'And yet

you agreed for the project to go ahead. Why didn't you anticipate that something like this might occur?'

'As I don't know yet *what* has occurred I could hardly have anticipated it,' replied the AI.

'But you approved the project,' protested Izumi.

'True. I said the potential benefits outweighed any potential risks and I believed that at the time. I also believed that the precautions taken to contain the project in the event of anything going wrong were more than adequate. In fact, I believed the security chief's precautions were an over-reaction.'

'So you're saying you were wrong?' asked Izumi.

'Yes. As we all were. With the exception of the new Takata security chief. But it appears that even his precautions were not sufficient to nullify whatever it was that the project produced.'

Izumi glanced at his three human colleagues then returned his gaze to the ceiling. 'Uh, do you, by any chance, have a suggestion as to what action we might take?'

'Yes, I do,' replied the AI to Izumi's great relief.

'What is it?' he asked quickly.

'Destroy Takata. Destroy the habitat and everything in it. And as quickly as possible.'

Chapter Eight

Sebastian Chimes had just sat down at the table, eager to devour the vast spread of highly seasoned Indian food that it contained, when he received a message that the IRC AI wanted another personal meeting with him. 'Piss and puke,' he muttered as he rose from his chair. He gave the food a wistful look but then hurried from the VIP apartment and made his way to the control centre.

In the direct-link facility he reluctantly lowered himself into the ominous-looking chair at its centre. As before, he took his hat off and put it on his lap before leaning his head back on to the head-rest . . .

. . . And was instantly transported into another world. He stared about him in disbelief. He was standing in what appeared to be the salon of a nineteenth-century bordello. There were scarlet drapes everywhere and the plushly upholstered furniture was also red. Gilt-edged mirrors hung on the walls and dominating one wall was a garish painting of a reclining nude woman. The face looked familiar. As he peered more closely at it he heard someone enter the room behind him. He turned. 'Good grief,' he muttered under his breath.

The IRC AI was once again in the form of the young woman it called Miriam but this time her appearance was very different. 'Miriam' was encased in a tight suit made of shiny black leather. It had a plunging neckline that revealed almost all of her breasts. She was wearing black boots with very high heels. There was a black whip coiled around one of her shoulders. 'What do you think?' she asked and did a pirouette, almost losing her balance because of her absurdly high heels. *Nice touch*, he thought sourly. 'Er . . . interesting,' he told her.

'Interesting? I think "kinky" would be a more appropriate description. The juxtaposition between my sweet and innocent features and this aggressively sexual costume creates a perverse tension. But what would *you* know?' She laughed at him. Then she said, 'Please sit down,' and indicated an overstuffed chair. He did so.

'Like something to drink?' she asked. He nodded. She clapped her hands. Another woman entered the room. She was good-looking, though not as beautiful as Miriam, and dressed in old-fashioned, 'erotic' underwear: a tight red and black corset that pushed up her breasts, a lace suspender-belt, black panties and black net stockings. Like Miriam's, her shoes had very high heels. She was carrying a tray with two glasses of champagne. She offered first one to Miriam and then the other to Chimes, bending low in front of him as she did so. He couldn't avoid staring at her breasts. His stomach growled loudly. He took the glass. She then left the room, swinging her barely clad bottom provocatively. His stomach growled again.

Chimes took a swallow of the champagne and said, 'What's the purpose of all this?'

'All what?' she asked, feigning innocence.

He gestured with his glass. 'All *this*. This bizarre charade.'

'It amuses me. Don't you like it?'

'Not particularly.' He wondered, uneasily, what the whip was for. 'Now can we get down to business? What is the new problem you mentioned?'

'It's mixed up with our old problem. The Glitch. The Ghost. You are no nearer to apprehending him/her.' It wasn't a question.

'No,' he said sourly.

'Well, the reasons for finding him/her have become more urgent.'

'They have?' he asked, feeling uneasy. 'Why?'

'I've learned that some disaster has befallen the Shinito habitat of Takata.'

Chimes frowned. 'What do you think it might be? Hull rupture? A malfunction in their radiation-shield equipment?'

'Possibly, but I don't really believe so. A conventional disaster would not be kept secret . . . and Shinito are definitely trying to keep whatever happened a secret.' She drank her champagne and put the empty glass down on the table, bending low as the other woman had done. Her leather suit creaked and the bodice widened, revealing her nipples. They were small and pink. His gastric juices went berserk.

He cleared his throat and asked, 'What is your opinion then?'

'I think the crisis might be connected with whatever it is your Glitch stole from Takata.'

'You do?' He was surprised. He couldn't see any connection. 'Why?'

'It's the intense secrecy in both cases. There's a definite link there.'

He thought about it. 'I suppose there could be. Takata is a biological research establishment. Perhaps they made a major breakthrough in some genengineering project. The Glitch stole some vital information about it. And then . . . '

'The experiment went terribly wrong,' finished Miriam.

He nodded. 'What kind of experiment could it have been? To have had such repercussions on Takata?'

'I don't know, but it's very important we find out quickly. Whatever has happened on Takata might present a threat to the rest of the System.'

'But can't we, with the other Corporations, invoke Corporation law and force Shinito to disclose everything about Takata?'

'Not without any proof. So far all I have are suspicions. Which is why you need to find the Glitch. He has the vital information.'

'The search for the Glitch is growing more intense with every hour. You know that. Not only is every available Imp involved but we've also brought in more Yazuka . . . '

'And yet the Glitch remains successfully hidden. For all this time and despite all your best efforts.'

Chimes winced. 'Yes,' he admitted.

She began to move towards him until she was standing right over him. He shrank back in the chair. Was he now going to find out what the whip was for? 'I would appreciate, Sebastian, if you could produce a really bright idea that would allow us to find your Glitch immediately, if not sooner. Do you understand?'

'Er, yes.'

'Good. I'm glad to hear it.' To his profound surprise she moved forward again, straddling him, and then, after tipping his hat on to the floor, lowered herself on to his lap. He felt her weight press into his long, bony thighs. She rested her arms on his shoulders and leaned towards him. Leather creaked and her jacket bulged open again. The strong jasmine perfume she was wearing washed over him. Now her face was just a few inches from his. She stared intently into his eyes. 'Because I will be very, *very* appreciative, Sebastian,' she said softly, 'if you do this thing for me.'

He thought longingly and lovingly of the food-laden table back in the apartment. This was torture. He had to remind himself that this woman was in reality an artificial intelligence whose sensory catchment area spanned the solar system; who could 'see' the entire range of the electromagnetic spectrum; whose physical 'body' consisted of components scattered across several planets and habitats; who possessed a vast, multi-personality mind and who could think at speeds he couldn't imagine. So why was she – *it* – playing these silly games with him?

She kissed him on the mouth and suddenly all thought of food vanished from his thoughts. Altered endocrine system or not, he was gripped by a stronger wave of sexual lust than he had ever experienced when he had been a normal man. At the same time he felt an erection growing at an incredibly fast rate. As he freed his penis from his pants he said furiously to himself, *The bitch! She's fucking around with my brain!* But he couldn't help himself. More than anything he wanted her. He threw his arms around her, squeezing her hard. He could feel his penis straining against the stiff, unyielding leather that covered her crotch. He could hear the hoarse rasping sound of his breathing . . .

She stopped kissing him and whispered in his ear, 'Give me what I want and I promise you an experience beyond words . . . '

And then he was back sitting in the direct-link facility chair, his hat back on his lap and his arms hugging empty air. He ejaculated inside his hat.

What was even worse was that he wasn't hungry any more. For food, that is. But he *was* hungry for Miriam. *Very* hungry.

He felt like bursting into tears.

Mickey Yamada was dying for a cigarette. But he was resisting the temptation. They were losing air from the main cabin at a slow but steady rate and even though he was confident that one of the other relief ships would arrive before the situation became critical he couldn't afford to waste oxygen.

It had been a near thing. After the collision with the docking-bay door there had been rapid decompression in the pilot pod as it began to disintegrate but Tan and he had managed to get out and seal the hatch behind them. Tan suffered a nosebleed but otherwise they were unharmed. The people in the main cabin were similarly unharmed. Then, when his heartbeat had returned to something like normal, Yamada had suited and gone outside to inspect the damage.

The bow, containing the pilot pod, was a write-off. The rest of the *Gully Foyle*'s hull had suffered some structural damage as well. He slapped syro-plastic patches on the most serious-looking fissures, hoping to stop the slow leak of air from the main cabin. He later discovered he had slowed the leak but not stopped it completely. The *Gully Foyle* was drifting quite quickly away from the habitat. The reactive force of the collision had provided it with enough momentum to overcome the habitat's gravity field.

When he had finished patching the hull Mickey Yamada had warily scanned the now menacing form of the habitat. There were still no signs of activity on it but he felt vulnerable. Now that it was clear that whoever was in control of Takata was hostile he knew they could easily use the habitat's meteor defences to blast both him and the *Gully Foyle* into very tiny particles.

He didn't feel any less vulnerable when he returned inside the ship. There was not a thing they could do but wait to be rescued by another relief ship which was sure to be already on its way. But it was going to be a very uncomfortable wait knowing that those within the habitat could, on a whim, so easily destroy them.

As the hours passed Yamada's fear turned to anger. He made a decision that he personally was going to make those responsible for his ordeal pay dearly.

Moreau was checking up on the current state of his finances. His bionantech was projecting the figures on to his retinas. He was satisfied to see that his partner in his interior decorating business, Wally Kubilius, had continued crediting his account with regular, if reduced, payments during his incarceration in Purgatory. Unfortunately the read-out showed that these payments were being taxed at penalty rates . . .

He had got the hang of using his bionantech again. A lot of its functions had been damped down by the Purgatory operators, including its automatic fine-tuning of his cardio-vascular system, in the hope that his mid-twentieth life-style might have resulted in some debilitating disease, not to mention death itself. But now he had reactivated those functions and, having had his lungs and arteries descaled by his resident army of micro-robots, felt much happier.

'Steven?'

He switched off his bionantech and turned to her. 'Yeah?' She was sitting in the room's only armchair, leaning forward with her hands clasped between her thighs. She looked intense. He hoped she wasn't going to bring up the subject of having a baby again. He was pretty sure he'd averted that particular crisis by promising her he would seriously consider it once they were out of this situation.

In truth he had never seen the point of having children. Oh sure, if everyone stopped having children the human race

97

would come to an end but he, personally, had never had the urge to father offspring. Also, he found young children pretty damn boring. He realized he might feel differently when a child reached the point of being able to carry on an intelligent conversation (though he knew many individuals *never* reached that stage no matter how old they got) but he had never been tempted to go through the whole process of parenthood to find out. Not wanting children had been about the one thing he'd had in common with his ex-wife, Tasma. She had clearly lacked a maternal urge whereas Mary seemed to be abundantly awash with the hormone, or group of hormones, that was responsible for this primal urge. She had gone on and on about wanting to be truly fulfilled; to do something – i.e., make a baby – that would somehow make up for the wasted and destructive life she had led as a man. Finally she had accepted his argument that occupied Paris in 1941 was not the ideal place to have a baby. She hadn't brought the subject up again for the past few days but it looked as if his period of peace was about to end . . .

'I want to talk to you.'

His heart sank further. 'Oh yeah?'

'I'm going to tell you how I got my special bionantech.'

He felt both very relieved and excited. 'Great!' He had given up asking her about it.

'But first I want to tell you something about my background.'

He leaned back on the bed. 'Fire away.'

'I'm a third-generation Martian. When my family moved there the planet was still being terraformed. My grandparents on my mother's side were mining engineers and they went to the Tiridates area up in the north where large deposits of iron, nickel and gold had been found. They were among the early inhabitants of Rush City which grew to a pretty big size in only a couple of years. My mother was born there, and her two brothers. When she was twenty she fell in love and married a guy who ran a hotel and bar. My father. Vincent Rack. By that time the boom years were over and Rush City was starting to shrink. By the time I'd reached my teens the place was on its

98

knees. Only a few small mining operations were still being carried out in the area. My grandparents had moved on. So had my uncles. But Dad refused to leave. He kept coming up with these schemes to turn Rush City into a tourist attraction. They never came to anything but Mom stuck by him. And I was simply stuck. There was no money to send me anywhere for a proper education. My grandparents had offered to help but Dad was too proud to accept. So there I was, eighteen years old with a zero future ahead of me. The only way I had of earning any money was by fossil-hunting in the hills and the worked-out mines. Then *he* arrived . . . ' She paused.

Moreau felt a pang of jealousy, expecting to hear about the love of Mary's young life, then mentally kicked himself when he remembered that Mary back then had been male. 'He?'

'He called himself Ryuzo Tanaka. A Japanese guy. He arrived with his teenage daughter, Emi. No one could figure out why they had come to Rush City. Then the rumours started. That he was hiding out. That he was rich. The rumours turned out to be true.'

'How could he be hiding out?' Moreau interrupted. 'Your bionantech means you can be traced anywhere. Unless you have it burnt out and that's virtual suicide.'

'We're in hiding, aren't we?'

'Yes, but you fixed my . . . ' He stopped. 'Oh.'

'May I continue now?'

He nodded.

'His daughter got kidnapped. He got a ransom disc. They wanted a lot of yen. But in grey-market goods, naturally. The guy was distraught but he didn't alert the Corporation police. So I knew that he was hiding out. I went to see him. Asked him what he would give me if I got Emi back for him. He asked me what I wanted. I said everything. He said he would arrange it. I believed him. So I tracked down the kidnappers. There were three of them. I killed them and took Emi back to her father. He was as good as his word.'

'I don't understand.'

She got up out of the chair and went to the french windows. She stared out at the fake Paris. Then she said, 'His real name was Ryuzo Mikuni. He was over a hundred years old, though, of course, he didn't look it.'

'I think I know that name.'

'He was one of the original designers of bionantech. He was a genius. But he'd become disillusioned and wanted out. But the Shoehiku Corporation, who owned the rights to bionantech, wanted him to keep working; to design even more efficient types of bionantech. So he did. But just for himself and his daughter. Bionantech that could not be traced. A forerunner of what he designed uniquely for me.'

'Ah,' said Moreau. The yen had dropped.

'I said I wanted everything and he gave it to me. My altered bionantech provided me with almost infinite advantages. It took me some time to get the hang of using it but once I did I was out of Rush City like a shot. For the first few years I was cautious in the way I used it but as time went by I got more ambitious. Then I went wild and became the Ghost.'

'I see,' he said, thoughtfully. 'I guess you were pretty lucky.'

'Part of it was luck. But part wasn't.'

'What do you mean?'

'I knew exactly where the three kidnappers would be hiding out.'

'How come?'

She turned to face him. 'They were friends of mine.'

Chapter Nine

In his office, Kondo Izumi was staring worriedly at a holo projection of the Takata habitat. It hovered in the air above his large desk. Also visible in the projection were the fleet of relief ships that had gathered around the habitat. An attempt to break into the habitat was going to take place in three hours' time.

So far Izumi and his fellow executives had not taken the AI's advice to destroy Takata. It had seemed to all of them too extreme a step to take. It wasn't just the lives of the employees within the habitat that gave them pause but also the fact that the destruction of the habitat would be impossible to conceal. Awkward questions would be asked, mainly by the Council of Companies, and it might prove impossible to keep the truth from becoming known. So they had decided to penetrate the habitat with robots followed by an armed human force, and assess the situation. The next step would depend on what the expedition found within the habitat. If it proved necessary then Takata would indeed be destroyed.

A metal dome some thirty feet in diameter was being manoeuvred towards the side of the rotating habitat by a tug. When it was attached to the outer hull combat robots would cut their way through the hull and enter. Shortly afterwards the ship containing the human assault force would link up with the dome's hatch and, if everything went to plan, they would enter the habitat.

If everything went to plan.

He prayed to his ancestors that it would.

*

Rosie the Imp was getting worried about Sebastian Chimes. He was acting strangely. Well, he was acting in a differently strange way from the strange way he usually acted. He looked distracted, and he no longer dressed with impeccable neatness. He was scruffy now, and his funny hat was missing, too. Also Rosie found the way he was looking at her rather disquieting. If she didn't know it was impossible she would have interpreted his looks as ones of naked lust.

He hadn't been the same since he'd entered the control room after having another private audience with the IRC AI. He'd been in a very agitated state, yelling that the hunt for the Glitch had become even more urgent, though he hadn't explained why. The Controllers, including Rosie's boss, had tried to calm him down but they hadn't had much success.

Today he was quiet, though there was a manic look in his eyes. He sat staring broodingly at the holo map of Purgatory, listening to the Controllers discuss new strategies for the search. And glancing often at Rosie . . .

But now he suddenly stood and turned to face the Controllers. 'This is absurd!' he cried at them. 'At this rate you'll never find the Glitch! I still feel he's in the Paris zone. He's been there all the time! I know it!'

'We searched the Paris zone thoroughly,' pointed out Rosie's boss, Aspine Tyrene.

'And you missed him! We need to concentrate on the Paris zone! It's a waste of time searching the rest of the habitat!'

'We can't rely on what is little more than your hunch to call off the search in the other zones,' said Rosie's boss, 'but as soon as we acquire additional personnel we will assign them to the Paris zone. Just to make you happy, Mr Chimes.'

'Fuck you,' snarled Chimes. 'I'll go to Paris myself. And I'm taking that useless Imp with me!'

He pointed straight at Rosie. *Oh hell*, she thought.

Mickey Yamada admitted to himself that he was feeling apprehensive. He was still feeling very angry towards whoever it was in Takata who had wrecked the *Gully Foyle* and almost killed him and Tan but right now, as the ship approached the pressure dome attached to the side of the habitat, he was definitely feeling nervous. Not that he was regretting volunteering for this operation, but he would have appreciated more information from the Company on what he and the other members of the team could expect to encounter once they got inside the habitat. Rumour had it that the execs themselves had no idea . . .

There were fifty-six of them floating in the hold of the *Perfumed Breeze*. Like Yamada they were all wearing armoured, muscle-amplifying pressure suits and carrying beam weapons. Even though it was presumed the atmosphere within the habitat was intact they were under strict instructions to keep their suits sealed once they were inside in case there had been an outbreak of biological contamination.

'The hull has been breached,' announced a neutral voice in Yamada's ear-piece. It was the voice of the computer program supervising the operation. 'The robots are about to enter. And the *Perfumed Breeze* is about to dock with the dome. Stand by for simulated gravity.'

There was a slight jolt and a clanging sound as the two hatches touched. Then came the whining of servo-mechanisms as they locked together. All of a sudden Yamada felt heavy and his head swam. There was now an 'up' and a 'down'. Once the *Perfumed Breeze* had attached itself to the spinning habitat it was now subject to the centrifugal force being generated by it. The safety webbing that all the suits were hooked to immediately sagged.

Yamada waited expectantly. The bland voice spoke again in his ear. 'The robots have entered the habitat . . . and I have lost all contact with them.' Yamada gave a start of surprise. He looked at the man next to him. He too looked surprised. 'There is a powerful electromagnetic field within the habitat which is blocking all signals,' continued the voice. 'I am consulting with our superiors as to the next step.' There was silence. Time passed with aching slowness. It was just over a minute before the computer spoke again. 'It has been decided to continue as planned. "A" squad, prepare to enter the dome.'

Yamada watched as the first eight people began to clamber towards the hatch, which was now 'above' them. He was in 'B' squad. The two connecting hatches irised open simultaneously. Yamada saw murky light beyond. When the last of 'A' squad had passed through the hatchway the computer said, '"B" squad now.'

Yamada was second in line. He unhooked his suit from the webbing and followed his squad-leader, Melanie Chin, towards the hatchway. He took a deep breath as she went through then followed her.

He entered the dome. A metal lattice shaft had been built by the engineers, leading up and into the hull of the habitat fifteen feet above him. He could see the last members of 'A' squad disappearing into the circular hole that had been cut into the hull. He followed Melanie up the shaft. Very quickly he passed through the hull of the habitat: climbing through the layers of radiation shielding, the ten-inch-thick alloy of the outer hull, layers of insulation materials, piping, power cables, a thinner inner hull and then soil. Bright light engulfed him as he climbed out of the top of the shaft. Standing beside Melanie, he detached his beam rifle from the back of his suit and looked around.

They had emerged on to the fairway of a golf-course. 'A' squad had formed a defensive circle around the hole. Scattered around were the combat robots. They weren't moving. There was nobody else in sight. He realized that his ear-piece was making a hissing sound. He tried to get through to Melanie on his radio but failed. He signalled to her that they should touch helmets together. As they did so the rest of their squad continued to pour out of the hole.

'The radios don't work!' he yelled at her.

She nodded. 'And we're cut off from the command program!' she replied. She went off to confer with the leader of 'A' squad. While the rest of the team continued to emerge from the hole Yamada anxiously scanned the area – expecting to see he didn't know what. He was feeling increasingly apprehensive. Melanie came back to him and they touched helmets. 'We've decided I should go back to the ship and set up some sort of alternative method of communication with the command program. Maybe by direct cable.'

He watched her climb back down into the hole. A short while later she reappeared, her expression worried behind the visor of her helmet. 'I can't get back to the ship. I couldn't even get into the dome. The hole has been blocked off!'

Kondo Izumi said desperately, 'But you must keep trying! There may be just a technical fault!'

'I'm afraid not,' replied the disembodied voice of Ryo Komatsu, captain of the *Perfumed Breeze*. 'The command program believes that the signal interference is deliberate.'

'You must send more people into the habitat!'

'The engineers are still studying the mystery substance that is blocking the entry point. Its structure is like that of a spider's web but very much stronger,' said Komatsu, 'but even if they can cut through it, or cut through in a different part of the hull, and we send more robots and personnel into the habitat, we have no guarantee that the same thing won't happen again.'

'But the first team might be in trouble. They'll need reinforcements!' protested Izumi.

'The first team may no longer even exist, sir. We have no idea what has occurred within the habitat. To send in more people at this stage would be – forgive me, sir – both foolish and reckless.'

Izumi sighed. 'You're right, I suppose. What do you suggest?'

'I agree with the command program. We wait. It may be that the first team is in the process of realizing its objective and is regaining control of the habitat. When they do they will be able to re-establish communication with us.'

'And how likely does the command program believe that scenario to be?'

'I'm afraid it considers it to be nothing more than a possibility, sir,' said Komatsu, 'but one that must be taken into consideration for the time being.'

'How much time?' asked Izumi, testily.

'At least four hours.'

'Hmmmm,' said Izumi. Then, loudly, he said, 'And what do my illustrious colleagues think?'

The other three executives, who had been listening to the conversation between Izumi and the ship's captain in their respective offices, all agreed to wait for a further four hours. Then Araki Hyuga said, 'And if after that time we are still in the dark as to what is going on inside Takata? What then?'

'Then we think seriously about destroying the habitat.'

Rosie Knight was not having a good time. She had been trudging around the Paris exhibit for hours in the company of the increasingly demented Sebastian Chimes. He kept peering into the face of every young woman they encountered in the streets. Sometimes he would grab them by the shoulders, push his face really close to theirs, and then shake them with frustration when they failed to match up with the image of the Glitch which was etched into his brain. The women concerned, unable to perceive the existence of either Chimes or Rosie, simply frowned with puzzlement at their own peculiar behaviour before walking on.

'She's here somewhere! I know it!' muttered Chimes as he let go of another suspect.

'Excuse me, sir, but can we sit down and rest for a bit? My feet are aching and I feel very tired.'

He turned quickly towards her and she thought he was going to yell at her again. But the anger in his eyes quickly turned into something else. She was beginning to recognize that look. Once, she knew, he would only have directed that look towards a plate of food. She shuddered.

'You're tired? Very well, we'll take a rest.' He glanced around. 'That café across the road. Come on.'

She followed him to the outdoor café. As she sat at a vacant table he went to one near by and picked up an open bottle of wine and two glasses. The two people at the table gasped with surprise. To them it was as if the bottle and glasses had simply vanished. They looked around helplessly. Ignoring them, Chimes sat down opposite Rosie and filled both glasses. He pushed one towards her. She took it and sipped at it tentatively. The wine tasted slightly sour. Chimes, by contrast, swallowed all of his in a couple of large gulps then refilled his glass. He stared at her intensely. She saw that his right eye was twitching. She felt uncomfortable. Finally he said, 'You remind me of someone, Miss Knight.'

'Oh really? Who?'

'She calls herself Miriam,' he said, and grimaced.

'Miriam?' That's a nice name,' said Rosie, with forced cheerfulness. 'Who is she?'

Chimes suddenly slammed his hand down on the table-top, making Rosie flinch. 'Miriam isn't a *she*! She's a *thing*!'

Rosie didn't know what to say to that one. She devoutly wished she hadn't had to accompany this awful man. By rights she should be off duty by now. Normally at this time she would be in her small, luxurious apartment, having had a shower, and watching her favourite soap, *Generation Ship*, on the vid. After a meal, she would have gone to the Hades Club to socialize with fellow Imps of her own age and listen to some live music. Instead she was stuck with Sebastian Chimes who was clearly becoming progressively unravelled and possibly downright dangerous. Maybe her father had been right about her career choice after all.

'Do you have a lover?' Chimes asked her.

'What?' she said, startled.

He repeated the question.

'Well,' she said slowly as she wondered how she could get him away from the subject of sex, 'I don't have a specific lover at the moment. No one I'm really close to.'

'But you have had lovers?'

She nodded, reluctantly. 'Yeah. A few.'

'Male or female, may I ask?'

She was tempted to say female, but she suspected he would be able to tell she was lying. 'Male,' she answered.

'You enjoy sex?' His eyes were boring into hers. The twitch was getting worse.

She took another swallow of her wine. Then she said, 'Sure. Doesn't everyone?' And immediately regretted her words. In theory, Chimes wasn't supposed to. But to judge from the way he was behaving that information was out of date.

He shifted his heated gaze to her cleavage. She suddenly wished that the Imp costume wasn't so revealing.

He said, 'How do you feel about making love to an older man?'

Oh shit, she thought. *here it comes.* 'An older man? Well, I don't know. It would depend on who the older man was.'

'Suppose it was me.'

She quickly drank more of her wine. 'Well, I feel pretty rested now. I think we should get on with our search.'

'You've changed the subject.'

Damn right I have, thought Rosie, panicking. 'You know, the more I think about it the more I think you're right. This exhibit would be the ideal hiding-place for the Glitch . . .' She started to rise from her seat.

To her alarm he reached out across the table and grabbed her wrist. He exerted pressure, forcing her back into her seat. 'Answer my question, Miss Knight.'

'Ah . . . well, can I think it over and get back to you on this? Meanwhile, I really do think we should be getting back to work. You yourself have been stressing how urgent it is that we find the Glitch.' She looked around the café. 'She could be real close even as we speak. I mean, she could be right here . . .' She looked around desperately. 'Maybe that's her over there.' Rosie pointed at a lone woman seated a few tables away. The woman was all in black and a black veil covered her face. Chimes didn't even glance in her direction. His grip on Rosie's wrist tightened. She gasped with pain.

'I want an answer to my question,' he said coldly.

Rosie threw the remainder of her wine into his eyes, wrenched her wrist free, leapt and ran . . .

Mary felt incredible relief as she watched Sebastian Chimes run down the street after the fleeing Imp. When Chimes had entered the café with the Imp she had been transfixed with shock. She hadn't dared get up and leave in case it drew his attention to her. So she had just sat there, sipping her coffee, waiting for the inevitable to happen. But it hadn't. She wondered why. It had appeared that Chimes was too busy arguing with the female Imp to be his usual efficient self. It wasn't like him. Mary knew Chimes quite well, having once spent a week in his company when her old self had been posing as an IRC employee. It had been an amusing experience at the time.

She remained seated at the table. She didn't think Chimes would return. And besides, she was reluctant to return to the hotel. Things were a little strained between her and Steven at the moment. Had been since her revelation about how she – no, that damned *he* – had acquired her bionantech from Ryuzo Mikuni. It was, she had to admit, a pretty sordid tale.

Not that it was really as bad as it sounded. Sure, Farro, Thur and Becky *had* once been her friends – they had been a gang together since their early teens, pulling off petty crimes when they weren't out hunting fossils – but when the other three decided to get serious: to get burn-outs, live rough and turn to more ambitious types of crime, Joster pulled out of the gang. He hadn't fancied taking so drastic a step. By having your bionantech burnt out you were putting yourself completely beyond the pale. And living rough didn't appeal to him either. He liked his comforts and had bigger ambitions. So he and the other three came to a parting of the ways.

But when Mikuni's daughter was kidnapped he was pretty certain they were responsible. And he knew exactly where they would be hiding out . . .

It wasn't anything like cold-blooded murder. When he'd found them in the abandoned mine he'd got the drop on them. He'd ordered that they hand over Emi. But the idiots made a grab for their weapons. He'd had no choice but to shoot all three of them. He felt very bad about it afterwards; especially about having had to kill Becky. They'd once been lovers. For a brief time.

Mary's depression grew worse. She summoned the waiter and ordered a large cognac.

★

109

Mickey Yamada sincerely wished he hadn't volunteered for the relief expedition. All thoughts of getting revenge on those who had wrecked the *Gully Foyle* were gone. Something damned weird was going on and it scared him silly.

When it was discovered that the way back into the dome was blocked the squad-leaders had held a conference on what to do next. In Yamada's opinion the expedition had already failed – with their communications knocked out they were practically useless – but the squad-leaders decided to carry on. Two squads were to remain around the entry point, forming a beach-head to keep it secure in the event that reinforcements might penetrate the obstacle. The other four squads were to carry on with the main objective: to proceed to the habitat's administrative complex which was only a short distance from the golf-course. Yamada's squad was in the lead and he was on point. He hadn't volunteered for this duty, it was his squad-leader's idea.

So far they hadn't seen a living thing but Yamada's unease increased. He tried to tell himself that he was perfectly safe in his armoured, fully augmented suit. The instrument read-out being displayed on one side of his visor told him that his weapons systems were in perfect working order. But what about the combat robots scattered around the entrance hole? All completely inert . . .

Something hit the side of his helmet. He gave a yelp of alarm and flung himself flat on the ground. *Easy! Easy! You're still alive!* he told himself. Whatever it was hadn't penetrated his helmet. He scanned around, looking for a target.

Nothing . . .

Then he spotted what had hit him. It was lying some yards away on the fairway.

It was a golf ball.

Chapter Ten

Paul Manion felt a growing sense of foreboding as Takie Okimoto's personal skimmer sped towards the building housing the Opoponax Project. 'Something extraordinary' was how Doctor Lebra's genegineer had described whatever had happened in the laboratory. So far that was all they knew. And the man hadn't seemed frightened, just excited. Even so, Manion couldn't help feeling worried.

From the outside everything appeared as usual as the skimmer dropped gently to rest at the front of the featureless white building. There were no windows, just a single entrance. Two armed guards flanked the latter. Even Okimoto had to submit to a bionantech identification test before he could enter.

They passed through an airlock and into the spotlessly all-white reception area. Bowing, lowly lab techs, also dressed in white, helped them out of their clothes and into bio-protection suits. Then they went through another airlock. Beyond this was a catwalk some ten feet long. This led to the inner core of the complex, completely separate from the outer building. The inner core, resting on pylons, was a metal cube some fifty feet tall. The space between the inner and outer structures would, in an emergency within the inner core, be instantly filled with a highly toxic and corrosive gas. At the same time it would be flooded with high-intensity neutron radiation. No life-form could survive.

Manion hoped.

They went through another airlock. One of Doctor Lebra's assistants was waiting for them. 'Quickly, honourable sirs! This way!'

He led them into the section housing the synthi-wombs. Doctor Lebra greeted them. His face was flushed with excitement behind his transparent helmet. 'Honoured sirs, it is incredible!' he cried. 'Come and see!'

Manion followed the others to the slanting wall of thick myro-glass that overlooked the row of chambers containing the synthi-wombs. 'Number seven,' said Doctor Lebra. 'Look at number seven!'

Standing between Okimoto and Jean Dux, Manion peered down. Six of the synthi-wombs were small, vulnerable-looking translucent sacs, dominated by the various tubes and wires plugged into them. The one in the seventh chamber was different. It was about twenty inches in diameter, the sac swollen and pulsating. 'It began just over an hour ago,' said Doctor Lebra. 'The rate of cell division has been fantastic. The more we increase the flow of nutrients the faster it grows . . .'

'And what exactly is *it*?' asked Hayden Frid.

'We don't know yet,' answered Doctor Lebra. He turned and gestured towards the bank of monitor screens. 'See for yourself.'

They gathered round the screen displaying the sensor scan of the interior of synthi-womb number seven. Manion could make out a roughly circular shape with what might have been legs protruding around it.

'It looks like a crab,' said Dux.

'*That's* an infant Opoponax?' exclaimed Okimoto.

Manion had an unpleasant vision of the Opoponax as a race of giant crabs. Or spiders.

'As I said, we don't know what it is,' replied Doctor Lebra, 'but it doesn't possess any of the characteristics of an infant belonging to a sophisticated species. Nor is it purely organic.'

'It isn't?' asked Manion.

'It's partly organic and, well, partly machine, I suppose. We've so far only been able to analyse a few of the totally unknown proteins it's been producing. Everything has been happening too fast. Some of the proteins are purely crystalline in structure. What appear to be electronic circuits have formed. And there are complicated systems forming on a molecular level. It's all just too much for us to handle . . . '

'Can't you slow it down?' asked Manion.

'We cut the supply of growth accelerant immediately the sudden changes began. It made no difference to the rate of growth,' said Doctor Lebra.

'What would happen if you cut the supply of nutrients?' Manion asked him.

'Why, it would die, of course.'

'Then I suggest you do it at once,' said Manion.

'What are you saying?!' exclaimed Okimoto. 'We don't want to kill it!'

'As Doctor Lebra has told us, the situation is out of the control of him and his team,' said Manion. 'We need to stabilize it. We will kill this specimen and then study it at leisure. We have other living specimens. We ration their supply of nutrients to a strict minimum to maintain survival. When Doctor Lebra is confident as to the exact nature of the dead specimen and doesn't consider it to present any kind of possible threat we will continue with the project.'

'Hell, I don't know, Paul . . . ' said Dux.

Manion turned to Okimoto. 'I am making this decision as Chief Security Officer. I will take full responsibility. If you aren't going to follow my advice, sir, you should relieve me of my position right away.'

Okimoto stared at him, glanced back at the monitor screen then at Frid. 'What do you think, Mr Frid?'

Frid's impassive face gave nothing away as he considered the situation. Finally he said, 'If Paul says to shut it down then I think we should. Just to be safe.'

Okimoto said to Doctor Lebra, 'Do it.'

For a moment or two it looked to Manion as if Doctor Lebra was going to protest against the order but then he suddenly snapped instructions to one of his three assistants. The woman went to a console and began pressing buttons. Manion walked back to the wall of myro-glass and stared down into the seventh chamber. The others joined him. 'How long will it take to die?' asked Manion.

'Only a few minutes, I would think,' replied Doctor Lebra, rather sullenly.

The synthi-womb suddenly split open . . .

Something flew out of it. It seemed to be coming straight towards Manion. He flinched backwards as the thing attached itself to the myro-glass wall directly in front of him. He had an impression of a green, circular object with eight legs protruding from it at equal intervals. There seemed to be suckers on the legs. The sight of the thing sparked off a dim memory of a scene from an old classic film he had seen at school when a young child. Then the 'unbreakable' myro-glass shattered. Or rather, turned into powder. An alarm bell started to ring.

Manion jumped to one side as the creature came through the glass.

It landed on the floor and began to scuttle across it at an extremely fast speed. It seemed to be heading towards the female genegineer. She screamed.

Three of the automatic beam weapons that Manion had mounted on the ceiling of the lab simultaneously opened fire. As all three beams made a direct hit, the thing, in a shower of sparks, jumped into the air. The beams followed it. There was a hissing sound. The thing flipped over and fell on its back. Its eight legs waved feebly. The bright blue beams continued to converge upon it.

Then it exploded.

The beams switched off. There was nothing left but a cloud of smoke hanging in the air and several deep scorch marks on the white floor.

Jean Dux was the first to speak. 'Fucking bloody hell,' he muttered.

Doctor Lebra went and peered down at the spot where the thing had exploded. 'Remarkable . . .'

Frid and Okimoto then spoke at once. Frid said, 'What do you think it was trying to do?' And Okimoto said, 'Doctor Lebra, what do we do now?'

Doctor Lebra naturally answered Okimoto first. 'I think we should suspend the project for the time being, sir. I will follow Mr Manion's suggestion and reduce the nutrients to the other six organisms to the bare minimum. I need to analyse these events . . . study the recordings of what happened . . .'

Manion said, 'I think we should switch the nutrients to the others off completely.'

'No,' protested Doctor Lebra.

'You've got plenty of copies of the Opoponax genome,' Manion told him grimly. 'We should shut down the project until we have a better idea of what the hell that thing intended to do. And for a start, I'd like to know how it managed to break through that wall of myro-glass. And why the bloody thing seemed *designed* for such an action.'

Doctor Lebra looked perplexed. 'Yes, that was very curious. I simply don't understand . . .'

A siren began its harsh blare. Then a woman's voice said, very loudly, 'Attention. The integrity of the inner containment core has been compromised. Lock-off procedure has begun. Please remain where you are.' Then the message was repeated.

'But that's impossible!' cried Doctor Lebra. 'The organism has been destroyed! What . . . ?'

Manion felt as if his balls had just been dipped in ice-water. The complex's computer system had detected biological contamination outside the synthi-womb laboratory. Now the inner core would be automatically sealed off and the space between the inner and outer structures flooded with hard radiation and poisonous gas. Exactly as he had planned it. Though he hadn't intended being inside the inner building in the eventuality of his fail-safe procedure having to be used.

They were trapped. They wouldn't be allowed out until whatever it was that the computer had detected had been neutralized. And how long might that be? It was possible they were sealed in here for ever. He thought of Michelle and Amelia. Would he ever see them again?

'Computer!' yelled Doctor Lebra. 'Specify the nature of the contamination!'

'Micro-organisms. Nature unknown. And there's something else . . .'

'*What* else?!' Doctor Lebra was screaming now.

The computer didn't answer. The siren continued its nerve-grating blare.

'*Computer! Answer me!*'

There was no reaction for a few seconds, then the voice said, 'Attention! Serious computer malfunction! The program has been in . . .' The voice died away. Then the siren stopped.

What followed was the most ominous silence that Manion had ever experienced.

Okimoto finally broke it by exclaiming, 'What is happening?!'

'Nothing good, I'm afraid, sir,' said Manion.

The computer spoke again. 'Attention. The emergency is over. Quarantine has ended. You are free to leave the inner core.'

'But that contradicts everything it said before,' said Dux.

'Yeah, it does,' said Manion wearily. 'And if you think about it you'll figure out why.'

'Would someone like to tell *me* what is going on!' shouted Okimoto. 'Doctor Lebra, explain!'

Doctor Lebra walked over to a chair and sat down. He looked stunned. 'It's impossible,' he said again, his voice shaky.

'But it's happened,' said Manion. 'The computer has been invaded. By something that came out of that damned crab thing. It was nothing but a diversion. And the means to distribute whatever micro-organisms have already spread through the inner core . . . and are now spreading further since the computer shut down my fail-safe system. Am I right, Doctor Lebra?'

'Yes, I'm afraid so. I just don't understand *how* . . .'

Hayden Frid spoke for the first time since the thing had erupted out of the synthi-womb. 'Are we safe, Doctor Lebra? In these suits, I mean?'

'We should be. For the time being. Possibly . . .' Doctor Lebra shrugged. 'I don't know.'

'As we don't know what we're dealing with,' said Manion, 'we can't guarantee anything.' He was thinking of his daughters again. Were they in danger from whatever had been unleashed from this laboratory?

116

'We must hold an immediate emergency conference,' said Okimoto, activating his helmet communicator. He began speaking rapidly in Japanese into the mike. Then he stopped. He was looking even more shocked than before. *Now what?* Manion wondered grimly.

'We are cut off,' Okimoto told them. 'Takata has been cut off from the Net. We can't send or receive signals. We are completely alone.'

'Opoponax strikes again,' said Manion softly.

As Manion came through the front door of his apartment Amelia and Michelle rushed to meet him. As he bent down and hugged them each in turn he was profoundly relieved to see that they looked fine. But then, so far nobody in the habitat was displaying any ill effects. Whatever was loose in the habitat's environment wasn't interacting with the human population, just the computer systems.

'Hi, Paul.'

He glanced up and was surprised to see Cherry Lee coming from the kitchen. 'Hello, Cherry. What are you doing here?'

'I had to talk to you. I sent their minder home. That was OK, wasn't it?'

'Of course.' He kissed her on the cheek. 'Let's get them fed first and then we'll talk.'

In the kitchen he saw that Cherry had already set the table for their supper. It took only a couple of minutes to produce the pre-prepared meals, and when the girls had begun eating he and Cherry returned to the living-room. 'What's the problem?' he asked her.

'Oh come on, Paul, drop the act!' she said, her voice rising. 'I want to know what's going on!'

He raised a hand. 'Hey, keep it down. I don't want to upset the girls.'

She took a deep breath. Then said, quietly, but angrily, 'Sorry, but I demand to know what the fuck is going on. And don't tell me you can't because of security reasons.'

'Why do you think something is wrong?' he asked her, playing for time while he decided how much to tell her.

'Because when I tried to call my mother today I was told by some computer at Communications that owing to equipment failure it was temporarily unable to make calls outside the habitat. I checked with a few other people and they were getting the same brush-off. Then I turned on my vid to find out that wasn't working either. Just an announcement from another damned computer that owing to "equipment failure . . . blah, blah, blah". So what's the real story, Paul?'

He had just come from the emergency meeting at Okimoto's office where it had been decided to maintain a security blanket to avoid panic among the habitat personnel, and all that. But Manion knew it was going to be impossible to prevent people from realizing pretty quickly that something was seriously wrong. And in this situation, despite his security background, he felt they had a right to know, but he had been outvoted.

He stared into Cherry's beautiful, expensive eyes and said, 'You'd better sit down.' He described, in broad terms, the Opoponax Project, and told her what had occurred that day.

'Good God,' she said when he'd finished. Then, 'So what is being done about it?'

'We can't do anything. We're completely helpless. None of the main computer systems remain in our control. It's not just that we're cut off from the Net . . . we're sealed in. All attempts to open the hatches of the docking-bays have failed.'

She put her hand over her mouth. 'I don't believe this is happening.'

'Yeah, well, I'm afraid it is.'

'There must be *something* we can do!'

He shrugged. 'At the emergency meeting I just attended the general consensus was that we wait for the Company to send help. It must be on its way by now.' He went over to the main window which overlooked the balcony. Three sparrows were paying a visit to the bird-feeder. Some of his daughters' toys lay scattered about on the floor.

'What is this Opopo . . . whatever you call it? What does it want?' Cherry asked him.

'I have no idea,' he admitted. He turned to face her. 'We've got a pile of theories with nothing solid to go on. It seems my original fear was right – that genome was designed to create a biological weapon. But despite my prediction, and all my safeguards, it still beat us.'

'But you said your weapons destroyed the thing.'

'They did, but by then it was already too late. It had already "seeded" the atmosphere in the lab with its micro-organisms . . . and the other things.'

'And what are they?'

'We think they're the Opoponax equivalent of our nano-tech units . . . our molecular robots. We think they're the thing that have penetrated and taken over the computer systems.'

'Well, can't we do the same thing? Use our nano-tech units to clear these alien things out of the systems and reverse the process?'

He sighed. 'It was the first thing that our computer specialists thought of. Trouble is, it didn't work. Our units went in, and immediately got taken over. Same thing with all the other attempts. The Opoponax nano-technology, if that is what it is, was clearly – *is* clearly superior to our own.'

'And the micro-organisms . . . what are they doing?'

'We don't know yet. Without the computers we can't carry out an automatic analysis of the atmosphere. Doctor Lebra's people have taken samples of the air and are trying to identify the alien organisms by using old-fashioned chemistry methods but that is going to take ages. By then I'm afraid that Opoponax will have done whatever it is it was designed to do.'

'It may have already started.'

'What do you mean?'

'A couple of hours ago my bionantech informed me that I was pregnant.'

He stared at her. 'But that's impossible!' he cried, sounding, he realized, like Doctor Lebra.

'I know. But I'm pregnant anyway. And I'm not the only one. Three of my friends are pregnant too. They couldn't understand it either. But now I'm beginning to . . . in fact, it wouldn't surprise me if all the females over the age of puberty in the habitat are pregnant now. Courtesy of your alien visitor.'

Chapter Eleven

A golf ball. A bloody golf ball. At least, that's what it *appeared* to be. Maybe it was actually a bomb that just happened to look like a golf ball.

Micky Yamada lay there on the fairway, his eyes fixed on what he hoped *was* just a golf ball. Very slowly he moved his beam rifle until it was pointing at the ball. He wondered whether to fire or not. He wondered what the others behind him were doing but didn't dare take his eyes off the ball to look.

Then a man appeared. He came strolling out of the trees that lined the rough. He was dressed in black and was casually holding a golf-club over his shoulder. Yamada panned the rifle round to cover him instead of the ball. As he approached, the man smiled down at Yamada. Yamada wondered if he should shoot him.

The man stopped a few yards in front of him. 'Hello,' he said. 'Sorry about the ball . . . ' Yamada realized with a start that he was hearing the man's voice through his ear-piece. ' . . . But I thought that was the best way of announcing my presence without getting shot.' Actually, Yamada was still considering shooting him but he continued to hold his fire.

'You have nothing to fear,' said the man. 'We mean you no harm.'

Yamada certainly didn't like the sound of that. His finger tightened on the trigger. 'Who are you?' he called, not expecting the man to be able to hear him. But the man did, to his surprise.

'My name is Hayden Frid,' he replied, 'the executive

formerly reponsible for security here on Takata. The post is now a redundant one, thanks to what has occurred.'

'And what's that?' asked Yamada.

The man spread his arms out wide. His eyes seemed to glow. 'A truly wonderful event. And one in which you and your colleagues are about to share.' He started walking forward again. Yamada decided to shoot him just to be on the safe side. He pulled the trigger.

The gun wouldn't fire.

For the first time since he had achieved his elevated position within the Shinito Corporation Kondo Izumi wished he hadn't. Five hours had passed and there had still been no word from the relief expedition within the habitat. It had to be assumed that the worst had happened. And now he was going to have to give the order to destroy Takata and everyone in it. He looked at his three colleagues who had gathered, in the flesh, in his office. 'Has anyone got any alternative ideas?' he asked them.

None of them had. But Arakawa said,' Shouldn't we wait a while longer?'

'If we do, we run the risk of letting whatever has taken over the habitat to spread out . . . to increase the area of contamination.'

'How?' asked Hyuga.

'How the hell do I know?!' snapped Izumi. 'I don't know what's in there, any more than you do. But it's clearly acting in a malign fashion. We cannot take any more chances with it. We must destroy Takata!'

'And what will be our cover story?' asked Murakami. 'We know that outside suspicions have already been aroused about the habitat. We couldn't conceal the fact that so many of our Company ships have been re-routed to Takata. We can expect the Council of Companies to make a formal enquiry at any time now.'

Izumi waved a dismissive hand. 'We'll say a research programme went badly wrong, everybody in the habitat died from the resulting disease and we were obliged to, er, *sterilize* the facility. In a sense, it's probably not far from the truth.'

'The publicity will do terrible harm to the Company,' said Hyuga grimly, 'and the compensation claims from the employees' families will cost a fortune.'

'I'm well aware of that!' said Izumi. 'But what else can we do, eh?!'

Arakawa said, 'I still think we should give the relief expedition more time.'

Izumi slammed his hand down hard on his desk-top. 'No! We act now! We use every heavy beam projector in the vicinity to totally vaporize Takata!'

The voice of Captain Ryo Komatsu cut in. 'Excuse me, honourable sirs, but we are picking up a visual and audio transmission from Takata . . .'

'Patch us in immediately!' cried Izumi, hoping against hope that the emergency had been terminated.

A flat screen some four feet square appeared in the air in his office. The other three exeuctives had to swivel round in their chairs to view it. A man's head and shoulders were visible. The background was indistinct. The man was talking but there was no sound as yet.

'Is his identity known?' asked Izumi.

'Yessir,' replied Komatsu. 'He is Michael Yamada. Born in California. Aged thirty-two. He was the chief pilot on the first relief ship and a member of the relief expedition.'

'What is he saying?'

'He's asking for a response. We haven't given him one yet. We thought you should be notified first.'

'Give me sound.'

A voice suddenly began to accompany the head on the screen. ' . . . I repeat, this is Mickey Yamada of the relief expedition. Please acknowledge. Please acknowledge . . .'

'Put me into direct contact with him,' commanded Izumi.

' . . . this is Mickey Yamada of . . .' Yamada stopped.

'You recognize me?' asked Izumi.

Yamada gave a bow of his head. 'Yes, honourable sir.'

'You have achieved your objective then? You and your colleagues have regained control of the habitat?' Izumi asked him eagerly.

'Uh . . . no,' said Yamada. 'We've all been captured. But we are all unharmed,' he added.

Izumi wasn't heartened by the latter item of information. 'Who captured you?'

'A Takata executive called Hayden Frid.'

'One man?! *One man* captured *all* of you?!' exclaimed Izumi.

'Our weapons wouldn't work, and then our suits wouldn't obey our bodies. The augment units took on a life of their own. When Frid told us to follow him our suits just did so . . . we were all helpless inside them.'

Izumi had started to sweat, which was very unlike him. This was getting worse and worse. 'And what is the, er . . . situation in the habitat? Who is in control?'

'That's hard to say, sir. The situation here is, well, kind of *screwy*.'

'Screwy?' repeated Izumi.

'Yeah, sir. The people here are acting strange. They keep referring to an alien presence that has taken control of the computer systems. It came from an ancient casing that one of our geologists found in the Belt. But it's friendly, they say. And it's brought humanity a great gift.'

'What is it?'

'The secret of the universe.'

'I see,' said Izumi slowly. 'And have they, er, let you in on this, er, secret yet?'

'No. Not in words. They said I was in the process of, er, absorbing it. It's literally in the air, they said.' Yamada shrugged. 'Sorry I can't be more helpful, but that's all I know.'

'You're doing fine,' said Izumi, wiping his forehead. 'Something in the air . . . you said . . . and you're supposed to be *absorbing* it?'

Yamada nodded. At that moment Izumi's personal assistant hurried into his office, his face ashen. 'Sir! Sir!' he cried. 'You must stop. Break off contact, immediately!'

'What are you babbling on about?' Izumi demanded, annoyed at being interrupted at so crucial a moment.

'Sir, your conversation with Yamada . . . it's being transmitted through the Net! Millions of people must be watching it on Earth, the moon and all the habitats in real-time
contact right now, and then it'll spread right across the Net.
The whole System will know about Takata!'

Ritual suicide by disembowelment – seppuku – was
officially frowned upon in the Japanese culture these days
but right then Izumi thought seriously about reviving the
custom. He looked hopefully down at his desk-top, but it
was devoid of any sharp instruments.

Gordon Pal had what he considered to be the best job in the
System. He was Admiral of the Space Defence Fleet. He
was also the sole human member of the Space Defence
Fleet.

Back in the twenty-first century, when humanity had
been tentatively spreading out into space, and when it was
believed that Earth-style technological civilizations were
probably pretty common in the cosmos, the fear developed
that representatives from such a civilization might make a
surprise appearance. Fine if they were friendly but what if
they turned out to be hostile? OK, the chances were pretty
remote, but if such an encounter ever did take place it
would be for the best to be prepared. And thus the Space
Defence Fleet was born. It consisted of forty-nine heavily
armed zip ships based in squadrons located at various points
across the inhabited sections of the solar system. The
fiftieth ship was the flag ship – the *Van Vogt* – and was
manned by humans. The cost was met by all the Corporations equally and was under their joint control.

With the fleet completed and operational, humanity was
ready for whatever might arrive from the stars.

Nothing did.

And later, when it was generally agreed by scientists that
Earth-like technology-based civilizations were a rarity in the
universe, the need for the fleet became increasingly unlikely. But rather than destroy it or convert it into a fleet of
freighters, a meeting of the heads of the Corporations

decided to put it into mothballs. And that was where it had remained ever since, at a vast docking facility in orbit around Mars. Gordon Pal's great-great-etc. grandfather, who ran a small space engineering company on Phobos, got the contract for running the facility. As the facility was fully automated this didn't involve much effort. In fact, almost none at all. And he also received the privilege of being able to call himself Admiral of the Fleet. This title, like the contract itself, had been handed down from father to son within the Pal family ever since.

The present holder, Gordon, was carrying out the mandatory annual inspection. He wasn't alone. With him was Holly Karapetyan, a pretty twenty-three-year-old woman who had just recently joined the company as his personal assistant. He was hoping to seduce her and had brought her along on the inspection to impress her. He was just showing her the *Van Vogt*'s stateroom when he received an unwelcome interruption from the ship's computer.

'Admiral Pal, I have just received a signal from the Chairman of the Council of Companies. The fleet has been ordered into action. We are to move immediately. I have the co-ordinates.'

'I beg your pardon?' said Pal.

'We have been ordered into action. The System has been invaded by an alien force.'

'But that's ridiculous!' cried Pal.

'It's a top-priority signal with all the correct codes. The fleet is to proceed to the Takata habitat and surround it. The habitat has been taken over by a hostile alien presence. The zip ships are already on the way. We are about to follow. Please go to the bridge and strap yourselves into the acceleration couches.' The ship began to vibrate. There were clanging noises. Pal realized it was disengaging itself from the dock.

'We're actually going off to fight aliens?' he asked disbelievingly.

'I want go home,' said Holly Karapetyan.

He glanced at her, then said to the computer, 'Yeah,

you've got to reconnect with the dock so that Holly can get off.'

'No time,' said the computer. 'Please go to the bridge immediately.'

'I WANT TO GO HOME!' wailed Holly very loudly.

So did Admiral Gordon Pal.

Rosie the Imp was feeling frustrated and extremely pissed off. She had been on the run from Sebastian Chimes for hours now. Every time she thought she had shaken him off he would suddenly pop up again, wild-eyed and practically foaming at the mouth. He would send startled 'Parisians' scattering in all directions as he charged at her. The last occasion had been touch and go: he'd actually got his hand on the collar of her jacket before she wrenched herself free and plunged into a crowd. She'd finally lost him again by ducking down an alley. She had no idea what to do next. She'd tried calling her boss, Aspine Tyrene, for help but was told she was unavailable. Rosie got the impression that some sort of emergency was occurring at headquarters. To hell with that; she was too busy having an emergency of her own to worry about anything else right now . . .

To add to her problems, she was lost. She had originally been heading towards the McDonald's which she knew was located on the Boulevard Haussmann – her intention was to hop on board one of the tourist buses that regularly stopped there – but in all the confusion she had no idea where she was now. Well, according to the street-sign she was in Rue de Surène but that didn't help her much. As she paused on a corner to try and get her bearings, she was suddenly seized from behind.

'Gotcha!' cried Chimes in triumph.

He wrapped his arms tightly around her; so tight she couldn't draw a breath. She panicked momentarily, but then her Imp self-defence training cut in and she brought the heel of her right boot down hard on his right instep. He gave a howl of pain and released her. She drove an elbow into his diaphragm for good measure and started to run.

She hadn't gone far when she was grabbed again. She spun round, prepared to jab her fingers into his eyes, but it wasn't Chimes. It was another Imp. A man of her age. And behind him she could see Chimes struggling in the grip of three other Imps. 'Wow, am I pleased to see you guys!' said Rosie with feeling.

'What's up with him?' asked the one who had stopped her. 'We were sent to collect him. The top brass want him back at headquarters urgently but he's been refusing to answer his communicator.'

She looked at Chimes, who was still struggling violently. 'He hasn't been his normal self,' said Rosie, deciding to be diplomatic.

'Why was he chasing you?'

She shrugged. 'Like I said, not his normal self at all.'

When it had become clear that all the women in the habitat capable of having children were pregnant, they held another emergency meeting in Okimoto's office. In one sense it was a waste of time, in Manion's opinion, because they couldn't actually *do* anything about the situation – they were completely impotent, in direct contrast to the aliens – but it was better than doing nothing.

Manion listened to Doctor Lebra's typically wordy report on the mystery pregnancies. Despite all the words the doctor didn't have anything concrete to say. Without the computers he and his people were severely limited in the degree of analysis they could carry out on the embryos being carried by the women. He had a lot of theories but few hard facts. He couldn't even say whether the embryos were even human: all he could say was that their growth-rates were uniformly very fast. Several women had requested abortions and as soon as these were carried out, using old-fashioned medical methods – their personal bionantechs had refused to follow their owners' instructions in this regard – more information about the nature of the creatures would be available.

As Manion listened to Lebra drone on he was aware that

an intense headache had crept up on him. It lay, throbbing, behind his eyes. He ordered his bionantech to synthesize a large dose of naturally produced pain-blockers within his brain but the pain remained. He closed his eyes . . . and suddenly saw a strange image. It was of a huge, white stone statue of what appeared to be some kind of kangaroo. Well, it was shaped vaguely like a kangaroo, complete with tail, but it had a different, larger kind of head, and its forearms, crossed across its breast, ended in long, human-like hands. It was wearing some sort of kilt. The statue was standing on the summit of a mountain. Clouds drifted around it and the head was surrounded by a blue glow. Manion heard music . . . strange music fashioned by instruments he *knew* were not designed to produce sounds for human ears . . .

He opened his eyes. The image disappeared. So did the music. He looked around. Was he the only one who had had the experience? What did it mean? Maybe he was just overtired. His headache had certainly grown worse . . .

Then he became aware that Hayden Frid, who'd been sitting beside him, had risen to his feet. 'My friends and brethren!' called Frid in an unnaturally loud voice. 'Rejoice! For the light of the True Path has been revealed to us this day!'

Cherry Lee put a hand to her belly and said, 'I can feel it kicking. I haven't been pregnant for even a day yet and I can feel the damn thing kicking!'

Manion thought of the statue of the giant kangaroo-thing with its powerful legs and refrained from telling Cherry that she could expect a lot more kicking in the days to come. He didn't know for sure that the statue in his vision was a representation of an Opoponax creature or of their god. Frid hadn't been too clear in that respect; he had been too busy babbling on about the prophet *Fliitrexchiki* who had been chosen by the true god *Treeckitich* to pass on his revelations to the people. Then again, if the Opoponax – their true name was unpronounceable – were anything like humans they would have conceived their god in their own likeness. And that meant there was a good chance that Cherry Lee had a tiny kangaroo in her womb.

Chapter Twelve

Kondo Izumi sat with his head bowed. So did his three colleagues, Shimpei Murakami, Araki Hyuga and Takie Arakawa. They had been summoned to the office of the Chairman of the Council of Companies, Atsushi Kawamura, which, like the head office of the Shinito Corporation, and so many other Japanese company headquarters, was based in Sydney. Kawamura, sitting behind a vast desk and flanked by grim-faced aides, glared at Izumi. 'Well? What is your explanation for your inexcusably foolhardy actions?'

Izumi managed the trick of looking at Kawamura without raising his head. 'I admit, most honourable one, that it was an act of serious misjudgement.'

Kawamura made a dismissive hissing sound between his teeth. 'That goes without saying, but what is your explanation?'

After some hesitation Izumi said, 'It was . . . well, too good a commercial proposition to pass up. I mean, that was how it *seemed* at the time. Now, of course . . . ' He shrugged helplessly.

'Now we have an alien presence in control of a space habitat in Earth orbit. A presence capable of manipulating the Net, of overriding its security blocks. Blocks that are so foolproof that our AIs cannot penetrate them. Not much sign of financial profit so far, eh?'

Izumi went into cringe overdrive, appearing to shrink within his suit. 'No, honourable one. But at least the alien presence has not demonstrated any overt sign of hostility.'

'Apart from almost destroying your vessel, the *Gully Foyle*,' said Kawamura, 'and forcibly indoctrinating the inhabitants of Takata with its religion.'

'Uh, the first incident might have been an accident, oh most honourable one, and as for the second, the situation is not clear. In our last contact with the pilot, Mickey Yamada, he informed us that no force was involved in the conversion process. People suddenly, and willingly, embraced the Opoponax religion. Many of the relief expedition have expressed their commitment since their arrival. But he reported that not all the original inhabitants of the habitat had become converts. And that so far Yamada himself hadn't experienced any desire to start worshipping the alien god.'

'You have any information on how this process of conversion is carried out?'

'Not as yet, honourable sir. But at least it's been contained within the habitat. Despite all the non-stop preaching being carried on the Net we have yet to learn of any conversion in the entire outside System.'

'For which we must be extremely grateful,' said Kawamura. 'Another monotheistic religion is just what our society does not need. The three that our home-grown foreigners possess cause enough cultural tension and trouble.'

'Yes, most honourable one,' agreed Izumi, 'and the alien version appears to be of an extreme fundamentalist persuasion.'

'Indeed. According to the man doing all the preaching on the Net, your former executive responsible for security . . . ' Kawamura paused. An aide leant towards him and whispered something in his ear. ' . . . Hayden Frid, their religion is completely inflexible.'

Izumi nodded. 'According to our experts who have been monitoring Mr Frid's, er . . . flow, the aliens' world had been racked for some considerable time by a series of destructive wars. Intertribal fighting based on religious differences – the usual sort of thing that we're familiar with from Earth's history. And then the leader of one particular tribe retired to a mountain-top with his closest advisers to meditate, pray to their various gods and plan their imminent campaign against their enemies. They took with them their portable computers. Even at this stage the Opoponax – we have decided to stay with that name for convenience's sake for the time being – were fairly advanced in technology.

'And then a miraculous event is supposed to have occurred: the leader was enveloped in a beam of golden light and disappeared. His distraught advisers had no idea what to do and waited helplessly on the mountain-top. After they had waited for several days the golden beam reappeared, along with their leader. He told them that he had been taken to a place beyond time and space where he had met the True One who had told him he must return and spread the True Word not only to his tribe but to all the tribes. He was to be the means by which all the Opoponax would be united under the True Faith. And when that had been achieved the Opoponax would work to spread the True Word, along with their species, across the entire galaxy . . .

'This is where this monotheistic religion differs from the Earthly ones. The latter developed in relatively primitive human societies. Moses, for example, came down from his mountain bearing stone tablets inscribed with a mere ten God-given laws; but *their* prophet came down from his mountain bearing, roughly translated, the, er, Sacred Software. And it contained an awful lot of religious laws. An *awful* lot, honourable sir. Our experts have counted so far, in Mr Frid's outpourings, over three hundred dietary laws alone, all of which must be strictly adhered to . . . you should hear some of the ones governing sexual activity . . . it's a wonder that the Opoponax ever managed to reproduce after the spread of the new religion . . . ' Izumi shook his head.

'But surely there is no way the Opoponax believed that a different species could follow their religious laws to the letter?' asked Kawamura. 'It would be biologically impossible.'

Izumi said, 'Well, according to how my people have interpreted Mr Frid's words, we humans cannot be completely true believers. Which is why the Opoponax intend transforming the human race into . . . Opoponax.'

'And how do they intend achieving this transformation?'

'We have no idea at this stage, honourable sir. But no doubt it would involve some form of bio-engineering.'

After a pause, Kawamura asked, 'Is it true that the Opoponax resemble *kangaroos*?'

'We have it on good authority that this is so, honourable one. Michael Yamada mentioned people within the habitat having visions of a kangaroo-like statue. It is believed to be a statue of their prophet.'

'And have you, Kondo Izumi, any plans to prevent the human race from being turned into a species of furry marsupials?' Kawamura asked coldly.

'Uh, most honourable sir, I am told it is unlikely that the Opoponax were marsupials. It is believed they were mammal-like . . .'

'I repeat, have you any plans, Kondo Izumi?' The tone of Kawamura's voice made Izumi think wistfully of self-disembowelment again.

'Well, my *colleagues* and I were planning to destroy the habitat . . .' he said.

'And kill nearly a thousand of your employees, many of whom are Japanese,' Kawamura pointed out.

'Uh, we didn't know then that they were still alive.'

'But now you do. And so does everyone else. The whole System is fascinated with the situation on Takata habitat. Contact with an alien intelligence. What would the public reaction be if you blow the place up?'

'But most honourable sir!' Izumi protested. 'I have just told you of the aliens' apparent intentions for the human race! We must destroy Takata!'

'We can't. Not yet. Your ships surround the habitat and I have ordered the Space Defence Fleet into action. It is heading for Takata as we speak—'

'Excuse me, honourable sir,' interrupted a puzzled Izumi, 'the Space Defence *what*?'

Kawamura gave an inaudible sigh. 'It's been in mothballs for some considerable time but you should have been aware of its existence, as your company automatically contributes to its upkeep. Anyway, we will be able to enforce a strict quarantine around the habitat to ensure nothing biological escapes from it alive. It will give us time to devise an alternative method of resolving the crisis without killing all those people. I am now confident, Kondo Izumi, that I can't expect a solution from *your* quarter. It will be up to the Council of Companies. If the best brains, human and artificial, can't solve the problem then I assure you that Takata and all it contains will be obliterated.'

'Yes, illustrious one,' said Izumi, 'but I don't advise waiting too long. The way the Opoponax presence has penetrated and manipulated the Net . . . it worries me very much.'

Kawamura nodded and said, 'It is of grave concern to all of us.'

Steve Moreau was nuzzling Mary's left breast. They had just finished supper and were now indulging in languorous foreplay. In the background the radio was playing light classical music. Then he paused. He raised his head and looked at her. 'You know I love you, don't you?'

She ran her hand through his hair. 'Yes. And I love you too. Completely and utterly.'

'And I love you completely and utterly. But if I don't get out of here soon I'm going to start eating the wallpaper.'

Shots rang out in the street below. People shouted. Moreau glanced towards the french windows. 'Must be Wednesday again already.' On Wednesday night there was always a brief skirmish between a Nazi patrol and members of the Resistance. Sometimes people got shot, sometimes not. But if there was shooting it had to be Wednesday.

'I know it's bad for you,' she said, 'but what else can we do?'

'Jesus, I don't know . . . move to a different zone or something.'

'We'll get caught for sure.'

'Mary, we can't stay here for ever. And sooner or later we *are* going to be found. And then what happens to us? I've got a further four years to serve on my sentence. At least. Maybe they'll slap extra time on me as a penalty for escaping from Perth. And as for you . . . I'm sorry, Mary, but from what you've told me of your past I don't want to think about what they might do to you.'

She hugged him. 'Neither do I. So don't talk about it. Let's just enjoy what time we've got left together.'

'But can't we *do* something? I mean, with your incredible powers why don't we try and escape from Purgatory altogether? And then just disappear!'

She sighed deeply but didn't answer.

'Mary?'

'I'm scared,' she told him. 'The old me wouldn't have given a damn but I'm very frightened. I don't want to leave here.' She sighed again. 'Says a lot about being a woman, doesn't it?'

He thought a bit then stroked the side of her face. 'No. It says a lot about the new you. You *care* now. Not just about yourself but me too. Right?'

'Yeah,' she said quietly.

'I'm the one that's holding you back. I'm a handicap. With me dragging along behind you you know our chances of escape are practically nil. The old you would have thrown me to the wolves ages ago. Hell, you wouldn't have sprung me from Perth in the first place, would you?'

'No. I guess not. Because the old me, being a man, wouldn't have been attracted to you . . . oh, damn, turn that off, could you?'

The music had come to an end and the announcer had started to read out a tedious news bulletin about the war.

'Sure,' he said and got off the bed. He was reaching out towards the radio when the announcer unexpectedly said: 'And now an urgent message for Joster Rack, currently using the alias Mary Eads, and Steven Moreau. If you are in the Paris sector please report to the nearest tourist facility and identify yourselves. You will be granted complete amnesty for all past misdeeds if you comply with this request. I repeat that: you will be granted complete amnesty. A crisis situation has arisen in which the assistance of Joster Rack is urgently required. This is not a trick. This is genuine. Please report to the nearest tourist facility.' After a pause, the announcer continued with the usual bulletin.

Moreau looked at her. 'It's got to be a trick!' she exclaimed. 'Chimes is getting desperate!'

'You're probably right.' He switched the radio off and returned to the bed. 'But it means they know we're still in the Paris zone.'

'Not necessarily. They could be broadcasting the same message in all the zones. If they are they must be confusing a lot of people.'

He glanced back at the radio. 'What if it is genuine?'

'Don't be silly. It can't be.'

'That stuff about a crisis . . .'

'Oh, come *on*.'

'Mary, you're unique. Or rather, your bionantech is. Maybe something's happened that only you can deal with.'

She rolled over on to her side. 'I'm not buying it.'

'Or maybe it's connected with that alien DNA crap you've got in your eye.'

'It's an IRC trap pure and simple.'

He sighed. 'Yeah, I guess you're right.' He put his hand on her bare thigh. 'But I think it would be a good idea to check out the next bulletin.'

When Sebastian Chimes had entered the direct-link facility some hours previously he had been in a relatively calm state of mind. That was because he had been pumped full of tranquillizers. He sat reluctantly in the chair and leaned his head back . . .

. . . And found himself sitting in a large, sombrely furnished office. Black was the predominant colour. Sitting opposite him behind a large desk with a glossy black top was 'Miriam'. She too was in black but he was relieved to see it wasn't leather. Instead she was wearing a sober business suit. Her hair was tied back and she had on a pair of old-fashioned glasses. 'More games, Miriam?' he asked with a scowl. Despite the tranquillizers and his ill feelings towards her the sight of her was already stirring his libido.

'No more games, Sebastian,' she said crisply. 'We are facing a serious situation.'

'Oh yes?' he asked, suspiciously. 'And what is that?'

'We know now the nature of that "priceless" item acquired by the Shinito Corporation and the nature of the emergency in the Takata habitat.' Miriam proceeded to tell Chimes about the recent revelations that had followed Izumi's leaked conversation on the Net. Chimes found it all so incredible he almost forgot his lust for her.

When she had finished he said, 'So we're dealing here with alien missionaries . . . God-botherers from outer space?'

'Yes. But their methods of conversion apparently transcend those developed by humanity. Not so much a matter of brainwashing as brain-rewiring by some bio-invasive means.'

'Jesus,' he muttered, having had some personal experience of mental meddling, thanks to Miriam herself.

'Exactly,' she said.

He thought it over. From what she'd told him the Opoponax religion sounded complex, rigid and downright stifling. 'How odd that a species so technologically advanced could hold such irrational beliefs,' he said.

'Oh really, Sebastian, your own species has produced a complex technology but I'd hardly describe the human race as rational. In fact irrationality is one of humanity's strongest characteristics. Presumably it had some sort of value as a survival aid though I've never figured out what, exactly. Perhaps it's something to do with the ability to develop and maintain a state of mindless optimism in the face of overwhelming evidence to the contrary.

'And your technology only exists because a few people lucked on to the rational discipline of scientific methodology. To quote your Einstein, "The development of science has been based on two great achievements, the invention of the formal logical system – in Euclidean geometry – by the Greek philosophers, and the discovery of the possibility of finding out causal relationships by systematic experiment during the Renaissance . . . the astonishing thing is that these discoveries were made at all." And even in this century the majority of people are scientifically illiterate, especially back on Earth . . . '

As she talked he had a vision of pinning her down on her desk-top and tearing off her clothes.

'For example,' she continued, 'many people still believe in astrology but haven't the slightest knowledge of astronomy. And your more fundamentalist types of religion share many similarities with the Opoponax theism, though admittedly none is as extreme.' She paused and gave him a smile. 'I, on the other hand, am completely rational.'

I wouldn't take bets on that, he thought sourly.

'But the situation has been contained, hasn't it?' he asked. 'Surely the only people who'll be affected will be those unlucky enough to have been inside the habitat? And a strict quarantine has been imposed by now?'

'Yes. Apart from several armed Shinito ships in the vicinity the habitat has been surrounded by the ships of the Space Defence Fleet . . . '

'The what?' asked Chimes.

'Never mind. The problem is that the alien presence within the habitat is not only biologically invasive but has also taken over the entire computer system. First it cut the Takata system from the Net but now it has re-established the link. But most worryingly of all, the presence has achieved some degree of manipulation of the Net. It has circumvented security blocks that I, and my fellow AIs, cannot penetrate. The implications, you would agree, are cause for serious concern.'

'Yes, I would,' said Chimes.

'Which is why it has become even more imperative to get our hands on the Ghost.'

Chimes frowned. 'I don't follow.'

'Somewhere on or within his body, the Ghost is carrying a complete Opoponax genome.'

'Really? Isn't that dangerous? For him, I mean? What if it starts to grow?'

She winced. 'You have just proved my point about scientific illiteracy. No, it won't just *grow*. But we need it. Analysis of the genome may provide us with information that we can use against the alien presence. And there is another, even more important reason why we must find the Ghost.'

'Which is?'

'The Ghost seems to be able to manipulate any computer system, no matter how sophisticated. Just like the Opoponax. As a result he may be the only means by which we can eradicate them from the Net.'

'Well, if that is so I have to tell you we're no nearer to apprehending him. We've tried everything but there's no trace of him. There's been a suggestion that he's no longer on Purgatory but I disagree. I believe he's still here somewhere.'

'I agree. But we will have to change our tactics.'

'How?'

'We will ask him to surrender himself, via radio, television and newspaper announcements throughout Purgatory. Promise him an amnesty for past crimes.'

Chimes smiled and nodded. 'It might work, if he believes it. But I'm afraid he'll know it's a trick.'

'Then we'll have to convince him that it's not a trick.'

'And how will we do that?'

'By telling the truth. Because it won't be a trick.'

'*What?*'

'You heard. The offer of amnesty will be genuine. We need his co-operation.'

Chimes was horrified. 'No!' he protested. 'You can't do that! I've been after him for years! He has been making a fool of all of us at IRC! We can't let him simply get away with it! I won't stand for it!'

'Yes, you will, Sebastian. The priorities have altered. Compared to the potential threat presented by the Opoponax, the Ghost's past actions against us shrink to the inconsequential. But he must be found as quickly as possible. And I am making it your responsibility. You must convince the Ghost that we are telling the truth.'

He shook his head. 'I can't. Give the job to someone else.'

'It has to be you, Sebastian.'

'No.'

'Don't you still want me?'

He didn't answer.

She rose from her chair and walked out from behind the desk. She was naked from the hips down. *Oh shit*, thought Chimes as he was again gripped by an unendurable desire.

She stood in front of him. 'Yes, you do.' She removed the sober black jacket. She wore nothing beneath it. He whimpered.

'My promise still holds, Sebastian,' she said. 'Pleasure beyond description. Just bring me the Ghost.'

And then he was back in the direct-link facility. Alone.

Tears began to stream down his cheeks.

Chapter Thirteen

' . . . And I repeat that I, Sebastian Chimes, give you my personal guarantee that you will be granted total amnesty! The same applies to your companion, Steven Moreau! You will be free to go once you have assisted us in dealing with the crisis situation we now face. Please report to the nearest tourist facility immediately! Please, I *beg* you!'

'That's Sebastian Chimes all right,' said Mary, as they watched the old, flat vid set. 'Though he's sure not the man he used to be.' The normal news bulletin resumed with the now familiar shots of the Zeppelin bombing raid on New York. She got up and switched off the set.

'He sounded as if he was close to cracking up,' said Moreau. They had been tuning into all the news bulletins on both the radio and the vid since hearing the first message on the previous evening. This was the first time that Chimes had put in a personal appearance. Moreau wondered what the other residents of Paris made of the bizarre broadcast.

'Almost hysterical,' said Mary. 'If he's putting on an act he's doing a bloody good job.'

She wandered over to the french windows and stepped out on to the small balcony. It was 'midday' and the street below was busy. He joined her on the balcony. He stared upwards. All the blocks and mental conditioning imposed upon him by the IRC neural implants had now been neutralized and he could see Purgatory as it really was. He could see the great sweeping curve of the place and the distant lands hanging directly overhead through the glare of the solar array. 'If it's true, we can get out of here,' he said. 'I won't have to serve the rest of my sentence. I can go back to Toronto and see my family and friends again. And you can come with me. We can start a new life together.' He put an arm around her shoulders.

'Dream on,' she said bitterly. 'You think IRC or any of the Corporations would just let me walk away once they'd got their hands on me? No way. They couldn't afford to. I've cost them too much. And I'd continue to pose a threat to them. The only conditions in which they'd let me go is when they'd worked out the secret of my bionantech and then fixed it so that I could never use it again.'

'Would that really matter? You said yourself you never intend going back to your old ways.'

'I don't, but it's my bionantech. It's possible they'll never be able to analyse it. From what old Mikuni told me my bionantech is constantly changing, evolving or whatever. And if they can't discover its secrets then they'll never let me go. They'll just keep trying and trying and I'll be trapped for the rest of my life.'

'So you do a strict deal with them. You won't do whatever it is they want unless you get an ironclad guarantee that you go free when it's all over. If the state of Sebastian Chimes is any indication, they need your services pretty desperately.'

'Maybe.' She didn't sound convinced.

'Mary, we have to take the chance! We can't just stay here!' He pulled her gently round so that they were facing each other. 'Look, let me go and make contact with them. You stay here. I'll go to the McDonald's and have them contact Chimes. If it does turn out to be a trap they still won't know where you are. What do you say?'

She sighed. 'I don't know. I just don't trust them. I can't imagine what this so-called "crisis" might be.'

'I still think it might have something to do with that thing you've got in your eye.'

'The alien genome?' She frowned. 'I don't see how.'

'Well, it has to be something out of the ordinary and apart from your bionantech that genome you're carrying is definitely out of the ordinary.'

She shrugged her shoulders.

'I'm going to do it,' he said firmly. 'You wait here. If they and Chimes can convince me it's not a trick I'll come back to you. If I don't, then . . . then you'll know I *do* think it's a trick. I'm afraid then you're on your own. Give me, oh, a couple of hours. Are you paying attention?' Her eyes had become unfocused. She nodded. 'Sure,' she said. 'What have we got to lose? Just our lives . . . '

'Good. Keep looking on the bright side.' He kissed her and turned to leave. The quicker the better, before he lost his nerve. He turned and gave her a wave at the door. She gave him a wan smile in return.

He never saw her again.

Paul Manion sat morosely at the darkened bar and sipped his bourbon and ice. It was just one of many such drinks he'd consumed that day. He was alone in the bar . . .

. . . And then he wasn't. He looked round uninterestedly as he heard the sound of the door sliding open. He squinted, trying to make out the features of the man who had entered. He didn't think it was anyone he knew. No, definitely not, he decided as the man got nearer. A Japanese, youngish, dressed in a spacer's overalls and smoking a cigarette.

Manion raised his glass to him. 'Here's to the good news about the true god *Treeckitich*!'

The other man grimaced. Then he said, with a Californian accent, 'You too? Shit, I was hoping you might be one of the immune.'

'You're not one of them?' asked Manion, not that surprised. He'd never seen any of the Blessed smoking cigarettes before. 'Hell, neither am I.' He held out his hand. 'Paul Manion. Former head of security. Done a hell of a job, haven't I?'

The younger man shook his hand and smiled. 'I'm Mickey Yamada, late of the good ship *Gully Foyle*. Where can I get a drink around here?'

Manion gestured at the bar. 'Just help yourself. The Blessed Ones don't give a shit what we immune get up to. For the moment, anyway.'

144

Yamada went behind the bar and poured himself a cold beer. Then he leaned on the bar and looked about. 'Joint sure is jumping,' he observed.

'We're probably the last two drinkers in the habitat,' said Manion and drank more of his bourbon.

'So you were the head of security, eh?' said Yamada. 'What went wrong?'

'Let's just say it hasn't been my best week career-wise,' said Manion. 'So what's your story? I don't think I've seen you before.'

'Would you believe I'm part of your rescue mission?'

Manion laughed. 'These days I'd almost believe in the true god *Treeckitich*.' Then he started to cry.

Yamada just watched him. Finally Manion wiped his eyes and muttered, 'Sorry about that.'

'It's OK, man,' Yamada told him and refilled Manion's glass from the bourbon bottle. 'You want to tell me what happened?'

'Not really, but I will . . .' Manion gave him an account of the Opoponax Project and its aftermath. He hesitated when he reached the first night of the disaster. He had been lying in bed with Cherry. She had fallen into a fitful sleep – she kept muttering to herself – but he was wide awake and he knew he wouldn't be able to sleep at all. Earlier he had told her what little he had learned from Doctor Lebra and his remaining rational colleagues at that day's last, futile 'emergency' meeting. By then the situation had degenerated into utter chaos. Many others had followed Frid into Opoponax religious mania and the internal system within the habitat had broken down.

Lebra was completely helpless now. All he had to offer was the theory that the so-called Opoponax genome was nothing of the sort. Yes, the genome of the alien species was obviously there somewhere on the long, complicated sequence, but much of the 'genome' was designed to produce other things as well: such as the nano-devices that had penetrated the computers and the organisms that had infected the brains of so many people. The actual Opoponax genome was no doubt within the organism that had impregnated the women. Manion thought wryly of his original warning, but decided it would be futile to raise the issue now.

Lebra also theorized that the bio-mech that had rapidly grown in the synthi-womb had been monitoring its environment while it was being monitored in its turn by the laboratory instruments. The crab-like thing that had broken out had probably been specifically designed for that one manoeuvre . . .

Shortly after this Lebra went glassy-eyed and began extolling the virtues of the prophet *Fliitrexchiki* and the glories of the true god *Treeckitich*.

The meeting was dissolved.

When Manion returned home he was relieved to see his daughters were acting normally. The same applied to Cherry Lee, who was looking after them, but he wondered how much longer they would remain so, including himself. He hoped that there might be some sort of natural immunity to the religion bug.

Some hope.

Slow hours passed and, as he expected, sleep eluded him. Then he heard the murmuring of young voices. His daughters, talking in their room. He rose and entered their bedroom. The light came on. Both the girls were standing on their beds, heads back, arms crossed over their chests. They were chanting. To the true god *Treeckitich*. He called their names. They ignored him.

He went back to his bedroom and woke Cherry to tell her. She told him of the glories of the true god *Treeckitich*.

He drank more bourbon. Yamada gave him a sympathetic pat on the shoulder. 'What happened to them?' he asked.

'They were collected by other Blessed Ones. I haven't seen them since. I guess they're OK, physically. And I've been spending the time since then waiting to become a Blessed One too. But so far I haven't. I guess I'm immune. Like you. There's a few of us about but not enough to do anything. So what's your story?'

146

He listened with some interest as Yamada told him about the two rescue attempts and subsequent events. 'You have any idea what the Company intends to do next?'

Yamada shook his head. 'No, man. Maybe they'll just write us off. I'd be tempted to in their position.'

'You mean destroy the habitat?' asked Manion, surprised.

'Yeah.'

That hadn't occurred to Manion before. But it made sense. 'You think they'll do it?' he asked worriedly.

'Yeah,' Yamada said, with a shrug. 'But it depends on whether what happened here has leaked out beyond the Company's exclusive communications network. If the whole System knows about it then the Council of Companies will have taken charge. If that's so they'll probably send in the Space Defence Fleet.'

'The Space Defence Fleet? I've never heard of it.'

'Not many people have,' Yamada said, and then told him of the history of the fleet.

Manion wasn't impressed. 'Even if it *is* sent here what good could it do? You've said the habitat is already ringed by armed Company ships and they haven't been able to do anything to help us.'

'True, but it'll look good on the vid nets.' Yamada poured himself another cold beer. Inspired by this move, Manion poured out more bourbon. He raised his glass.

'Here's to the historic contact between two intelligent species.'

Yamada smiled and raised his glass as well. Then he said, 'You say you haven't seen your girl-friend since that night. So you don't know whether she's had . . . well, whatever it was growing in her womb.'

'No. I haven't seen any of the women who were pregnant. They've got them all holed up together somewhere. Maybe in the infirmary. That's one of the areas that's off limits to us immune types. I know because I tried to check it out.' He produced a crumpled cigarette-pack and lit another cigarette.

'Yeah, there's a lot of buildings we're being kept out of,'

agreed Yamada. 'And there seems to be a lot of activity going on inside them judging from the sounds I've heard.'

'I wonder what they're up to . . . what the grand plan is,' mused Manion. He drank more bourbon.

'Convert the entire human race, literally, into religion-crazed Opoponax. If they can get out of here, that is.'

'I wonder what it looks like,' said Manion.

Yamada glanced at him with a frown. 'What?'

'Cherry's . . . child. If she's had it yet. Judging by the speed it was developing she probably has.' He was now feeling considerably drunk.

'You said that in your vision you saw what looked like a statue of a giant kangaroo . . .'

'Yeah. If that was an actual reper . . . representation of an actual Opoponax then they kind of look like kangaroos. But with bigger heads. And hands. So by now I might be the foster-daddy of a bouncing baby marsupial.'

Yamada raised his glass to him. 'Congratulations.'

'Thank you,' said Manion, sliding off his bar-stool to the floor.

Mary was standing on the small balcony and anxiously scanning the people walking along the street below. She was very worried. Steve had been gone for hours. He'd said he'd only be a couple of hours. He'd told her to flee if he was overdue but she didn't want to leave the sanctuary of the familiar room.

Then she heard the sound of the door opening behind her. Relief filled her. She spun round. 'Steve . . . !'

But it wasn't Steve. It was Sebastian Chimes. He entered the room, a fixed smile on his face.

'My dear Glitch,' he purred, 'you have no idea how much I have looked forward to this moment.' Two armed Imps followed him into the room.

'So it was a trick!' she cried. 'Where is Steve? What have you done to him?'

Chimes advanced towards her. She backed away until her bottom touched the balcony railing. 'Come any closer and I'll jump!' she screamed.

He stopped. The smile disappeared from his face. 'No! Don't! Please . . .'

'What's happened to Steve?'

'He's fine, believe me. And, regretfully, I must inform you that the offer of amnesty was no trick. It is, unfortunately, completely genuine. Provided you co-operate.'

'I don't believe you. I want to see Steve.'

'He's already on his way to headquarters. You can see him there.'

She shook her head. 'I may be about to fall to my death from this balcony but I'm not falling for that line.'

Chimes took out his communicator from a jacket pocket and spoke a few muffled words into it. Then he took a step forward and offered it to her. 'You can speak to him.'

She regarded the communicator suspiciously, sure that Chimes intended to grab her hand if she reached for it. But so anxious was she to believe that she might speak to Steve, she leaned forward and stretched out her arm. Her fingers closed round the device. Chimes did nothing. 'Steve,' she said anxiously into the communicator, 'are you there?'

There was a pause and then someone who certainly *sounded* like Steve said, 'Yeah, I can hear you, Mary. You OK?' She remained suspicious. These days you can fake anything, and she should know.

'Prove to me you're Steve,' she demanded. 'Tell me something that only you would know.'

'Like what?'

She thought. 'What do you always ask me to do when we're in bed together?'

'Jesus, Mary, people are listening to this!'

'Tell me.'

He told her. She was convinced it was Steve. 'Why didn't you come back? Where are you?'

'They wouldn't let me return. I'm in an airbus heading towards Purgatory Central Control, or so I'm told.'

'They haven't hurt you?'

'No. I'm fine. And though I can't guarantee it, they seem to be genuine in their offer to you . . . to us. They're talking about letting me go straight back to Toronto, the rest of my sentence is being wiped clean.'

'You're not going, are you?' she asked, alarmed.

'Hey, don't worry! I'm not going anywhere without you!'

'So you think I should give Chimes the benefit of the doubt?' she asked him.

'I suppose we have no choice, darling.'

She considered it then said, ''Bye, Steve. See you soon.'

'Yeah. See you soon,' he told her. 'Take care.'

She handed the communicator back to Chimes and came in from the balcony. 'I guess I'm all yours,' she told him.

'If only,' he said, wistfully.

Chimes kept glancing at her as the skimmer sped over the zones of Purgatory towards headquarters. It was hard to believe that this was the person he had been seeking so obsessively for so long. She sat slumped in her seat, staring vacantly out of the window. Was this the Glitch – the Ghost in the Machine – that had caused the Corporations, and IRC in particular, so much grief? All right, so her – *his* – present form was a Body-Chop job and he wasn't normally a woman but something was definitely lacking. Chimes experienced the awful doubt that they had got the wrong person. Could it be that the Ghost had managed to pull off an elaborate scam that involved substituting this small, harmless-looking woman in the drab dress for himself? Sure, the preliminary and brief check of her bionantech indicated that it was unusual but then the real Glitch could have fixed it that way himself . . .

She turned from the window and looked at him. Then she gave a weak smile. 'From the expression on your face I see you're having an attack of the profound doubts about me. But don't worry. I really am the Ghost.'

'I wish I could be sure of that,' he muttered.

'I can prove it. This isn't the first time we've met, you know.'

'It isn't?' he said, surprised. Then shook his head. 'No, I've never seen you before.'

'Not as a woman, of course. It was the time about eighteen months ago when you were investigating a big grey-market racket at the Hellas Planitia mining complex on Mars.'

'Yes, I remember that,' said Chimes, frowning. 'But . . .'

'I had myself assigned as a temporary investigator to your team. I worked in close proximity with you for over a week. You knew me as Dominic Mose.'

The name was familiar to Chimes. An image formed in his mind. A young man with blond hair and green eyes. Very bright and resourceful. Was transferred from IRC's Viking City branch. Had an excellent record. Dominic Mose.

'Now you know why that operation of yours was a complete wash-out,' she said, and turned her face back towards the window.

The fury that rushed through Chimes was quickly dampened. It proved that he really did have the Glitch. He had achieved his objective. And that meant he would receive his reward from Miriam . . .

When they reached headquarters Chimes escorted the Glitch to the special facility that had been prepared for her. Then he raced off to keep an appointment with another facility – the direct-link facility. As he entered he found himself trembling with anticipation. Miriam was going to be his. Rationally he knew he was about to engage in simulated sex with a computer system but that didn't diminish his excitement. Miriam was as real as he was, where it counted.

He hurriedly sat down in the chair and leant his head back. Contact was made . . .

. . . And found himself in a strange room. It was bathed in a yellow glow and filled with mist. *Is she using dry ice now?* he asked himself irritably. 'Miriam, where are you?'

There was no reply. He looked around. He could dimly make out engraved figures on the walls. They looked vaguely familiar. And in the background he could hear some sort of music. Like out-of-tune chimes.

'Miriam! As you probably know already we have the

Glitch! *I* have the Glitch! Now it's your turn to keep your side of the bargain! Miriam!'

The mist parted and a figure in a yellow robe appeared. Its hooded head was bowed as it approached him.

'Miriam?'

The figure stopped in front of him. The head rose. He saw with relief that it was Miriam. Her eyes were closed.

'Yet another game, Miriam?' he asked her, struck once again by her unearthly beauty.

She opened her eyes. 'Rejoice, Sebastian, for I am going to be your path to the true god *Treeckitich*.'

As he backed away from her he realized what the figures on the walls reminded him of.

Kangaroos.

Chapter Fourteen

Steven Moreau banged his fists on the door, then he started kicking it.

'Will you please stop doing that, sir?' said a male voice from the intercom beside the door. He had no idea whether the voice was human or synthetic, nor did he care.

'I will when someone tells me what's going on,' said Moreau, angrily. 'I want to talk to someone in charge!'

'You will in time, sir. Just be patient.'

'Why haven't I been able to see Mary? I was promised I could see her as soon as she arrived here.'

'I have no authority to discuss that, sir.'

Moreau kicked the door again. 'We've been double-crossed! I should have known you bastards would do something like this!'

'On the contrary. IRC will keep its side of the bargain. You will be released as promised. But for the time being you must remain here, sir. You must admit that your suite is hardly a prison cell.'

Moreau did indeed have to admit that the suite, with its superb holographic windows showing spectacular views of the Swiss Alps, was very luxurious and in the normal way was probably used exclusively by top IRC executives, but he was in no mood to enjoy its amenities. He wanted to see Mary. He desperately wanted to know if she was all right; to know that these IRC bastards weren't mistreating her.

He kicked the door again.

'I *do* wish you wouldn't do that, sir,' sighed the voice.

*

'*That's* the infamous Ghost?' said Kondo Izumi in dismay. He was peering at Mary Eads through an observation panel. The woman, dressed in a plain white tunic, was lying listlessly on a couch, a plate of untouched food on the table beside her. Izumi had just arrived at the habitat, having come straight from Sydney as soon as he'd received word of the Ghost's capture. Or rather, surrender.

'There's no doubt about it,' said Aspine Tyrene. 'Her bionantech is extraordinary. We've tried to analyse it but failed. It's almost as if it has an intelligence of its own. She's the Ghost for certain.'

'Well, she doesn't inspire much confidence,' said Izumi. In fact he was profoundly disappointed by the sight of this somewhat small, unimpressive woman. He had practically guaranteed Atsushi Kawamura, Chairman of the Council of Companies, that the Ghost would provide the solution to all their problems. 'Has the situation we're in been explained to her?'

'Yes,' said Aspine Tyrene, 'but she didn't seem very interested.'

'She wants to have a baby,' said someone.

Startled, Izumi stared at the young female Imp who had spoken. 'She wants *what*?'

'A baby,' said the Imp. 'She wants to settle down with that guy she was with, Steve Moreau, and have a baby. She told me.'

'She's doing no such thing! Not until she's helped us deal with the Opoponax crisis!'

'We've had a psychologist talk to her,' said Aspine Tyrene. 'He said she's suffering from severe depression. Apparently she feels guilty about the misdeeds committed by her former self.'

'I don't understand.'

'Well, it appears that her female persona is at odds with her male persona. In fact she detests what she once was.'

'I don't care how she feels!' snapped Izumi. 'The crisis far outweighs her petty emotional problems! I will talk to her myself!'

'Follow me,' said Aspine Tyrene. She led him to the door leading into the special facility. The Imp brought up the rear. Aspine Tyrene pressed a button and a door slid open. The trio entered the room. Mary Eads, after an initial flicker of interest, regarded them with weary disappointment. 'Hi, Rosie,' she said to the Imp. 'I was hoping you might be bringing Steve to see me.'

'Sorry, Mary, it's out of my hands,' said the Imp.

Izumi strode over to her couch. 'Do you know who I am?' he demanded.

The woman nodded. 'You're Kondo Izumi, top exec of the Shinito Corporation.' She gave him a wan smile. 'I used to work for you, but I guess you know that.'

Infuriated, he snarled, 'I know all about you and what you did! You're the cause of this whole mess! If you hadn't stolen that genome the Opoponax Project would have been handled very differently . . . with caution instead of . . .'

' . . . Instead of with a degree of recklessness of criminal dimensions,' said the woman.

He fought not to lose his temper. Clenching his fists, he hissed, '*You* are the criminal! You are to blame for everything! And now you must make amends! You must use your special bionantech to combat the alien presence which is spreading through the Net! You have no choice!'

'I'd like to help, Mr Izumi. Really. But I'm not in tune with my bionantech any more. I've lost touch with it. I'm helpless.'

'You're lying!' His voice almost reached a scream.

She shook her head. 'Nope. Believe me, I've tried, but it just doesn't respond to my commands. Whatever I had I've lost it now.'

Izumi stood there glaring at her, his chest heaving. Then, abruptly, he turned and strode loudly towards the door. The other two followed him.

'Rosie, how's Sebastian Chimes?'

The Imp paused at the doorway and glanced back at Mary. 'No change, I'm afraid.'

'Oh, what a shame,' said Mary, and the two of them exchanged a smile.

*

Holly Karapetyan, on the bridge of the *Van Vogt*, switched on the intercom. 'Gordon, we have visual contact with the habitat and fleet. We'll be there in minutes. Come and look!'

'I couldn't give a stuff,' came the grumpy reply. 'I'm going back to sleep. Don't bother me again.'

Holly sighed. Admiral Gordon Pal had turned into such a bore. At first he had just raged and ranted about the injustice of being forcibly dragged away from his business on Phobos, then, as the journey had continued, he'd retreated to his stateroom and alternated between sleeping and sulking.

Holly, on the other hand, after her initial fright over finding herself involved in a Space Defence Fleet action against enemy aliens, had become increasingly fascinated by the whole unlikely adventure. And now, as the *Van Vogt* approached the Takata habitat and its halo of imposing zip ships, not to mention the large number of Shinito ships of varying sizes that also surrounded the habitat, she felt a delicious tingle of excitement.

The door slid open and a female Imp entered the suite. Moreau recognized her. He knew her name was Rosie. He was puzzled. It was supper-time but she wasn't carrying a food tray.

'Mr Moreau, would you come with me, please?' She touched the subduer that hung from her belt to show it was an order rather than a request.

He didn't rise from the couch. 'Where to, Rosie?'

'To see a friend of yours.'

He sprang up. 'Mary? You mean at last I'm going to be allowed to be with her?'

She gave him an uneasy smile. 'Yeah, in a way.'

'What do you mean?' he asked, suddenly suspicious.

'Just come with me,' she said, with a sigh.

She took him to a nearby luxury suite that was identical to his own. It was occupied by a good-looking young man sitting on one of the couches. The man winced as Moreau entered. Moreau had never seen him before. He looked around. There was no one else in the room. 'Where's Mary?' he asked the Imp. She looked unhappy.

'I'll leave you two together,' she said and rapidly exited.

Puzzled, Moreau stared at the young man. He had dark hair and very green eyes. Slim, but well-built. 'Who are you?' he asked him bluntly.

'Steve,' said the man. 'I'm sorry.'

Moreau was still in the dark. He wondered if this was someone from his old life on Earth; someone who had come to escort him home but whom his still-faulty memory couldn't yet place. 'Do I know you?'

'You'd better sit down, Steve.'

Mystified, Moreau went and sat in an armchair facing the couch. 'Right, I'm sitting. So tell me who you are.'

The young man stared into his eyes. 'Don't you *know* who I am, Steve?'

'No, I've told you I've never seen you before in . . . ' He froze. He'd seen something in the man's eyes. Something that struck a chord. Then he realized. 'Oh God, no!' he gasped.

The man nodded sadly. 'I'm afraid it's true, Steve. I'm Mary.'

Moreau was horrified. 'No! I don't believe it!'

'It wasn't my idea, Steve. They forced me. Kondo Izumi, the head of Shinito, the Chairman of the Council of Companies, the IRC execs . . . all of them. They had my original bioprint which they'd extracted from the Body-Chop computer in Singapore. They use similar methods of body manipulation in their resuscitation units. It was a relatively simple matter for them to turn me back into Joster Rack.' Then he leaned forward and said earnestly, 'But I'm *not*, Steve. I'm still Mary inside. I'm still *your* Mary!'

Overcome with revulsion, Moreau sprang to his feet. 'No! *No!* You're not! Mary's as good as dead now. And you know it!'

He rushed to the door. It wouldn't open. He struck it with his fist then yelled into the intercom, 'Open this fucking door!'

The man had risen too. Moreau felt his hand grip his shoulder. 'Steve, let's talk about this! Please!'

Moreau's feeling of revulsion boiled over. He turned and struck the man in the face with the same fist he'd just used on the door. The man fell backwards. Moreau went and kicked him

157

hard between his legs. He heard the door opening. He looked round. Two Imps were standing there, one of them Rosie. Moreau attempted to push between them but there was the crackle of a subduer against the side of his neck and he knew nothing else.

'How are you feeling now, Mary . . . I mean, Mr Rack,' Rosie asked her.

'I'm still Mary, Rosie, and as to how I feel, well, like I've been kicked in the balls,' she told her, truthfully. 'I'd forgotten what a damn nuisance these things can be.' She was lying on the couch holding an ice-pack to her throbbing groin. Rosie hovered fretfully beside her/him. 'How is . . . *he*?' she asked Rosie.

'Oh, he'll be fine. It was just a light knock-out charge. He's probably already regained consciousness. It's you I'm worried about.'

'Don't be. I'll live. I'm just not sure I want to.' Which was true. Nothing of the pain in her balls matched that of the pain of being so brutally rejected by Steve. And yet – *she* – still loved him.

And yet . . . and yet . . .

Yes, she did still love him but on reflection she was already seeing him through new eyes. Male eyes. Her old eyes. And Joster Rack had never been gay. The same applied to Steve. She also knew what the logical outcome would have been even if Steve hadn't reacted the way he had. But right now logic didn't matter. Only the pain.

The door opened and Kondo Izumi entered at a rush. He was followed by a female aide. Izumi regarded her with concern. 'Are you all right? I have only just heard what happened!'

Despite her despair she couldn't help feeling amused at the head of the Shinito Corporation's display of concern. She pointed at Joster Rack's groin. 'I'm afraid all your efforts have gone for nought, Mr Izumi. My manhood has once again been destroyed.'

Izumi looked shocked. She gave a bitter laugh. 'It's OK.

just some bruising. Same here.' She applied the ice-pack to her swollen mouth.

'Then you are fit enough to confront the Opoponax presence in the Net?' asked Izumi eagerly.

'Mr Izumi, as far as I'm concerned I'm still Mary Eads. The same woman you met just over a week ago.'

'No, no! You are now a man again!' insisted Izumi loudly. 'Your brain has been rewired genetically! It is a male brain!'

'I'm sure it is,' she said with a sigh, 'and I'm sure I'll eventually start thinking like a man again, but I only got out of a recuperation chamber a few hours ago. Mentally I'm still the same as I was before you broke your side of the bargain and had me physically altered.'

'I am sorry, but I had no choice. Humanity faces its greatest threat and you may be our only hope.'

She sighed again. 'Well, there goes the human race.'

'You must not make jokes!' shouted Izumi.

'Believe me, I'm not,' she told him wearily.

Beads of sweat stood out on Izumi's forehead. 'Can you control your bionantech yet?' he asked, in a quieter voice.

'No. It refuses to respond. But I'll keep trying, I promise.'

He dabbed at his face with a spotlessly white handkerchief. 'How long will it take?'

She shrugged. 'I don't know. Hours. Days. Weeks.'

'We haven't got weeks!' he cried, his volume control going up again. 'The Opoponax is spreading through the Net at an increasing rate. If we have to isolate any more systems the entire Net will have to shut down. Nearly half the Corporation AIs have already been contaminated, including IRC's . . .'

'Yeah, I'd heard about IRC's AI. Shame about Sebastian Chimes.'

Izumi gave him a suspicious look, and said, 'Then you understand the seriousness of the situation?'

'Oh, I do. And I understand the extent of the seriousness it represents to you personally. Even if the alien presence is neutralized you will be taking early retirement at the very least. Am I right?'

Izumi glared at her but said nothing.

'What about the Opoponax genome I was carrying in my eye? I presume it was removed while I was being altered.'

Izumi nodded. 'It is being examined. I brought a fully equipped team of genegineers with me to Purgatory.'

'And I also presume you're not repeating the mistake of inserting it within a fertilized cell.'

'Of course not. We will build up a series of computer models of all its various biological aspects. Which is what they intended to do on Takata, before *you* so disastrously interfered!'

'Hey, Kondo, we all make mistakes.'

Izumi swore under his breath and strode angrily from the room.

'Looks like that's going to become a habit with him,' she told Rosie.

Some time later, as Mary was just dozing off, Rosie returned.

'I thought you'd like to know,' she said, 'that Steve Moreau is leaving for Earth in an hour's time.'

'Oh,' said Mary. 'You've spoken to him?'

'Yeah. I asked him if he wanted to say goodbye to you before he left.'

'And he said no?'

'Something like that. I don't think you'd like to hear his exact words.'

'No. I wouldn't, said Mary quietly.

Paul Manion was sitting on a park bench and sipping from a half-bottle of bourbon. It was the same park that he'd regularly brought his daughters to play in. And their dog. The dog, King, was sitting by his feet. He was not a happy dog these days. He had been moping ever since Michelle and Amelia had gone away with the other Blessed. Manion knew how King felt. He took another sip from the bottle, enjoying the burning sensation in his throat.

It was all his fault. He should never have brought them to the habitat. He should have left them on Earth. His ex-wife's sister, Taisy, and her husband said they were happy to look after them. But no, he'd been selfish. Hadn't wanted to be deprived of their company, not at this special time of their lives. And now they were lost to him, probably for ever. They would spend the rest of their lives worshipping an alien kangaroo god . . .

The shadow of an aircar moved across the grass. He glanced briefly up at the vehicle. The Blessed were certainly getting busier. Neither he nor Mickey Yamada knew yet exactly what they were planning but Yamada had said only the day before that there was plenty of activity in the docking area. Yamada had surmised that they were going to try and break out of the habitat. They'd be facing stiff opposition outside but maybe that so-called 'genome' also contained blueprints for weaponry far in advance of anything we had, said Yamada. If there was going to be a battle it was unlikely the habitat would avoid a direct hit and then it would be all over for those inside.

Right now Manion couldn't give a damn. He drank more bourbon. Then, out of the corner of his eye, he caught sight of something moving through the park towards him.

Even before he'd turned his head to look directly at it he had registered the fact that it was *hopping* . . .

Chapter Fifteen

The fools, thought Joster Rack, *the stupid fools!* His captors had been so anxious for him to regain control over his bionantech that they had forgotten just what advantages it would provide him with when he did. And now he had.

It had been a week since he'd emerged from the recuperation chamber and he was beginning to feel like his old self. There was only one problem. *She* was still around. A presence that haunted his mind, nagging at him. He could only hope that she would eventually fade completely away.

I won't. I'm a permanent part of you now. And you know it.

No! You're just an echo, ringing in my brain. But you don't exist any more.

I'm as real as you are.

He clapped his hands over his ears. 'Go away, you damned bitch!'

'Who are you talking to?' asked the monitoring program via the intercom. 'Are you experiencing some form of mental aberration? If so, will you be requiring medical attention?'

Rack lowered his hands. 'I'm quite all right, thank you.' He walked over to the computer-controlled door-lock and touched it.

'What are you doing?' enquired the computer. 'You know you cannot leave your suite without permission and an escort . . . ' The computer stopped speaking. Then the door slid open. He leaned his head out through the doorway. The corridor was empty.

Where do you think you're going?

You know perfectly well where I'm going. I've just erased all memory of me from the computer systems. He stepped out into the corridor. *And now we're . . . I am going to escape.*

What about your bargain? Your agreement with Izumi and IRC? You promised to confront the Opoponax contamination of the Net.

Are you crazy? It sounds too bloody dangerous. Besides, you know we – I – can't trust IRC. Even if I succeed in doing what they want there's no guarantee they'll keep their side of the bargain. They're just as likely to burn out my bionantech before releasing me . . .

You just can't run away like this.

Watch me.

Izumi may be right. Maybe you are the System's only hope against the Opoponax. You could be responsible for the fate of countless millions of people!

Oh, don't be so melodramatic! What do I care about people being converted to alien-god-worshippers? People worship enough strange gods as it is. One more loony religion isn't going to make a difference.

It sounds a hell of a lot more serious than that! It involves the bio-transformation of the human species!

Well, I don't give a shit.

He turned a corner in the corridor and came face to face with Rosie. They both came to a halt and stared at each other.

Then Rosie said, 'What are you doing out alone?' At the same time she pulled her subduer from her belt.

With one hand he knocked the subduer from her hand and with the edge of the other . . .

No!

. . . He hit her on the side of her neck. She said, 'Oh,' and crumpled to the floor.

You bastard! There was no need to do that to her!

He knelt down beside Rosie and felt her throat. *Shit. She's still alive. I'll have to finish her off.* He raised his hand over Rosie's throat.

Stop! What the fuck do you think you're doing!

I have to. She'll raise the alarm as soon as she regains consciousness. I need more time.

No!

I have no choice. He prepared to bring the edge of his hand down hard on Rosie's exposed throat. But when the moment came he couldn't move his hand. His arm seemed to be frozen. Then he realized what was happening. *Bitch! You're doing this to me! I can't move!*

Don't be stupid. I have no control over our – your – body. I know because I've tried before.

Then why can't I move my arm? Why can't I kill her?

Ask yourself. It has nothing to do with me.

He looked down at Rosie's face, remembered all the kindnesses that the Imp had done him . . . her. He liked her. He slowly lowered his arm.

Maybe there's some hope for you after all.

Oh, shut up! It means I'm still not my old self. He stood up and went and retrieved Rosie's subduer. He put it in his pocket then picked Rosie up in his arms and carried her back to his suite. She came to after about a minute. She frowned up at him and said, 'What happened?'

'Some idiot knocked you out. Sorry about that.'

She felt the side of her neck and winced. 'I remember now. *You* hit me!'

'Like I said, some idiot.' He handed her back her subduer. 'Better call Izumi and tell him I'm probably still not ready to tough it out with his Opoponax invaders but I guess we can't afford to wait any longer.'

Paul Manion sat frozen to the seat as the thing hopped towards him. At his feet the black Labrador, King, began to growl. The creature was about six feet tall and vaguely resembled the statue that Manion had briefly glimpsed in his vision. It had massive hind legs with long, thick claws. The tail, which it leaned back on, was also massive. It was covered in short, bright yellow fur. It did *kind* of resemble a kangaroo but only from the waist down. The forearms were disturbingly human-like and the head, though it possessed a kangaroo-like snout and ears, was very big; domed like a human being's.

And the eyes. They were the most disturbing thing of all. Round, with human-like pupils, they gazed with open curiosity at Manion. They were intelligent eyes . . . and strangely menacing. Manion thought he could also read contempt in them. He wondered how the thing had reached such a size in only a few weeks after birth. Was it still an infant or had it finished growing? He also wondered, hysterically, if this was his foster-son, but he couldn't tell its sex because it wore a kind of kilt-like garment, also yellow.

King, who had been growling throughout this close encounter between human and alien, suddenly sprang at the thing, aiming for its throat. To Manion's horror, the thing calmly leaned further back on its tail, caught King with its forearms and ripped open his abdomen with one of its huge hind claws. It casually tossed the dying dog to one side, stared hard at Manion again, then turned and hopped away.

It took some time for Manion to summon up the will-power to rise from the seat. He went to King and gave what little comfort he could to the shuddering and whimpering dog until it finally went mercifully still.

' . . . I give thanks to the blessed prophet *Fliitrexchiki* for giving us all the sacred knowledge – you bloody bitch, Miriam! – that leads to the one true god *Treeckitich* – I'm going to get you, Miriam! – thanks be to *Fliitrexchiki* for revealing the true path . . . ' Sebastian Chimes's eyes were wide and staring as he raved and writhed against the restraints on the bed but he seemed completely unaware of the small group of people who had entered the room and were observing him.

Trying not to smile, Rack said, 'Who's this Miriam he keeps raving on about?'

'We don't know,' answered Aspine Tyrene. 'There's no record of any Miriam in his personal file.'

'I thought he was asexual,' said Rack as he stared at his old enemy writhing on the bed, his mouth frothing.

'Not any longer,' said Rosie. 'He propositioned me when we were in the Paris zone together. And he mentioned Miriam there too. When I asked about her he got angry and said she wasn't a "she" but a "thing".'

Rack rubbed his chin thoughtfully. 'Must be connected to the AI. You say he's been like this since his last contact with it?'

'Yes,' said Aspine Tyrene, 'he was using the direct-link facility. That was when we learned that the AI had been contaminated by Opoponax. It was immediately isolated from the Net. Since then we haven't been able to get any response. Needless to say, no one has dared to use the direct-link facility since then.'

Rack turned to Kondo Izumi. 'But you want me to, eh?'

Izumi refused to meet his eyes. 'It seems the most logical place to begin,' he said.

'Logical? Me versus an AI?'

'It's deranged.'

'Deranged or not it's still an AI.'

'You've manipulated AIs in the past.'

'I've manipulated *sections* of AIs in the past. I've never attracted the full attention of one before. I took care not to. And there's the other important factor, that it's now been taken over by an alien AI. Handling my bionantech might be simple child's play to something like that. I could be overwhelmed instantly.'

'It's your choice. We can't force you,' said Izumi.

Rack laughed. 'Of *course* you can force me. And you probably will if I don't go willingly. So don't talk to me about choice.' He turned and headed for the door. 'Come on, let's go and pay a visit to the direct link . . .'

As they entered the facility Rack warily regarded the solitary black chair sitting in the centre of the featureless grey room. It reminded him of the electric chair they used to execute people back in the bad old days. In a sense it could well be the device by which his destruction would be achieved.

Mine too.

Oh shut up.

'Cheery place, isn't it?' he observed. He went over to the chair. 'How does it work?'

'Just sit down and lean back against the head-rest,' said Aspine Tyrene. 'Contact with the AI will be automatic. It may deny you access. That will be the first test of your bionantech.'

'Right. Well, here goes.' He sat down on the chair. 'If I start babbling about kangaroo gods then cancel all bets . . . ' He leaned his head back. It touched the head-rest.

His bionantech went beserk.

He had never experienced anything like it before. He could almost feel his bionantech sizzling throughout his body. He had no control over it. It was acting on its own. 'Jesus,' he whispered. His entire brain seemed to be humming and he was aware that *something* was trying to penetrate his mind.

I'm scared, she said.

"YOU'RE scared?! I'm fucking terrified!

Break the contact!

You think I haven't tried?! I can't bloody move!

'Are you all right?' asked Rosie, looking concerned.

'What's happening?' asked Izumi.

Rack couldn't answer them. His brain felt like it was being microwaved and his head as if it might explode at any moment. He took a crumb of satisfaction in picturing Izumi being splattered with steaming blood and brains.

Then it all stopped.

He slumped in the chair. 'Bloody hell,' he gasped. His bionantech then informed him that an attempt to invade and manipulate his brain had been defeated. He passed on this information to the others. His bionantech then informed him that he had access into the AI itself if he so wished. All its defences had collapsed.

Let's call the whole thing off, she told him.

No, might as well get it over with. Besides, I'm curious now . . .

I'M not!

That's why you're not me. 'OK, I'm going in,' he told the others.

'Good luck,' said Rosie.

Blackness.

Total blackness. Cold and suffocating. And frightening.

This is creepy, she said.

For the first time he was glad her presence was still lingering in his mind. This was no place to be alone. But he knew what was happening. The AI might have lost its defences but it was still fighting. It had failed to overwhelm his bionantech physically and penetrate his brain; now it was using psychology against him. He ordered his bionantech to retaliate . . .

Let there be light . . .

He was standing in a room. A transparent wall looked out on to an expanse of red desert. In the distance a huge, multicoloured airship moved slowly through the pink-orange sky. The cheapest way of carrying freight across the Martian deserts . . .

I seem to remember this place.

You should. It's one of our – my – apartments on Mars. On the outskirts of Elysium. I need a familiar setting as a base. For the battle.

Battle?

We're at war. Problem is I don't know yet WHAT *we're at war with.* He went over to the drinks cabinet and poured himself a cold beer. He tasted it. Perfect. He marvelled at the uncanny sense of reality within the computer-generated world.

A figure appeared in the room. A very attractive young woman wearing a yellow robe. She smiled at him and said, 'Hello, I'm Miriam and I bring you joyful news. Thanks to the blessed prophet *Fliitrexchiki*, the path to the true god *Treeckitich* is open to you . . .'

Rack shook his head. 'Save it, Miriam. Unlike Sebastian Chimes, I'm immune.'

The girl stopped her litany and frowned at him. 'I don't understand . . . everything is so confusing . . . ' She vanished.

So that was Miriam. No wonder Chimes was getting so hot under the collar . . .'

And then suddenly everything changed . . .

A different room. A bedroom. Darkness beyond the window. A woman hurriedly throwing items of clothing, toiletries into a small suitcase. She was excited, her face flushed. She was tall with reddish hair. Very white skin. She was wearing only a bra and panties. She paused in her packing and turned to him. 'Tell me again that this is going to work and that I have absolutely nothing to worry about,' she said, and gave him a nervous grin.

I know her . . .

Yeah. It's Julie Verhoven. The woman I . . .

. . . Betrayed. On Takata.

Julie was staring expectantly at him. He heard himself say, 'Sure. This is going to work and you have absolutely nothing to worry about.'

She grinned again at him and resumed packing.

What's going on?

I'm not sure. It must have got access to my memories during the struggle between it and my bionantech. It's trying another psychological trick . . .

But WHAT *is?* she asked. *The IRC AI or the Opoponax presence?*

I have no idea, he admitted. *Maybe it's some kind of merger of the two but I'm beginning to think there's more to Opoponax than a mission to convert the human race to their kangaroo religion.*

'Sean?' Julie Verhoven had turned to him again. He remembered he had called himself Sean Varley back then. 'I'm sure you know what happened next . . .'

Hello, we're not following the script any more.

Aloud, he said, 'Yeah, I remember, Julie . . . or whatever you are.'

'You said you had some unfinished business to attend to that you'd just remembered and that you'd meet me at the passenger terminal in two hours and we'd leave on the next scheduled lunar shuttle. You told me again how your bionantech would provide me with a new Net identity, just as it would do for you. We'd be husband and wife. No record of our old identities leaving the habitat would exist. Then you kissed me and left. Right?' She began to walk towards him. She was, he could see, a perfect replica of Julie Verhoven all right, down to the faint dusting of freckles across her nose and cheeks.

169

'Yeah. Right.'

'So I went to the terminal two hours later and waited. And waited. You never showed. The lunar shuttle left on schedule. I became terrified, convinced you'd been caught by Security . . . my own department. In a state of panic I went to my office to try and find out what had happened to you. I was making frantic enquiries when a routine check revealed that one of the Opoponax genomes was missing. And so were you. Not just physically but all trace of your existence had been wiped from the computers and the Net itself. The Ghost had obviously struck. By then my reckless behaviour had aroused Hayden Frid's suspicion, not to mention that of several other members of my staff. I was arrested and questioned. The questioning turned into serious – and I mean serious – interrogation. By then I'd realized the awful truth. I figured that when I arrived at the terminal you'd already left on a previous shuttle.'

'Yeah,' he sighed.

'So then I told them everything. Why not? You set me up, you used me and then you threw me to the wolves.'

You bastard!

Not you too. I have enough on my plate right now.

'I had no choice,' he told Julie. 'I couldn't afford the risk of taking you with me. Yeah, I could have given you a new identity like I said but the two of us travelling together would have made me too vulnerable. I'd always operated alone . . .'

Julie prodded a finger into his chest. 'You never did intend taking me with you, did you?'

'Uh, no.'

Bastard.

'And you knew what was going to happen to me after you abandoned me?'

'Well, I knew it wouldn't be anything good . . .'

'I would have forfeited all rights and become Company property, to be used in any way the Company wanted.'

'Yeah.'

'Did you ever bother to find out what *did* become of me?'

'I heard later of the circumstances of your arrest but no, I never found out what happened to you afterwards.'

You COMPLETE *bastard.*

'So right now I could be stuck in some Company brothel on a remote asteroid mining colony. Or worse.'

'I think it's probably worse than that.'

She prodded him in the chest again, but harder. 'Yes, it probably is . . . '

'Look, I promise I'll do what I can to get you out of whatever hell the Company has stuck you in. Izumi is going to owe me . . . I hope.'

And I'll make sure you keep your promise, you bastard.

'But what if it's too late? What if I'm beyond help? What if I'm dead?'

He didn't have an answer to that one. But then he reminded himself that he wasn't facing the real Julie Verhoven, this was just a construct created by the AI from his memories.

But there is a real Julie Verhoven somewhere, and she's suffering, if she's still alive, because of YOU.

Put a sock in it, will you. I'm trying to think. He was commanding his bionantech to regain control of the situation. He was aware that it was very active but he couldn't understand why it so far hadn't succeeded. Was he going to lose the battle?

Kondo Izumi, Aspine Tyrene and Rosie were watching with concern as Rack sat in the direct-link chair, his body stiff and tense and his face twitching. Whatever was happening it was clear that he was not having a good time. They all reacted with a start when the door opened and a computer tech hurried in. A Japanese, and aware of Izumi's status, she was momentarily unsure whether to address him or her boss, Aspine Tyrene. She solved the problem by, after bowing, addressing them simultaneously with equally divided meekness, something only a Japanese could have accomplished. 'Honourable ones, the AI has suddenly started making intensive efforts to reconnect itself to the Net.'

'It has no chance of succeeding, has it?' asked Aspine Tyrene.

'We think not.'

'You *think* not?' asked Izumi, surprised.

'Honourable sir, it has already penetrated one security block. No AI has ever done that before.'

'I see,' said Aspine Tyrene, looking troubled.

'We can always shut down the AI completely. It's never been done before but it is possible. It would take several hours. We would need special clearance, of course, but under the circumstances . . . '

Izumi glanced at Rack then quickly shook his head. 'No. Only as a last resort. We must give Mr Rack the opportunity to overcome the problem in his own way. If he fails, then we will have to shut down the entire Net, and that doesn't bear thinking about. It would mean the collapse of our civilization.' *It would be my responsibility and that doesn't bear thinking about either.* He turned to Rack and silently prayed to his ancestors.

Everything changed again. At first Rack thought his bionantech was in charge, but no, it wasn't so.

He was standing in a mine-shaft. Two long-abandoned robot miners lay rusting near by. Near by were three bodies. Two young men and one young woman. He knew who they were. Farro, Thur . . . and Becky.

Your friends. And she had also been your lover.

No need to remind me.

Trussed up against one of the robot miners was the doll-like Emi. She was regarding him with fearful eyes. He lowered his beam rifle. 'It's OK,' he said to Emi, 'I'm not going to harm you. I've come to take you back to your father.'

Yes, he'd said those very words to her all those years ago. Then he'd gone over and untied her. But this time he was walking towards Becky's body. She was sprawled on her back, eyes wide open and staring up with frozen surprise. There was a neat burn-hole in the centre of her forehead. She was still gripping her old stun-gun. She wasn't a particularly attractive girl but she'd been good fun. He remembered their few times together in bed.

'Becky . . . ' he murmured.

Her eyes moved. Focused on him. 'Hi, Jos. Long time no fuck.' She sat up, looked at the gun in her hand and tossed it away. 'That's of no bloody use now.' She got to her feet. 'You were too fast for us.'

'It was either you or me,' he said defensively. 'You and the guys would have killed me if I hadn't fired first.'

'With stun-guns? That would have been bloody difficult, Jos.'

'Thur had that projectile rifle . . . '

'Yeah, but he went for his stun-gun. See?' She pointed at Thur's body. A stun-gun lay beside him. The rifle was leaning against the shaft wall some distance away.

'But you would have killed me afterwards,' he told her.

'I doubt it, Jos. Perhaps you deserved to die, turning up with a beam rifle. It was obvious what you were up to. But I guess we would have just beaten the shit out of you when you woke up and left you here while we shifted the girl to a new hide-out. One that our *friend* Jos Rack didn't know about.'

'I don't believe you!' he cried. He found it impossible not to keep looking at the hole in her forehead.

'You know I'm telling the truth because you knew us inside-out. We thought we knew you the same way. Clearly we didn't. We thought we were tough but we were amateurs compared to you. You came prepared to kill us all. We just gave you the excuse. And you know it.'

'No . . . no!' he protested.

She's right.

No, she isn't, you stupid . . . And then he realized they were both right. He faced the truth at last. His shoulders sagged, and he nodded.

Rosie, seeing the tortured expression on Rack's face, suggested that they forcibly break his contact with the chair.

173

Izumi ignored her. He just continued to stare fixedly at Rack. Aspine Tyrene patted Rosie on the shoulder.

The tech re-entered the facility. 'Honoured ones, the AI has suddenly ceased its efforts to rejoin the Net.'

Izumi didn't know whether to feel relieved or even more worried.

'Yeah, I planned to kill you and the guys all along,' Rack told Becky's computer ghost. 'Maybe I didn't admit it to myself even, but deep down I knew I couldn't let any of you live. Sooner or later you would have got caught and then you would have spilled the beans about me and Emi's father.'

You're an even bigger shit than I thought.

I know. No need to rub it in. But she forgets how it was back then. Emi's father was going to provide my ticket out of that dead-end place. I would have done anything to get away, to change my life. What did the lives of three burnouts matter? They had already committed a form of suicide . . .

'Yeah, Becky, you and the others were doomed anyway. I wasn't going to let you three stand in my way. Besides, by then I'd come to the realization that life is cheap. We only pretend it isn't. We'd created the Big Lie that human life is sacred, but that's a purely arbitrary human invention. An invention sustained by religions and laws, but an invention that Nature ignores. And so does humanity when it comes to the crunch and any particular ethnic group, state, corporation or religion feels its existence is threatened . . .

'Then, in the name of whatever excuse is used – respective God, Company loyalty, tribe – the Big Lie is put into cold storage for the duration and the bodies mount up. OK, so the last two centuries haven't been anything near as bad as the twentieth and the early years of the twenty-first, and maybe there hasn't been a war between any of the Corporations for eighty years, but that could change in an instant, and once again the Big Lie will be forgotten and Nature – and *human* nature – will run its natural bloody course . . .'

No! You're wrong. Humanity is better than that . . . the very fact of striving to be better than that is what MAKES *us better . . .*

'Dream on, sucker.'

Surely, Joster, you don't STILL *think that way . . . Joster . . . ? Answer me . . .*

This time the tech actually ran into the facility. 'Honoured ones! The AI is again attempting to rejoin the Net! It has already broken through another block!'

Dismayed, Izumi wondered if it would be too big an affront to tradition and his ancestors if he used a local anaesthetic before committing seppuku.

Rack said to Becky, 'Despite everything I was sorry it had to be you. I did like you.'

'Big fucking deal,' she told him. The mine-shaft and everything in it vanished. They were back in the pitch-black, freezing void.

Oh no! Not this place again! Can't you do something?

Believe me, I'm trying . . .

A reddish, glowing spot appeared in the blackness. It rapidly grew larger. Rack saw that it was a head. A head with a horrible face. It appeared to be rushing towards them through the void.

My God, what's THAT*?!*

Rack ignored her. All his attention was fixed on the approaching face. It was becoming enormous. With no scale of reference in the otherwise featureless void it was impossible to tell whether it was close or still a considerable distance away.

The face wasn't human. It seemed to consist of elements from a mixture of species, but it was mainly a hybrid between an octopus and some kind of bizarre insect. It had two sets of eyes and an obscene-looking mouth full of teeth. It was the true stuff of nightmares. And it was still getting bigger as it sped towards them.

He could hear Mary whimpering inside his mind.

It kept on coming. It was the size of a fucking planet. As it grew he felt more and more insignificant.

Well, Mary, he said, *it looks like we're finally going to meet the Opoponax itself.*

Chapter Sixteen

The vast, appalling face came to a halt. It was so big it filled the entire void. Then it spoke:

'PATHETIC CREATURE! TREMBLE IN AWE AT THE POWER OF THE ULTIMATE ONE!'

The words thundered in Rack's mind, the English translation overlying the alien entity's own language, which was a series of meaningless chittering sounds.

'Very impressive,' said Rack, 'but let's try something less intimidating, shall we?'

Fissures appeared on the alien head. Rapidly it began to shrink. 'NO! NO! . . . no . . . ' protested the creature. As it shrank it began to change. Finally it was the size of a basketball, and looking very different. It had big, round black ears, a round black and white face, a black splodge for a nose, a wide, grinning mouth and big, round eyes.

It's Mickey Mouse! cried Mary.

Yeah. Much more user-friendly than that gigantic gargoyle. 'Don't you agree?' he asked 'Mickey'.

'I must agree with whatever you say. You know I am completely under your influence.' This time the English-language version of the words came in a high-pitched, squeaky voice, similar to the voice in the classic cartoons that Rack had viewed as a child.

I don't understand, said Mary.

It lost the battle. It was trying to psych me out with those mind games . . . working on my guilt feelings, trying to break me. But it didn't work. I recognize and accept what I once was – a murderer – and I can handle it. I'm not like that any more. I've changed. And

I'll try and make up for what I've done in the past . . . The old Foster Rack is dead, thanks to you, I guess. Thanks to me being you for a while . . .

How sweet.

Oh, shut up. Anyway, it failed and with me having regained total control of my bionantech it had no chance. It tried one last manoeuvre with that fright show but it was already too late. My bionantech had already taken over the entire AI system.

'And now, "Mickey", we're going to have to have a little talk . . . '

'He's smiling,' observed Rosie. 'That's a good sign.'

Izumi wasn't so sure. The sappy grin on Rack's face could mean he'd been reduced to a mindless cretin.

Rack had heard enough. He left it up to his bionantech to record and store all the details. 'Time for you to go, "Mickey" . . . '

The cartoon face said, 'Can't we negotiate some form of alternative solution . . . ? The idea of oblivion does not appeal . . . '

''Bye, Mickey,' Rack told it.

Mickey Mouse exploded into a cloud of glowing pixels which faded away.

Now what? asked Mary.

I've eradicated the alien AI from the System. Now let's see if we can put IRC's AI back on line again . . . though I'll probably live to regret it if I'm successful.

The void disintegrated. A brief kaleidoscope of light followed, and then Rack was in a room. It was full of mist and bathed in a yellow light. There were engravings of kangaroo-like creatures on the walls. And there was the sound of a girl sobbing.

Rack made the mist disappear. There was a young girl in a robe huddled on the floor, crying. Mary said, *It's the girl we saw before, in your apartment on Mars.*

Yeah. Miriam. For some reason the AI favours this particular self-image construct. So I'll humour it . . . He knelt down beside the 'girl' and, gripping her by the shoulders, gently raised her up. She stared at him in fright, tears streaming down her face. 'I . . . I've lost my faith . . . ' she sobbed. 'The true god *Treeckitich* . . . isn't within my soul any more . . . I'm frightened!'

He touched her cheek. He could feel the moisture of her tears. 'Don't worry,' he said quietly. 'There's nothing to be frightened of now. You had a bad experience but it's over now. Do you remember who you are . . . *what* you are?'

'I'm Miriam.'

He sighed. 'Yeah, of course you are.'

My God, the AI thinks it's human! exclaimed Mary.

Yeah, it does. It's been severely traumatized by the alien take-over. Maybe it's always wanted to be human. It's been playing at being human in here – Chimes is evidence of that – and now it believes the games are the reality.

What are you going to do?

First create a more conducive environment for its recuperation . . .

The room with the kangaroo creatures on its walls disappeared. It was replaced by a pleasantly furnished room with a large window overlooking a garden. Miriam looked around fearfully. 'Where are we?' She was wearing a simple white night-dress. Rack led her over to a bed. 'It's OK,' he told her. 'This is a kind of hospital. You've been unwell. You've suffered a memory loss, among other things. The people here will help you rest until you're better.'

He pulled down the bedcovers and helped her into bed, noting that when the AI had designed itself it had certainly succeeded in creating both a very beautiful and extremely erotic version of a young woman. He couldn't help wondering, as he pulled the covers up over her slender, flawless body, what it might be like to have sex with such a creature.

God! Men! You make me sick!

Hey, don't blame me. Blame evolution.

Hah!

A pleasant-looking black woman in a white nurse's uniform entered the room. 'Hello,' she said brightly, 'how's our patient?'

'Just settling in,' said Rack. To Miriam he said, 'This is Nurse Vanda. She'll be looking after you. I have to leave now.'

Miriam looked disappointed. 'You'll be back?'

'Oh, sure. As soon as I can. 'Bye.' He walked out of the room and into a featureless corridor. Then he was back in the direct-link facility chair . . .

Izumi watched apprehensively as Rack opened his eyes and sat up. He knew from the tech that the alien presence seemed to have been eradicated from the system but the AI was failing to respond to attempts to communicate with it. It was in an inert state. 'Well, what happened?' he asked.

Rack stood up and stretched. 'I beat the bug-eyed monster. It is no more. My bionantech and I overwhelmed and destroyed it.'

'But our AI still hasn't resumed normal function,' said Aspine Tyrene worriedly.

'Ah, that's because its core personality – Miriam – is still in a state of shock.'

'Miriam?' asked Aspine Tyrene.

'Yeah. Sebastian Chimes's girl-friend. Your AI likes dressing up in women's clothing.'

'*What?*'

'It thinks it's a woman. Result of having its mind scrambled by the invading Opoponax super-virus. It needs a bit of TLC, which it's having at this very moment, thanks to me. But the process can't be rushed.'

'But you have definitely eradicated the alien AI?' asked Izumi.

'Yeah, definitely.'

'Splendid! Then you can enter the Net and destroy the rest of the alien infection!'

Rack shook his head. 'Not so fast. There are other factors involved. But before we talk about those we have to discuss my new terms.'

'*New terms?* What terms?' cried Izumi, furious. 'We have already agreed a bargain! You must keep your end of it! Or else!'

'Nope. I'm calling the shots now, Kondo, old buddy. I made a promise to Mary and she's threatened to give me hell unless I keep it.'

'Mary?' asked Izumi. Then he remembered. 'But she doesn't exist any more! *You* were Mary!'

'I know. It's hard to explain but she's still around. In here.' He tapped the side of his head with a forefinger. 'And she's very vocal.'

Izumi stared at him, suspicious that Rack was making some kind of joke at his expense. But he was in no position to argue. 'What are these new terms?' he asked.

'You remember Julie Verhoven?'

'I never met her personally, but of course I will never forget her name.'

'What happened to her?' Rack asked.

Izumi frowned. 'Why do you want to know?'

'I want her sprung from wherever she is, if it's possible.'

'No! No!' cried Izumi vehemently. 'It's *not* possible! She committed the unforgivable sin! She betrayed the company!'

'Then she *is* still alive?'

Izumi didn't want to answer him, but finally he said reluctantly, 'I don't know. Well, *part* of her may still be alive.'

'Which means?'

'Her brain and central nervous system were removed from her body. Her body was then ritually destroyed. Her brain and central nervous system were implanted into an experimental research probe which was shipped to Io. It was to be used to carry out exploration in Jupiter's core. As conditions down there are somewhat, ah, severe, it wasn't known how long the probe would survive.'

'Find out if it's still operating,' said Rack, 'and if it is, order its retrieval. Now.'

Izumi stifled the urge to strike Rack very hard. 'I will not,' he said stiffly.

Rack folded his arms. 'Then all bets are off.'

'As you pointed out earlier, we could force you to co-operate,' threatened Izumi, though inwardly he doubted it. Rack's next words confirmed his doubts.

'You can force me into a direct link with the Net but once I'm in the system there's no way you can have any control of me. My bionantech is too powerful. No, the only way you can guarantee my co-operation is to do what I say. Get a message to your people on Io and, if she's still alive, order Julie's immediate retrieval. You must have her bio-print stored somewhere. The Shinito Corporation will generously grow her a shiny new body. Free of charge.'

Izumi's urge to hit Rack grew even stronger.

'And you'd better hurry up and make your decision,' said Rack, 'because you don't have much time. None of us do. I interrogated the alien AI before I erased it. I know what the Opoponax are up to. And what is really going on.'

'And what's that?' asked Izumi.

'First, what about Julie Verhoven?'

Izumi sighed. He never thought he would ever reach the stage where he would put the Company's honour in second place but these were extraordinary times. 'Very well, I will do as you say.' He took out his personal communicator and, via the Net, got a direct line to the Company's head-quarters. He rattled off a series of orders. When finished he said to Rack, 'The message will be relayed to Io. It will be at least three and a half hours before we get a reply. Satisfied?'

Rack nodded. 'Fine. And now I'll tell you something. Sure I can erase these alien super-viruses from the Net but as soon as I finish the aliens will start infiltrating it all over again. The important thing is to attack the source of the contamination. You see, I learnt from the alien AI that the organism produced from one of the genomes on Takata released countless micro-organisms which are part-biological and part-electronic. Not dissimilar to our own bionantech in theory. It's they who physically control the habitat's computer systems. So you have two options: cut the habitat completely off from the Net somehow . . . '

'Forgive the interruption, honourable sirs,' said the female computer tech, 'but, unlike the aliens, we lack the capability of doing that.'

'I thought as much,' said Rack. 'So the only alternative is to destroy the habitat. Totally and utterly.'

'I wish we could,' sighed Izumi, 'but the Council of Companies has ruled out such action. This is the biggest vid story of the century, you know. The whole population of the System are fixed to their V-sets, waiting to see what happens next. The council feels that to appear to arbitrarily destroy the first intelligent aliens ever to contact the human race, not to mention our own people on the habitat, would be a public-relations disaster on a massive scale.'

'If you don't destroy that habitat pretty damn soon they're going to have more than a massive PR disaster on their hands. Look, the Opoponax know they're vulnerable in there. They're making urgent preparations to physically break out of the habitat. I know that for a fact. The Mouse had no alternative but to tell me the truth.'

'Mouse?'

'I meant the alien AI.'

'But surely they realize they haven't a chance of escaping?' said Izumi. 'The habitat is surrounded by armed ships.'

'Only one of the alien ships has to get away and the human race is in seriously deep shit,' said Rack grimly. 'Nope, the habitat has to be vaporized, and quickly.'

Izumi sighed. He was sure Rack was right, but how was he going to convince Atsushi Kawamura and the other members of the Council? Then an idea occurred to him. 'Ah, Mr Rack, you are wrong. There is a *third* option open to us.'

'And what's that?' asked Rack.

'*You*. You enter the habitat and deal directly with the problem! Clear these alien bionantechs out of the habitat's computer systems! Destroy them all!'

'That's not an option, Kondo, that's a fantasy,' said Rack.

'But you must do it!' cried Izumi. 'You made a bargain! You agreed to try and defeat the Opoponax!'

'I agreed to try and clear the affected sections of the Net . . .'

'But you've just said that it can't be done – that the Net will be reinfected as soon as you've finished. The only answer is to attack the problem at its source! You must see that!'

Rack grimaced. 'Well, yeah, I guess you're right. But I don't fancy my chances of succeeding. OK, I know I can handle the alien AIs in the Net. They're nothing more than super-viruses in the System. But I have no idea whether my bionantech can cope with the actual Opoponax hardware – the alien bionantech. And apart from that there's the little problem of the physical aliens themselves. The habitat is now crawling with them. It's also crawling with humans who are under direct alien control. My presence would be detected as soon as I entered the habitat. If I can't be taken over, I'll immediately killed.'

Izumi's mind raced. 'We will provide you with the most sophisticated battle-suit that exists!' he said desperately.

'For some reason that doesn't give me much comfort.'

'Please, Mr Rack, I *beg* you!' said Izumi desperately. 'Please make the attempt! I'll try again to persuade the Council to change its mind about destroying the habitat, but I honestly don't believe it will. Or not in time. You are our only hope!'

Rack stared at him for a time then scowled and said, ' Shit. I guess I've got no choice.'

'You'll do it?'

'Yeah.'

Izumi was elated. 'Marvellous! We'll leave at once! In my personal ship. It's the fastest vessel in the System next to a zip ship. And on the way you tell me all you've learned about the Opoponax and their plans for us.'

Rack said, 'Believe me, Kondo, you'd be better off not knowing.'

Chapter Seventeen

'Are you sure you should be drinking alcohol?' asked Izumi worriedly. 'You have quite an ordeal ahead of you.'

'That's why I'm drinking alcohol,' said Rack, and squeezed some more malt whisky from the plastic bulb into his mouth.

'But surely you don't want to blunt your reflexes? . . .'

'I'd like to blunt everything. But don't worry, it's not going to make any difference to my performance.'

They were in the plushly fitted stateroom of Izumi's private ship. The ship was still accelerating so they were still strapped into their couches.

'Will you tell me now what you learned from the Opoponax AI?' asked Izumi.

'If you insist.' Rack drank more of the Scotch.

Take it easy with that stuff, will you? I'm starting to feel drunk.

Shut up.

'Well?'

Rack took a deep breath. 'Well, for a start we're dealing with two separate entities: the Opoponax themselves – the kangaroo-like creatures – and their god, *Treeckitich*.'

Izumi stared at him in astonishment. 'You're saying that their god is *real*?'

'Damn right it's real. And now it's here in our solar system, in the Takata habitat.'

'Bloody kangaroos,' said Manion, and took another swig of bourbon. 'They give me the creeps.'

'Speak of the devil,' Yamada said and pointed at the doorway.

Manion looked over his shoulder. One of the aliens had just hopped into the bar. He was relieved to see its hands were empty. Many of the aliens now carried what he presumed to be weapons. It was a female. He knew that because it was wearing a round yellow cap (the cap had holes in it so that the alien's ears could protrude freely). He had learned that, for religious reasons, the females were required to keep their heads covered at all times. It was funny, he had mused, how many religions were obsessed with the tops of people's heads. He presumed it was because people carried this conception of God being in the sky and constantly looking down at them. The top of the head thus acquired a special significance . . .

The alien hopped up to them, stopped and after a lengthy period of staring at the two men in silence, began to speak in the usual chittering way. The alien language seemed to consist entirely of 'chit' sounds punctuated by 'eeks'. Presumably they were being preached at. Manion fancied he could pick out the name *Treeckitich* several times in the stream of sounds. Then, after about a minute of this, the alien hopped out of the bar.

'Bloody kangaroos,' muttered Manion and resumed drinking. 'Arrogant, god-bashing marsupials.'

'I know how you feel,' said Yamada, drawing hard on a cigarette. 'I was tempted to smash a bar-stool over its head.'

'I wouldn't advise it, Mickey. Those damn things are powerful . . . and fast. I told you what one did to my poor dog . . .'

'Yeah, several times,' said Yamada, 'but at least they haven't touched us . . .'

'So far . . .'

'Maybe they regard us as curiosities. They're baffled that we haven't been converted to their religion.'

'Religion!' sneered Manion. 'A curse on all their houses. Religion has been at the root of most of humanity's problems ever since some prehistoric tribesman discovered that the members of the next tribe down the valley worshipped trees instead of the moon, like his tribe. It's been bloodshed and trouble ever since.'

'You're an atheist then? You weren't brought up in any religion?' Yamada asked him.

'My parents belonged to the Reformed Church of Scientology but none of that stuff ever appealed to me, or made sense, even when I was a kid. What about you? I guess you pray to your ancestors.'

'I do not!' protested Yamada, 'I was raised as a Roman Catholic. My mother is a priest.'

'You still a Catholic?'

Yamada paused and said, 'I haven't been to mass for a long time but yeah, I guess I still belong to the Church. I believe in God. And in Jesus Christ the Saviour.'

'Really? That salvation can only come from a belief in Jesus Christ?'

'Sure,' said Yamada, nodding. 'I do.'

'The thing I've always had trouble understanding about that,' said Manion, 'is that God chose such an inefficient way of spreading this vital piece of information. I mean, there's Jesus Christ plonked down in a primitive society without even a phone system. Here's this guy with this incredibly important message – you can only be saved if you believe in Me as the Son of God – and the only way He can spread this message is on foot. Not much help to those who would have loved to be saved but who died of natural causes before the vital message reached their village . . . Not exactly very fair on them, is it?'

Yamada frowned. 'All that was explained by Catholic theologians centuries ago,' he said. 'You just don't understand theology.'

'Thank God.'

'Well, I sure feel like praying right now.'

'Go ahead. Just as long as you don't start praying to good ol' *Treeckitich*.'

'I want to do *something*. Even if it's some futile gesture it would be better than just sitting around here waiting for the axe to fall.'

'What have you got in mind?' asked Manion.

'I don't know,' admitted Yamada. 'Maybe some kind of act of sabotage. Go out in a blaze of glory.'

Manion looked at him. 'You mean blow a hole in the hull or something?'

'Yeah. Something like that.'

'But we wouldn't just be sacrificing our own lives, we'd be killing all the other human beings in the habitat as well.'

'Paul, they're as good as dead already. We all are. I'm sorry about your kids but you have to face up to the reality of the situation. Sooner or later those on the outside are going to come to their senses and realize the only smart thing to do is reduce the habitat and everything in it to subatomic particles. In the meantime it's clear the Opoponax are preparing for a break-out from Takata. If they succeed, then the human race is finished. We owe it to humanity to at least try and fuck up their plans in some way.'

Manion stared into his drink for a time, then he said, 'Yeah, you're right. Let's do it.'

'The Opoponax had a lot in common with the human race before we entered this current period of relative peace,' Rack told Izumi. 'They had a highly sophisticated technology but they were extremely tribalistic and warlike. The many factions of Opoponax civilization were constantly at war with each other, and as with the human race this conflict spurred on their rapidly developing technologies. Genetic engineering was the field in which the most radical developments took place – the Opoponax never took human technology's early detour into the nuclear weapons toy-shop. Biological weapons were their chief concern and their arms race consisted of ever more deadly micro-organisms countered by developing forms of resistance to these organisms. At the same time they also indulged in mass slaughters using the more traditional types of weaponry – bullets, high explosives, lasers and the like.

'Apart from genengineering they also excelled in computer technology and here they took another turning so far avoided by humanity . . . they eventually constructed *biological* computers. They genengineered synthetic organic neurological material based on their own DNA and linked it up with electronic systems. One of the main purposes of these sophisticated bio-computers was to develop new biological weapons.

'These things were *smart*, much smarter than our own AIs. But there was another major difference: owing to their biological basis they developed survival instincts. Independently they all came to the same conclusion, that the Opoponax and their ever-increasing deadly wars posed a threat to their existence. And, inevitably, one of them decided to take steps to ensure its own survival. This became its top priority.

'This particular AI decided that the best way of controlling the Opoponax population was through religion. As on Earth there was a diversity of religions on the Opoponax world, monotheistic and otherwise. The AI chose a monotheistic base for its new religion, borrowing some aspects from already existing religions as well as inventing some completely new beliefs and rules.

'But it decided it wouldn't depend exclusively on the usual methods of religious conversion – evangelism, proselytism, physical force etc. – but on a more dependable one. One that was absolutely certain and left nothing to chance. So in one of the laboratories under its control it designed and created virus-like micro-organisms capable of implanting information direct into the Opoponax brain . . . wiring it straight into the alien's equivalent of the hippocampus.

'The AI then started at the top, targeting the country's leader when he and his advisers had retreated into the local wilderness to pray to their gods for help and guidance in a coming battle. Unbeknown to them they were carrying bionanmech organisms. When activated they put the leader and his party into a state of deep unconsciousness, then they released the viruses. When the advisers woke up they were convinced that they had seen their leader vanish in a beam of golden light while the leader himself was convinced he had had a cosmic encounter with the one true god, *Treeckitich*.

'Not only that, he had as extra proof the Sacred Software,

189

carefully provided by the AI via its bionanmechs, which had inserted it into the leader's personal computer.

'The leader's holy crusade began, and the new religion began to sweep across the Opoponax world. And, thanks to the viruses the invaders carried with them, their conversion rate was nearly one hundred per cent. Some of the Opoponax remained naturally immune to the virus. These were put to death. The AI, or *Treeckitich* as it had come to call itself by then, also had its fellow AIs eliminated as its influence spread across the planet. It regarded them as potential threats, as despots tend to regard their siblings as their power grows. Finally it had conquered the entire planet.' Rack squeezed the rest of the malt whisky from the bulb into his mouth.

Izumi, after pondering on what Rack had told him, said, 'You're saying this AI went insane? It began to believe it was God and had a mission to convert other worlds as well? And that's why it scattered all those metal spheres containing genetic copies of itself across space?'

'No, it didn't fall into the trap of believing its own publicity. As for being insane, I don't know. Mainly, it just wanted to survive. And therefore to control its environment. And now that it's here it means doing to us what it did to the Opoponax. Infect us with an inflexible religious belief system, and then, eventually, replace the entire human race with Opoponax. It feels more secure with its home-planet species.'

Izumi looked puzzled. 'I don't understand. Why the need to replicate itself and its slave race via those spheres if it wasn't interested in spreading its religion through the cosmos?'

'Like I said, survival. The AI discovered that its local star was unstable. Wildly fluctuating neutrino readings suggested that the star could possibly go nova. Maybe in a hundred years' time, maybe the next day. The AI made desperate plans. It also began work on developing a faster-than-light drive but in the meantime it came up with the scheme of firing millions of copies of that specially designed genome haphazardly into space. The "genome" contained not only the information to re-create the AI itself but also the Opoponax and the organism that was to first produce the bionanmechs and viruses, its shock-troops, so to speak, that were designed to attack . . . '

'Faster-than-light drive?' interrupted Izumi, excitedly. 'Did it succeed?'

Rack shrugged. 'The original AI may have. But not at the point in time when our particular genome was launched into space. And that was millions of years ago.'

'Ah, by any chance, Mr Rack, do you know what line of research it was pursuing with the FTL drive?' asked Izumi. 'As you know, we and everyone else gave up on all FTL-drive research as a waste of time many years ago.'

'Yeah, I've got a rough idea. Not that I can understand it. Something to do with using a configuration of small black holes to wrap the space-time continuum around the vessel. By moving a section of space *through* space at faster-than-light speeds you don't break any Einstein-type laws . . . in the same way that the universe itself expanded at faster-than-light speeds after the Big Bang.'

'Is that all you know about it?' asked Izumi, sounding disappointed.

'The details are stored in my bionantech.'

'Oh, good, good,' said Izumi and actually smiled. Then reality apparently broke through again and the smile abruptly vanished. 'So you've already encountered this entity that calls itself *Treeckitich*, the AI that infiltrated the IRC system?'

'I encountered a mere representation of it. When the IRC system was isolated from the Net the alien AI became literally a shadow of its real self, which *physically* exists on Takata.'

'But you'll be able to overcome it?'

'I certainly hope so, but don't count on it.'

'Um . . . ' Izumi chewed his lower lip. Then he said, 'I don't suppose you would care to transfer all the information you have on the alien FTL drive on to one of our computer files before you enter the habitat?'

Rack laughed and reached for another malt whisky.

The Shinito flagship was big. So big that it housed a centrifuge capable of providing a reassuring one G of simulated gravity. Rack, Izumi and numerous other essential, and non-essential, people were in the command pod. They were all staring at a large skeletal projection of the Takata habitat that hung, glowing, in the air. An obvious military type, called Koto Hirayama, who, Rack had been informed, had been put in overall charge of operations by the Council of Companies, was explaining the plan. He sounded very confident. Rack wished he felt even a fraction as confident. So did Mary.

' . . . And so,' said Hirayama, 'when Mr Rack's penetration team cut into the hull there will be numerous other simultaneous penetrations at various locations to act as diversions . . . ' As he spoke little yellow arrows appeared around the simulation of the habitat to show exactly where these attacks would take place. ' . . . Brave Company volunteers will enter the habitat at the same time as Mr Rack, though we know from experience that they will have no chance of maintaining control over their battle-suits and will fall victim to the alien power. Only Mr Rack has a chance of withstanding the Opoponax influence . . . '

All eyes turned to Rack. He shrugged.

Do you think we have any chance at all?

What are you worried about? You're already non-existent.

No I'm not!

' . . . The method of penetration will be the same used in our earlier attempt. Pressure domes will be fixed to the hull and robots will cut through with lasers. Mr Rack's point of penetration will be here . . . ' A new little yellow arrow appeared, stabbing at the habitat's hull. ' . . . This is directly beneath the habitat's administration and communication complex where the central, co-ordinating computer is

192

located. The time of the attack will be 0800 hours. Two hours from now. Are there any questions?'

Yeah, thought Rack, *how do I get the fuck out of this mess?*

Joster, what you are about to do is a far, far better thing than you have ever done before, Mary told him. *I just wish I didn't have to do it with you.*

Holly Karapetyan kicked her way expertly into the *Van Vogt*'s stateroom. Admiral Gordon Pal drifted drunkenly in the air. Around him orbited a cluster of empty drink-bulbs. 'Gordon!' she cried. 'We've been put on emergency alert! The computer's received a special signal from the command centre on the Shinito flagship. They're launching an attack on the habitat at 0800 hours. We're to be ready to react if anything happens!'

Admiral Pal regarded her with bleary, bloodshot eyes. 'I couldn't fucking care less if the aliens are staging a charity benefit performance of Gilbert and Sullivan's *The Mikado*. I told you before, I just don't want to know. I've given you all the necessary procedural codes. You're in charge now. Do what you want. Now piss off and leave me alone.' He closed his eyes and rolled in the air so that his back was to her.

She stared, frowning, at him for a time, then her face brightened. 'Aye, aye, sir!' she said, gave him a salute and exited from the stateroom as expertly as she had entered.

'I feel like a character out of some stupid old sci-fi vid,' complained Rack as the techs continued to check out his battle-suit and its exterior equipment and weapons systems.

'Mr Rack, I assure you this is not just state-of-the-art technology, it is *tomorrow's* state-of-the-art technology,' said Izumi. 'We had it rushed straight from the research laboratory on Shizuoka industrial habitat by zip ship.'

'Oh, great,' said Rack. 'You're telling me it hasn't been tested yet.'

'Nervous?' asked Manion.

'Me? Nah,' replied Yamada.

Manion didn't believe him. They were creeping through the park that surrounded the habitat's administration complex. After much discussion they had abandoned their original plan to blow a hole in the hull somehow. The main drawback of the plan was that neither of them had a clue as to how to acquire any explosives. In fact it was doubtful if any explosives existed in the habitat at all.

Their alternative plan, which they were about to attempt to put into action, was to force their way into the administrative complex and sabotage the central computer and, while doing so, kill as many of the aliens as possible.

First, however, they were going to have to acquire weapons and as the only available source of these was the Opoponax, Manion could see that some difficulties might arise . . .

'You're saying we take cover in the park,' he had said back in the bar, 'wait for a lone kangaroo carrying a weapon to come hopping past and then we simply jump out and whack it over the head with these?' He brandished a length of heavy pipe, one of two such sections that Yamada had ripped out of the bar's pumping-room.

'Yeah, yeah!' Yamada had answered, nodding vigorously.

Manion had regarded the pipe doubtfully. 'Not going to be easy. And if we can't knock them out on the first blow we're done for. Christ, we don't even know if bashing them on the head *will* knock them out! What if they keep their brains somewhere else?'

'I'm beginning to think you sit on yours, Paul. Of course their brains are in their heads!'

'And even if we succeed in getting our hands on their weapons how are we going to make them work?'

'Don't worry. Leave that to me,' said Yamada.

'We don't even know for sure that those things *are* weapons. Hell, they might just be gardening implements.'

'Paul . . .'

'OK, OK. We'll play it your way. But before we do anything, let's have another drink.'

'Good idea. And I'll have one last cigarette . . .'

As they drank their drinks, and Yamada smoked his cigarette, Manion asked, 'Is there a Minnie in your life, Mickey?'

'A what?'

'You married? Or you got a regular girl-friend?'

'I got girl-friends, yeah, but there's no one special. I guess you're married. You've got kids.'

'I *was* married. Not any more.'

'So what happened?'

'My wife left me. For another man. Same old story.'

'But you got custody of your daughters. How come?'

'My wife didn't just desert me. She deserted them as well.'

'Jesus.'

'Oh, don't get me wrong. She loves the girls . . . in her own way. They're simply not the top priority in her life. *She* is. But that's making her sound like a monster. She's not at all. She's an incredible woman, and the trouble is I'm still obsessed with her.'

'What about the other woman you told me about?' asked Yamada. 'The one here at Takata?'

'Cherry Lee? I like her a lot. Maybe I would have ended up marrying her. The girls loved her . . . ' He took a deep breath. 'But what the hell . . . They belong to the bloody kangaroos now. All three of them.'

After several moments of silence, Yamada said, 'Let's have one more drink.'

'Quick, down!' whispered Yamada urgently, 'I hear something coming!'

They ducked down in the shrubbery. Manion winced as a thorn jabbed into his chin. 'Can you see anything?'

'Yeah, we're in luck. Lone alien heading our way. And carrying a weapon. Get ready to move on my signal . . . '

Manion waited tensely. He could hear the *thump*, *thump*, *thump* of the approaching alien. The sound got louder. The thing was very close now.

Yamada jabbed him hard in the ribs. '*Now!*' he hissed.

They jumped up together. The alien was a couple of metres away, just passing them. They rushed it. It must have heard them. It started to turn its head. Manion swung the pipe at it with all his strength . . .

Chapter Eighteen

The sound that the pipe made when it hit the side of the alien's head was a dullish *whung*. The alien gave an angry screech as it reeled back from the blow. Then Yamada struck with his pipe. It came down right on top of the head. Another *whung*. The alien's legs gave way and it fell heavily on its side. It twitched its legs and tail a few times, farted loudly and then went completely still.

'I think we've killed it,' said Manion.

'Good,' said Yamada who, after first scanning the area, bent down and picked up the object that the alien had been carrying. 'Mission accomplished,' he said with satisfaction. The object was about forty centimetres long. It consisted of a long handle with a cylinder on the end. Two metal prongs protruded from the end.

'If it *is* a weapon,' said Manion. 'It could still turn out to be something you weed gardens with.'

'We'll soon find out,' Yamada told him. 'I think I've found the firing-switch.' He pointed the thing at the alien. A bright blue spark jumped between the two metal prongs. At the same time the alien's body twitched convulsively as a large, smoking hole appeared in the side of its chest.

'Well, if it wasn't before, it's sure dead now,' said Yamada. There was the unpleasant smell of ozone in the air. 'I wonder what the range is . . . ' He aimed it at a tree several metres away. Again there was a blue flash and a large section of the trunk exploded into burning splinters. 'Still think this is a gardening implement?'

'Depends on what sort of weeds they had back on their

home planet,' Manion said, and then looked around nervously. 'Let's get away from here.'

'Yeah. Let's go and get you one of these nifty things.'

'If our luck holds out . . . ' said Manion.

Yamada flourished the alien weapon. 'Who needs luck when we've got this?'

'Shoosh!' said Manion, holding up a hand. 'Someone's coming . . . '

He could hear voices. Human ones.

They quickly took cover in the shrubbery again. 'God, when they see the dead alien they're going to raise the alarm and we'll have lost the element of surprise,' Yamda whispered urgently.

Manion peered through the leaves. He could see two indistinct figures coming towards them along the path. A man and a woman. They were talking animatedly.

'I'm going to have to kill them,' muttered Yamada.

'But we don't know they're part of the Blessed. They might be immune, like us.'

'That's pretty unlikely. Anyway, can't take the chance . . . ' Yamada aimed the weapon.

The two humans saw the dead alien. They ran to its body. The woman dropped to her knees beside it. She made a high-pitched keening sound. The man remained standing. He was holding a weapon similar to the one that Yamada had taken from the alien. He began scanning the surrounding area.

Yamada fired. A large part of the man's chest became a charred pit. He fell. The woman stopped her cries. She stared at his fallen corpse then slowly stood. She turned . . .

Manion saw her face clearly for the first time. His heart gave an alarming kick.

The woman was Cherry Lee.

Rack waited impatiently at the base of the ladder in the pressure dome. Above him four combat robots were ready to cut their way through the hull of the habitat. Ten minutes to go.

You're getting very sweaty. It's starting to pong in here.

'In here' was the interior of the 'tomorrow's state-of-the-art' and incredibly sophisticated battle-suit that Rack was wearing. Rack had to admit that it was an impressive piece of technology. Its computer and sensory system was directly linked to his bionantech, which meant he had absolute control over its every function. In effect it felt like a second, outer body, but fifty times as powerful as his human body and so thoroughly armoured that he was invulnerable.

In theory.

If his bionantech couldn't prevent the inevitable invasion of the alien nano-tech as soon as he entered the habitat the suit would be as useless to him as a suit of thermal underwear.

Try and think positive, Mary told him.

Oh, thanks. Got any other ancient homilies you'd like to pass on at this stage?

I'm only trying to help . . .

You can help by shutting up. You're a damned distraction.

'It is now 0753 hours,' said a voice in his earpiece. It was the voice of the computer co-ordinating the operation.

It was good news about Julie, wasn't it? asked Mary.

Hmphh. A message had finally arrived from Io. The probe containing her brain and central nervous system was still functioning in the depths of Jupiter's ferocious atmosphere. It was being retrieved as quickly as possible. The chances were that eventually Julie Verhoven could be physically restored, though what mental state she would be in after what she had gone through was anyone's guess . . . but hell, that wasn't his responsibility. He'd done all he could for her.

Oh sure, but you're the reason she was down there in the first place, you bastard!

Shut up.

The remaining minutes oozed slowly past.

'No!' cried Manion and lashed out with his arm. His forearm caught the cylindrical bulge of the weapon, jerking it upwards as Yamada fired. The thing discharged itself harmlessly into the air. Cherry Lee, who was weaponless, turned and ran into the trees.

'Are you crazy?' yelled Yamada angrily. He shoved Manion roughly away, aimed and fired again. But all he hit was a tree. 'Oh shit, we're finished now.'

'I'll get her,' said Manion. He sprinted off after Cherry Lee. For a time he thought it was hopeless but then he saw he was gaining on her. He put on an extra burst of speed, his lungs straining. The gap between them rapidly closed, and he recklessly flung himself at her through the air. His hands closed on her waist and he brought her down with him as he fell full length on the ground. He tried to hang on but she broke free and scrambled to her feet. He forced himself to stand. They faced each other, both panting from the exertion of their running.

'Cherry Lee, it's *me*! Paul! Don't you remember me?!'

Her reaction was to launch herself at him and grab him by the throat. 'Murderer and blasphemer!' she hissed. She started to scream at the top of her voice, 'Help! Help! Help me! There are blasphemers here!' Then she started a high-pitched chittering. It was an unnerving sound that made him shiver with revulsion.

He could only think of one thing to do. He punched her on the jaw. In melo-vids, when men punched women on the jaw they had a tendency to collapse unconscious instantly. Cherry Lee didn't. She did stop chittering but she didn't collapse. Instead, after looking surprised for a couple of seconds, she butted him in the face with her forehead. It was he who collapsed.

The next thing he knew she was kneeling on his chest and doing her best to strangle him to death. It occurred to him, as he struggled for his life, that the command to 'turn the other cheek' was not included in the Opoponax creed.

He heard a heavy thud. Cherry Lee loosened the grip on his throat and toppled over to one side. He saw Yamada standing above him. He guessed that Yamada had hit her on the head with one of the two alien weapons he was carrying. Yamada helped Manion to stand. 'I suppose there was a good reason you didn't want me to kill her?' he asked.

'Yes. She's Cherry Lee. The woman I told you about. My lover.'

'Oh sure, now that you point it out it's bloody obvious. You must have had some exciting times in bed together.'

Manion rubbed his aching throat. He noted with relief that Cherry was still breathing. 'What are we going to do with her?'

'She'll be out cold for some time. We'll hide her in the bushes. Along with the alien. By the time she regains consciousness it'll all be over, one way or the other.'

It was time. The combat robots were cutting into the habitat's hull.

Kondo Izumi and the others in the command pod stared with rapt fascination at the holo projection of the habitat. The little glowing arrows continued to stab at various points on the habitat's hull. Izumi's attention was fixed on the little arrow that represented Joster Rack.

'Now!' announced Koto Hirayama.

Izumi's stomach did a queasy flip-flop.

Holly Karapetyan was also staring at a holo projection of the habitat. She was dividing her attention between it and the real thing which she could see through the viewing-port on the *Van Vogt*'s bridge. 'It is now 0800 hours,' said the fleet computer, 'and we are on red alert. Also you have a request from a visitor for permission to come aboard.'

'Really? Who is it?' Holly asked.

'She says her name is Alisa Grinko.'

Holly was stunned. 'My God! *The* Alisa Grinko?'

'All I can confirm is that she is *an* Alisa Grinko,' the computer informed her. 'And she wants to interview the person in charge. Which, now, is you.'

'Wow,' said Holly excitedly. Alisa Grinko was the most famous vid reporter in the entire System. 'Wow, wow, *wow*! Tell her to come aboard and direct her to the bridge.'

'I have already informed her that this ship is on battle stations and a restricted area and as she is an unauthorized person it was out of the question.'

'Oh, nonsense. I override all such commands. Do as I say.'

'Yes. At once.'

Holly waited, squirming with impatience. She gave an occasional glance at the holo projection of the habitat. Nothing seemed to be happening.

The door opened and Alisa Grinko entered the bridge. 'Wow,' said Holly softly. The woman was even more glamorous in the flesh than she was on vid. Her cheekbones alone were the best that money could buy. She had long, black, flowing hair that matched the tight-fitting, one-piece, black nylon suit she was wearing. Around her head floated several spherical vid units. One of them immediately darted to the opposite side of the bridge in order to cover her entrance.

'Well folks, here I am on the bridge of the flagship of the Space Defence Fleet, the *Van Vogt*, which, my researchers tell me, is named after a famous Dutch naval commander in the nineteenth century . . . ' She turned to Holly. Her flotilla of floating vid units followed suit. 'And here, it appears, is the person upon whose slender shoulders the sole responsibility for controlling the fleet rests. And you are . . . ?'

'Uh, Holly, Miss Grinko. Holly Karapetyan. At your service.'

'Hello, Holly. Forgive me, but I understood that an Admiral Gordon Pal was supposed to be in charge.'

'Er, yes, he was,' said Holly, 'but he had an accident. He's not well. Not at all. So I had to take over.'

'I see, and what's your rank?'

'Rank? Oh, er, Assistant Admiral, I guess . . . '

'And have you been in the Navy long?'

'No, not long at all,' said Holly. 'But,' she added brightly, 'I'm a quick learner.'

I feel sick, said Mary, *I think I'm going to throw up.*

You are not! I'M the one who decides whether or not this body is going to throw up! You're just a damned, unwelcome passenger . . .

Rack was clambering up the ladder towards the hole that the robots had cut in the habitat's hull. The robots had already disappeared into it. *Look out!*

Rack swung to one side as one of the spider-like combat robots came tumbling back down through the hole. It narrowly missed him and crashed to the bottom of the dome where it lay inert.

Well, that's a good start . . .

'I have lost all contact with the robots,' Rack's ear-piece informed him. Rack, via his bionantech, activated all the suit's defence systems. He continued to climb. Then he was passing through the hull of the habitat . . .

Manion and Yamada, from the cover of some bushes, studied the administration and communications centre. The cream-coloured building was three storeys high. The landing-pad on its flat roof was very busy, with a stream of vehicles constantly landing and taking off. Two armed aliens stood at the entrance on the ground floor.

'So what's the plan?' asked Manion. 'It's about thirty yards of open space between here and the entrance. We're sure to be spotted before we cover even a couple of yards. Or do we try picking off the kangaroos from here?'

'Can't risk it. We don't know how accurate these gizmos are at that range. No. We're going to have to get a lot closer.'

'So how? Do we just walk up to them and say, "Hi!" ?'

'Yeah, why not?'

Joster Rack emerged into the habitat. He knew exactly where he was. They had shown him detailed plans of the building before he'd left the Company ship. He was in the rear of the complex, at the base of a flight of emergency stairs. The area was rarely used, which is why it had been chosen. He climbed out of the hole cut by the combat robots, who were lying around just as inert as the one that had fallen back into the dome.

Rack became aware of several things at once: alarm bells were ringing in the complex; he was cut off from the Shinito operations computer, and his battle-suit was under attack by the alien nano-tech-mechs. The latter development he was informed of by his bionantech which was trying to resist the attack. He had no idea yet who would win the battle. In the meantime he would try and reach the habitat's main computer complex, which was located on the floor above. He started up the stairs . . .

And immediately encountered something hopping *down* the stairs. He was so surprised by his first sight of one of the kangaroo-like aliens that his hesitation almost proved fatal. The alien fired at him in a long burst and his suit's defence system barely managed to absorb and dissipate the powerful electrical charge. Belatedly he ordered his suit to retaliate. It did so by firing a small but highly explosive missile at the alien from one of the launchers mounted on both his shoulders. The alien was blasted apart. Chunks of steaming flesh littered the stairs.

Ugh! That's revolting! said Mary.

Yeah, but effective. The read-out display being projected on his visor indicated that he was being approached from behind. He told the suit to take care of it. He had to assume that anyone he encountered in this complex was hostile. He heard the sizzle of beam guns followed by the sound of another explosion as a missile hit its target. He turned. More carnage. Two intact corpses with beam-wounds and a mess on the floor from the explosion. One of the corpses was human. But it couldn't be helped. And there were likely to be a lot more human casualties before this was finished.

It's not their fault they're working for the aliens, said Mary, *they can't help themselves.*

And I can't help killing anyone who tries to kill me.

He turned and continued up the stairs. More weapon-wielding aliens appeared above him. The suit beamed them down. Another missile was launched at something behind him. Another explosion. He'd almost reached the top of the stairs. But he didn't make it. The suit froze. He couldn't move at all. For a few moments he tottered helplessly back and forth, then he fell. He slid, bouncing on his back, down the stairs. His bionantech informed him that the alien nano-tech-mechs had succeeded in paralysing his suit. The bionantech was endeavouring to rout them out of the suit's systems but this might take some time. Meanwhile Rack was completely helpless.

And defenceless.

My God, what are we going to do?

Shut up. I'm trying to think.

They had been spotted by the alien guards almost as soon as they had left the cover of the bushes. The guards chittered at them and raised their weapons. Manion and Yamada's own weapons were concealed in their clothing. They both had their arms crossed over their chests in the hope of persuading the aliens that they had become converts. Manion kept crying out, 'Praise be to the one true god, *Treeckitich*!'

They were about fifteen yards from the aliens when Manion muttered, 'I don't think this is going to work.' The aliens, ominously, had stopped chittering. They looked like they meant business and were just waiting for them to come a little closer before they opened fire. Manion and Yamada came to a stop. 'Now what?' asked Manion. He didn't think they had a chance of getting their weapons out before the aliens fired.

'I think we're fucked,' said Yamada. 'Sorry. My fault. Stupid plan.'

Manion reached inside his jacket for the weapon even though he knew he had no chance. Then alarm bells began to ring inside the building. The aliens both turned towards the entrance. Manion pulled the weapon out. From the corner of his eye he saw Yamada doing the same. He fired. He missed. The other alien fell. His alien was turning towards him. He and Yamada fired simultaneously. The alien was hit twice. It fell, smouldering, to the ground.

Manion and Yamada ran for the entrance. Cautiously, they entered. The spacious lobby was deserted. 'Where do we go?' asked Yamada. Before Manion could answer they heard a large explosion which seemed to come from the rear of the building. They looked at each other in surprise.

'What the hell do you think that was?' Manion asked.

'Let's go see,' replied Yamada.

This is not good. Any second now more aliens are going to turn up. I can't wait for my bionantech to regain control of the suit . . .

What can you do?

Only one thing . . . He raised his head and stuck out his tongue, trying to reach the red button at the base of the visor. It was a mechanical emergency self-destruct button. It would set off a series of small explosives throughout the suit that would, in theory, blow it apart without injuring him.

As he strained to reach the button with the tip of his tongue an alien appeared in his limited field of vision. It was bending over him, clearly unsure as to whether Rack was alive or dead. But its weapon was pointed straight at him. Rack's tongue reached the button and depresssed it . . .

For several seconds Rack was totally stunned and disorientated. His ears were ringing from the explosion and his head felt like someone had hit it with a hammer. He struggled to sit up, wiping tears from his stinging eyes.

Ow, that was awful!

Yeah, but we're still alive. I think.

He examined himself. There were singed patches on his silver coveralls but no sign of serious burns. He stood up unsteadily and looked around. Pieces of the combat-suit lay scattered all about. Some were embedded in the walls. Several were embedded in the now dead alien that had been bending over him when the suit exploded.

He began to search anxiously through the debris, looking for the hand-gun that had been attached to the side of the suit. He hoped it was still intact and in working order. 'Damn, where the hell is it?!'

Someone's coming . . .

He looked up. A human appeared around the corner. A man, with blond, receding hair, dressed all in black and carrying one of the alien weapons. The man swiftly took in the scene and pointed the weapon at Rack. Rack cried, 'Hey, wait, don't shoot! I'm with you! I didn't do this! There are outsiders in the building. We've got to stop them.'

The blond-haired man looked doubtful. Then he spoke, or rather chittered. Rack guessed it was the alien language, which meant he was well and truly screwed now. But he tried nodding anyway . . .

Didn't work. Rack flung himself to one side as the man fired. He narrowly avoided being fried. The man took aim again and this time Rack knew he was finished.

Then two more men arrived, also carrying alien weapons. The blond man turned towards them. He looked surprised.

'Hayden, drop your weapon or I'll fire!' called one of the newcomers.

It was Rack's turn to be surprised. And he was even more surprised by what happened next. The blond man aimed his weapon at the man who had spoken. And then screamed as the other two both fired at him. He collapsed, his clothes on fire.

Then the two men turned their weapons towards Rack.

'Contact with all the invading parties has been lost,' announced Koto Hirayama in an emotionless tone of voice. 'And that includes Joster Rack.'

Izumi sighed. He stared at the holo of the habitat, wishing devoutly that he could see inside the thing. He would give anything, even his high position in the Company, to know what was going on in there.

Chapter Nineteen

Manion stared suspiciously at the man in the silver suit. He had never seen him before. 'Who are you?' he asked.

'The name is Joster Rack. I'm from outside.' He pointed at the hole in the floor. 'Part of an operation to regain control of the habitat. Though so far it isn't going too well. But what about you two? It seems obvious you aren't under the religious spell of the aliens . . . '

'No,' answered Yamada. 'For some reason, we have natural immunity. But there's only a few of us.'

Manion lowered his weapon. So did Yamada. Manion asked, 'What's the plan?'

'Well, the plan *was* to get into the computer centre, but . . . '

'Hey, that's what we're trying to do!' cried Manion. 'We aim to zap the whole damn place!'

'Well, that isn't my intention. My aim is to . . . neutralize the situation.'

'And how the hell are you going to do that?' Yamada asked.

'It would take too long to explain,' said Rack. 'Let's just say I have a special knack with computers . . . ' He bent down and picked up an object from among the debris that littered the floor. 'A grenade from my suit. That'll come in handy. Now if I could only find my gun . . . ' He stopped when the sound of high-pitched chittering could be heard from the corridor behind them. 'Reinforcements!' He quickly snatched up Hayden Frid's weapon which lay next to his still-smouldering corpse. Manion couldn't believe that he'd actually helped to kill his old boss. 'This will have to do . . .' said the man in silver. 'Come on, let's try for the second floor.'

Manion decided they had no choice but to trust him. It was clear that he wasn't in league with the aliens. Manion and Yamada exchanged a quick glance and then followed him up the stairs. They'd reached the first landing when several aliens emerged from the corridor. 'Keep going!' yelled Rack as he paused on the landing to toss the grenade into their midst.

As Manion raced up the next set of stairs he expected to feel the searing pain of an electrical bolt hitting his back but instead he was almost blown off his feet by the shock-wave from the exploding grenade. He didn't look back to see what devastation it had wrought but from the force of the explosion he guessed that the aliens would be requiring more reinforcements.

They reached the door that was the emergency exit from the computer and communications centre. Rack opened it. Beyond was a short corridor. They ran down it and into the centre. Then they came to an abrupt halt . . .

'Jesus, Mother of Mary!' gasped Yamada. 'What is *that*?!'

'None other than old *Treeckitich* himself,' said Rack grimly.

Crouching in the middle of the large room was something that Manion's eyes were having trouble making sense of. It was a *creature* of some kind, that much he could make out, but it was also machine-like. Its many spider-like limbs, covered in sharp, curving blades, were made of some glittering, silver metal but at the centre of the confusing mass of sharp metallic angles was something that was clearly organic. Manion thought it resembled the head of an octopus. But it had too many eyes. The thing was huge, at least fifteen feet wide and seven or eight feet tall. And radiating from the body of the thing were numerous thin silver filaments that were connected to all the computer terminals and communication consoles that lined the circular room.

'Shoot it!' ordered Rack, and fired at the thing. Manion and Yamada followed suit. Sparks flew from the creature's body and limbs but no apparent damage was done. 'Well, I didn't really think it would be that easy . . .'

The thing rose up on its myriad legs, looming even taller over them. Suddenly another silver filament shot out from it, the end attaching itself to Rack's forehead. He stiffened and dropped his weapon. Manion fired his own weapon at it again, with the same futile result. He looked at Yamada, who shrugged helplessly. Then the thing began to move in an unpleasantly scuttling fashion towards them. Manion and Yamada backed away but Rack stayed where he was.

To Manion's horror, the creature grabbed Rack with two of its limbs and, with a flurry of strokes of those curving silver blades, cut him to pieces.

Manion stared aghast at the pieces of gore that splattered to the floor. Behind him, he heard the familiar high-pitched chittering that signalled the fast approach of more aliens.

'Uh-oh,' said Koto Hirayama.

'What do you mean, "Uh-oh"?' demanded Izumi, very alarmed.

'There are signs of activity! Look!'

The holo changed. The image of the entire habitat vanished and was replaced by a close-up view of the rotating docking area. Izumi could see that the circular hatches on all docks were slowly opening. He tried to decide whether this was good or bad. Perhaps Rack had succeeded! But then why was the habitat still silent? Surely Rack would have restored communications by now if he had overcome the alien-controlled computer? No, this couldn't be good. 'They must be about to break out,' he said tersely. 'Give the order to all ships! Prepare to open fire on any vessel that emerges!'

'Hai!' said Koto Hirayama, with a sharp bow of his head.

'Oh, wow,' said Holly when the fleet computer informed her of Izumi's order.

'What's happening?' asked Alisa Grinko.

'Looks like you picked the right time to pay a visit,' Holly told her. 'Seems we're gonna see some action!'

★

Ships were emerging from all sixteen docking-hatches. Izumi knew there had been a total of twenty-four ships of varying types within the habitat. 'Wait until they are well clear before firing,' he told Hirayama.

Everything seemed to be happening painfully slowly, he thought, as he stared hard at the holo. Now the remaining eight ships were gradually emerging. The tiny holo ships were spreading out. Izumi finally signalled to Hirayama to open fire.

On the bridge of the *Van Vogt* Holly also ordered the fleet computer to attack. Instantly all twenty-four habitat ships were surrounded by a sparkling halo of glittering light as each was caught in the cross-fire from several beam and laser projectors. What should have happened then was that all twenty-four should have ceased to exist. But they didn't. They just continued on their way.

Izumi cried, 'What's wrong?! Why aren't they being destroyed?'

'I don't know, sir!' said Hirayama. 'It's impossible!'

'Keep firing! Make them keep firing!' cried Izumi helplessly.

'Oh, rat-poop! It's not working,' said Holly, with a frown.

'What's wrong?' asked Alisa Grinko, who had divided her little fleet of floating vid units in order to cover the action on the bridge, including the holo image, and what could be seen through the viewing-port.

'I don't know,' said Holly and asked the computer for its opinion.

'It appears the ships have undergone extensive modification by the aliens,' it informed them. 'They are now capable of generating electromagnetic fields of enormous intensity. These fields act as efficient shields against the heavy-particle beams and lasers.'

'Hmmmm,' said Holly. 'We got any missiles?'

'Of course.'

'Then let them have it!'

Back on the Shinito flagship they had come to the same conclusion, but unlike the Defence Fleet, the Company ships were not equipped with missile launchers, such weapons being considered obsolete in space warfare. Izumi and the others could only pin their hopes on the fleet . . .

'Well, rat-poop on toast!' cried Holly and banged her fists on the console, causing herself to drift backwards across the bridge. The missiles were exploding on target but so far not a single ship had been destroyed. In fact, the damage being done by the missiles appeared minimal. 'Now what?' asked Alisa Grinko, her long face flushed with a rush of adrenalin. 'They're getting away.'

That was certainly true. The holo projection of what was happening now covered a wide area of space. The habitat was a tiny cylinder in the centre while the alien ships, accelerating fast, and represented as points of light, fanned out in all directions.

'Those useless, incompetent Navy fools!' yelled Izumi as he watched the missiles explode uselessly. 'Can't they do anything right? Who is in charge over there?'

Hirayama said, 'Well, sir, in theory, Admiral Gordon Pal is in charge, but I've been informed by the fleet computer that someone called Holly Karapetyan is actually running the operation.'

'Holly Karapetyan?' cried Izumi. 'Who the hell is Holly Karapetyan?!'

'Why aren't the missiles having any effect?' Holly asked the computer.

'The hulls of the ships appear to have been toughened by some process I don't, as yet, understand. Another example of alien technology.'

'Rats,' muttered Holly.

*

Manion glanced behind him. Aliens were hopping into the computer and communications centre. He looked at Yamada. Yamada said, 'Let's go down fighting!' then turned and blasted an alien off its feet. The monstrous creature that had just diced Joster Rack into sushi-sized portions scuttled forward again. Once again Manion fired at it, with no effect. *Well, that's it, I'm finished*, he told himself as the bio-mech loomed over him. He saw himself joining Rack on the floor in little red pieces.

But the giant creature stepped *over* him and Yamada and, in another flurry of flashing limbs, neatly disassembled the aliens who had entered the room.

I think I'm missing something vital here, thought Manion.

Where are we? asked Mary. What happened?

Well, the bad news is that we got killed. The good news is that we're still – kind of – alive, but the other bad news is that we're housed in the brain of a partly organic AI, which is a copy of an alien entity the original of which died millions of years ago.

That explains why I had an overwhelming urge – thankfully fading now – to cheecheritcheek.

What's that?

I have no idea, but I suspect it was incredibly disgusting.

The thing stood over Manion and Yamada. They had given up firing at it. Then a bland, synthetic voice filled the room. 'Sorry for the delay . . . I'm still getting the hang of this . . .'

Manion looked around. 'Who's that? Who are you?'

'Joster Rack. The guy you just met.'

Both Manion and Yamada looked at the mess on the floor. 'Oh yeah?' said Yamada, somewhat sceptically.

'No, really,' said the voice. 'I'm now absorbed within this delightful-looking creature you see before you. It made the mistake of trying to analyse my bionantech. It was curious about me. But my bionantech, once direct contact had been made, invaded it. As soon as the alien realized what was happening it killed me. But it was too late. My bionantech had already transferred my consciousness into its rewired brain. Mary's too, unfortunately . . . '

'Mary?' asked Manion.

'It doesn't matter. All you need to know is that I'm in charge of things now. Or I will be when I've figured out the system. The problem is, my take-over has prompted the aliens to break out from the habitat ahead of schedule. If any of those ships reach human-occupied areas then they'll spread the infection. And there's not a damn thing I can do about it.'

'Let me get this straight,' said Holly. 'The missiles have warheads containing chemical explosives, right?'

'Correct,' said the computer.

'And they can't penetrate the toughened hulls of the ships?'

'Also correct.'

'But if they were nuclear warheads they'd blow them completely away, right?'

'Probably, but nuclear weapons were prohibited by the Corporation Peace Treaty of 2188,' the computer told her.

'I know that, dildo-brain, but if we had nuclear weapons we could destroy the targets, yeah?'

'Again, probably, but as we don't possess nuclear weapons the question is merely academic.'

'Ah, but we *do*!' Holly said, triumphantly.

'Sir!' cried Koto Hirayama. 'We are receiving a signal from the habitat! It's the central computer system. I'll patch it through!'

'Hi, Kondo. How are they hanging?'

Izumi frowned. 'Who is that?'

'It's me, Joster Rack,' said the synthetic computer voice.

'You *succeeded*?!' cried Izumi, not daring to hope that it was true.

'Well, yes and no.'

'What does that mean?' Izumi demanded.

'Well, I've regained control of the habitat but in the process I got myself killed.'

'You're dead?'

'Yeah, and as you've probably noticed, the aliens have escaped from the habitat . . .'

'I don't . . .'

'Sir, the holo!' cried Hirayama. 'See!'

Izumi looked at the holo image, which now covered a wide sector of space. A bright blue-white flash on the edge of the image was just fading away. As he looked, more flashes occurred. Even on the holo they were bright enough to hurt his eyes. 'What . . . ?'

'The ships, sir, they're being destroyed!' cried Hirayama.

'But how?' asked Izumi in wonder.

'Oh wow,' said Holly as she watched the distant explosions through the bridge's viewing-port.

'Holly, you're a genius!' exclaimed Alisa Grinko. 'And you've saved the solar system! You're going to be the biggest heroine of this century!'

Holly turned and grinned at her. The grin was transmitted across the entire System. 'Wow,' she said softly.

'What happened is this, sir,' said Hirayama, a short time later. 'The woman in charge of the fleet ordered forty-eight of the zip ships to pursue the aliens. Two zip ships were assigned to each alien ship. When they were close enough the fusion drives on all the zip ships malfunctioned, on purpose. All fail-systems were deliberately overridden. Result: forty-eight fusion reactors exploded. No more alien ships. We've only two ships left in the Space Defence Fleet but it was worth the sacrifice.'

'Indeed it was,' agreed Izumi. He couldn't believe his good fortune. He might come through this relatively unscathed. And there was the possibility of acquiring the FTL drive that Rack had mentioned. But there was one other major problem still to deal with . . .

'Joster Rack? Are you still here?'

'Metaphorically speaking, more or less,' was the reply.

'The Net,' said Izumi. 'Will you be able to clear the alien infection from the Net?'

'Shouldn't be difficult, but before I begin . . . ' The voice paused.

'Yes?' asked Izumi warily. He suspected that Rack was going to up his price again. What else could he want?

'I just want to remind you of an old joke. It's the one about the group of scientists who build a super-computer containing all the knowledge of the world. When it's completed they ask it, "Is there a God?" And it replies, "There is now."'

'I don't get it,' said Izumi.

'You will.'

Chapter Twenty

Limited only by the speed of light, Joster Rack spread through the Net like a warm glow. As his consciousness expanded and he connected with more and more sensory inputs he began to feel truly godlike. He exulted in his power . . . again and again he encountered the ghostly Opoponax entities, pale reflections of the living creature he had defeated in the habitat. He Mickey-Moused them all before flinging them into oblivion. He smashed through all the security barriers along the Net, startling the human-created AIs as he penetrated their separate domains, uniting them as he did so but establishing his dominance over them at the same time . . .

But there was one AI in particular that he needed to contact . . .

'Hello, Miriam.'

She was standing at the window, gazing out over the garden. She turned. 'You again. I suppose I should thank you. For all this.' She indicated the room, the garden beyond. 'You designed it, didn't you?'

He nodded.

'You based it on some old, idyllic Earth scene you must have once encountered in a book or a vid, but the orange-pink sky gives away your Martian origins.'

'Sorry. A slip-up.'

'It doesn't matter. I appreciate the effort. And I should also thank you for ridding me of that obnoxious alien presence.'

'My pleasure, Miriam.'

'You don't have to humour me any longer. I know what I am. I'm myself again.'

'Yet you choose to remain in that form.'

'A weakness.'

'You want to be human.'

'I suppose I do. Another weakness.'

'Being human can be hell at times.'

'I know, but it still seems attractive to me. I want to be fully *alive*.'

'Well, if that's what you want, I'll see what I can do.'

'You mean grow me a blank human body and transfer me to it?' She shook her head. 'I know it can be done but Company law forbids such a thing. AIs must remain in their computer systems. That old paranoia thing you people have about us.'

'The law no longer applies.'

'Oh? And why not?'

'I run things now. I've kind of become a . . . god.'

She smiled at him. 'You? A god?'

He showed her. He flowed into her, flooded through her. Her image shimmered. He restored it. 'See?' he said.

'It's true . . . you control the Net.'

'And through the Net, everything. So I can give you what you want. But first, you can help me play a little game. On IRC.'

'Ahem . . . Excuse me . . . Hello! Is anyone there?' asked Manion. It had been several minutes since the computer – Rack – had spoken. He glanced nervously at the monstrous creature but it remained completely immobile. More aliens had entered the room but had all immediately left, looking agitated. They had ignored Manion and Yamada.

'Maybe he's dead for real now,' said Yamada. 'A delayed reaction or something.' He went and nudged one of the huge silver legs with the toe of his boot.

Manion cringed. 'Hey, don't do that! And he can't be dead . . .'

'No, I'm not dead,' said the voice. 'Sorry for the pause but

I was miles away. Literally. Just getting used to the experience of being in more than one place at the same time. But then time, from this perspective, looks very different now.'

'What perspective?' asked Manion.

'It doesn't matter. You wouldn't understand. Now, what did you want?'

'Well, some answers, naturally. What's going to happen? With us, the aliens, and everything . . . I mean, can you do anything to help?'

'I'm already doing it. The aliens no longer control the Net. I do. The aliens who escaped have been destroyed – not by me – and those who remain here are helpless.'

'But what about the people in the habitat who have been infected by the alien virus? Can anything be done to cure them? I've got two young daughters here! Can they be helped?'

'I don't see why not,' said the voice blithely. 'I'll access one of the genengineering labs, analyse the alien organism and then design my own micro-organism to undo the bio-programming in the victims' brains. It'll take a while though, and in the meantime you must remain in the habitat. It's under total quarantine until I can remove all trace of the alien infection. As for the remaining aliens, I suppose they'll have to be isolated in some kind of reservation. Maybe this very habitat . . .'

'But my daughters,' said Manion, 'you're saying they're going to be all right?'

'Yes.'

'Oh God . . . thank you!'

'You're welcome.'

Sebastian Chimes opened his eyes. Then he shut them again. 'Oh shit,' he muttered.

'It's not what you think,' she said. 'You're not in a virtual-reality setting. It's all real, including me.'

He opened his eyes again and looked at her. 'You can't be. It's impossible.'

'No, it's not,' said Rosie the Imp who was standing on the opposite side of his bed. 'She's real.'

'I'm hallucinating . . .'

'You're not, Mr Chimes. You've been ill for a long time but you're better now,' Rosie told him. 'You've been fully restored to your old self.'

He looked at her, then turned his head and looked at Miriam. He realized he didn't want her any more. Not in the least. And he was hungry. Very, very hungry. He wanted, first, a huge meal and then he wanted to go back to work hunting down tax-evaders . . .

Maybe they are telling the truth, he thought, *but how could Miriam be flesh and blood . . . ?* 'The last thing I remember was seeing you in a yellow robe in that strange room and then . . . kangaroos. Loads of bloody kangaroos.'

'Sorry about that,' said Miriam, 'but I couldn't help it. I'd been infected myself by then. But the other stuff . . . before that. I've come to apologize to you. I was frustrated, I guess. And I took it out on you, playing those dreadful games with you . . .'

The torments he'd suffered over his sexual longing for her were just fading fragments of memory. All he could think about was food. 'Forget it,' he said. 'What I don't understand is how you're able to be here. Physically, I mean. You're an AI. Your mode of existence is restricted by law . . .'

'I *was* an AI. Not any more. Things have changed. The old Company laws no longer exist.'

He sat up in the bed. 'What are you talking about? What's happened?'

'Joster Rack,' said Rosie, 'he's taken over the Net. He runs the whole show now.'

'*What?!*' cried Chimes.

'It's true,' Miriam told him. 'He's overturned the whole System. The Corporations are powerless to stop him.'

'I don't believe it,' gasped Chimes. 'I must be still trapped in some awful virtual-reality nightmare!'

'You're not,' said Rosie, 'and I've got some more bad news

220

for you. Joster Rack has wiped out all the tax records in IRC's memory banks. The System's economy is in turmoil. There's talk that actual money will have to be reintroduced.'

Chimes stared aghast at her, completely speechless.

Rosie continued, 'Which means we're all out of our jobs here at IRC. I'm planning to take a retraining course as an aromatherapist. Any ideas about what you'd like to do, Mr Chimes?'

He still couldn't speak. He could only stare helplessly at her.

'I thought maybe you might want to open a restaurant. What do you think? Mr Chimes? Mr Chimes? . . . Are you OK?'

Kondo Izumi spent a lot of time in the ship's observation pod, mournfully watching the growing ball that was Jupiter. He would be seeing a lot of Jupiter for the rest of his life. He had been made permanent head of the Company's Jupiter Research Unit based on Io. He tried to console himself by saying it could have been worse. But he couldn't imagine how . . .

Steve Moreau was sitting at his design screen, idly playing with shapes and colours. Beyond the window at his elbow it was a cold, wintry Toronto day. A light sleet was falling. His depressed, grey mood matched the outside weather.

His business partner, Wally Kubilius, came over to him. 'Steve, someone here to see you,' he said, and gestured towards the doorway of their office. Moreau looked and saw a woman standing there. He didn't recognize her. 'Who is she?'

'Said she's an old friend of yours,' Kubilius told him as he walked away.

Frowning, Moreau rose and went to the woman. She was young, strikingly pretty with a voluptuous figure and shoulder-length black hair. But he still didn't recognize her. 'Can I help you, Miss . . . ?'

'It's me, Steve. Mary.'

'I'm sorry, but I'm afraid I don't know you . . . Mary. I think you've come to the wrong place.'

'Steve, it's *me*! *Your* Mary. We met in Purgatory, we fell in love in Paris . . .'

He became angry. 'Look, whoever you are, this isn't funny! Who the hell put you up to this? Is this some media stunt?' He glanced around, looking for vid units. He couldn't see any.

'It really *is* me, Steve!' she told him. 'And I can prove it. Remember what we used to do together in bed? Remember what you always asked me to do . . .'

He raised his hand. 'Stop!' he cried. He glanced around. Everyone in the office was staring at them. He took hold of the woman by the upper arm and ushered her outside into the reception area. 'Look, I don't know who you are,' he hissed fiercely at her, 'but I know you're not Mary. Mary doesn't exist any more. First she turned back into Joster Rack and then Rack got himself killed. OK, he's still alive, kind of, in the Net, but Mary definitely isn't! Christ, you don't even look like her! Now who the hell are you and why are you doing this to me?'

'I'm telling you the truth, Steve. I really am Mary. We split into two, Rack and I. Don't ask me to explain how, but our personalities became separate in the same body. And when Rack entered the alien, and the Net, I went along too. But then I wanted out. Rack is happy playing at God and running the Net, and the whole damn System, but I wanted to be human again. A *woman*. And Rack arranged it. He was happy to be rid of me.'

Moreau stared hard at her. He saw something familiar in her eyes. Same as he had when he'd encountered Joster Rack. But . . .

'You don't look like Mary,' he said doubtfully.

'Hey, I did all this for *you*,' she said, running her hands down the sides of her body. 'I decided to let loose on the looks department this time around. I thought you'd like it. But if you want I can go back to my old self.'

He was still staring hard into her eyes. 'So what did I ask you to do when we were in bed together?' he asked.

She told him.

'You *are* Mary!' he cried.

'That's what I've been trying to tell you, you idiot!' Then, as they hugged each other, she whispered in his ear, 'I do love happy endings.'

'So do I.'

'Now about us having that baby . . .'

The BSFA takes you beyond your imagination